DEAD AS A DOORNAIL

CHARLAINE HARRIS

DEAD AS A DOORNAIL

Copyright © Charlaine Harris Schulz 2005
All rights reserved

The right of Charlaine Harris to be identified as the author
of this work has been asserted by her in accordance with the
Copyright, Designs and Patents Act 1988.

First published in Great Britain in 2007 by
Gollancz
An imprint of the Orion Publishing Group
Orion House, 5 Upper St Martin's Lane, London WC2H 9EA
An Hachette UK Company

This edition published in Great Britain in 2011 by
Gollancz

A CIP catalogue record for this book
is available from the British Library

Printed in Great Britain by
Clays Ltd, St Ives plc

The Orion Publishing Group's policy is to use papers that
are natural, renewable and recyclable products and made
from wood grown in sustainable forests. The logging and
manufacturing processes are expected to conform to the
environmental regulations of the country of origin.

www.charlaineharris.com
www.orionbooks.co.uk

This book is dedicated to a wonderful woman I don't get to see often enough. Janet Hutchings (then an editor at Walker, now editor of *Ellery Queen Mystery Magazine*) was brave enough to take me on many years ago after I'd taken a long sabbatical from writing. God bless her.

ACKNOWLEDGMENTS

I didn't thank Patrick Schulz for loaning me his Benelli for the last book—sorry, Son. My friend Toni L. P. Kelner, who pointed out some problems in the first half of the book, is due a big hats-off. My friend Paula Woldan gave me moral support and some information on pirates, and was willing to endure me on Talk Like a Pirate Day. Her daughter Jennifer saved my life by helping me prepare the manuscript. Shay, a Faithful Reader, had the great idea for the calendar. And in thanking the Woldan family, I have to include Jay, a volunteer firefighter for many years, who shared his knowledge and expertise with me.

1

I KNEW MY BROTHER WOULD TURN INTO A PANTHER before he did. As I drove to the remote crossroads community of Hotshot, my brother watched the sunset in silence. Jason was dressed in old clothes, and he had a plastic Wal-Mart bag containing a few things he might need—toothbrush, clean underwear. He hunched inside his bulky camo jacket, looking straight ahead. His face was tense with the need to control his fear and his excitement.

"You got your cell phone in your pocket?" I asked, knowing I'd already asked him as soon as the words left my mouth. But Jason just nodded instead of snapping at me. It was still afternoon, but at the end of January the dark comes early.

Tonight would be the first full moon of the New Year.

When I stopped the car, Jason turned to look at me, and even in the dim light I saw the change in his eyes. They weren't blue like mine anymore. They were yellowish. The shape of them had changed.

"My face feels funny," he said. But he still hadn't put two and two together.

Tiny Hotshot was silent and still in the waning light. A cold wind was blowing across the bare fields, and the pines and oaks were shivering in the gusts of frigid air. Only one man was visible. He was standing outside one of the little houses, the one that was freshly painted. This man's eyes were closed, and his bearded face was raised to the darkening sky. Calvin Norris waited until Jason was climbing out the passenger's door of my old Nova before he walked over and bent to my window. I rolled it down.

His golden-green eyes were as startling as I'd remembered, and the rest of him was just as unremarkable. Stocky, graying, sturdy, he looked like a hundred other men I'd seen in Merlotte's Bar, except for those eyes.

"I'll take good care of him," Calvin Norris said. Behind him, Jason stood with his back to me. The air around my brother had a peculiar quality; it seemed to be vibrating.

None of this was Calvin Norris's fault. He hadn't been the one who'd bitten my brother and changed him forever. Calvin, a werepanther, had been born what he was; it was his nature. I made myself say, "Thank you."

"I'll bring him home in the morning."

"To my house, please. His truck is at my place."

"All right, then. Have a good night." He raised his face to the wind again, and I felt the whole community was waiting, behind their windows and doors, for me to leave.

So I did.

Jason knocked on my door at seven the next morning. He still had his little Wal-Mart bag, but he hadn't used anything in it. His face was bruised, and his hands were covered with scratches. He didn't say a word. He just stared at me when I asked him how he was, and walked past me through the living room and down the hall. He closed the door to the hall bathroom with a decisive click. I heard the water running after a second, and I heaved a weary sigh all to myself. Though I'd gone to work and come home tired at about two a.m., I hadn't gotten much sleep.

By the time Jason emerged, I'd fixed him some bacon and eggs. He sat down at the old kitchen table with an air of pleasure: a man doing a familiar and pleasant thing. But after a second of staring down at the plate, he leaped to his feet and ran back into the bathroom, kicking the door shut behind him. I listened to him throw up, over and over.

I stood outside the door helplessly, knowing he wouldn't want me to come in. After a moment, I went back to the kitchen to dump the food into the trash can, ashamed of the waste but utterly unable to force myself to eat.

When Jason returned, he said only, "Coffee?" He looked green around the gills, and he walked like he was sore.

"Are you okay?" I asked, not sure if he would be able to answer or not. I poured the coffee into a mug.

"Yes," he said after a moment, as though he'd had to think about it. "That was the most incredible experience of my life."

For a second, I thought he meant throwing up in my bathroom, but that was sure no new experience for Jason. He'd been quite a drinker in his teens, until he'd figured out that there was nothing glamorous or attractive about hanging over a toilet bowl, heaving your guts out.

"Shifting," I said tentatively.

He nodded, cradling his coffee mug in his hands. He held his face over the steam rising from the hot, strong blackness. He met my eyes. His own were once again their ordinary blue. "It's the most incredible rush," he said. "Since I was bitten, not born, I don't get to be a true panther like the others."

I could hear envy in his voice.

"But even what I become is amazing. You feel the magic inside you, and you feel your bones moving around and adapting, and your vision changes. Then you're lower to the ground and you walk in a whole different way, and as for running, damn, you can *run*. You can chase. . . ." And his voice died away.

I would just as soon not know that part, anyway.

"So it's not so bad?" I asked, my hands clasped together. Jason was all the family I had, except for a cousin who'd drifted away into the underworld of drugs years before.

"It's not so bad," Jason agreed, scraping up a smile to give me. "It's great while you're actually the animal. Everything's so simple. It's when you're back to being human that you start to worry about stuff."

He wasn't suicidal. He wasn't even despondent. I wasn't aware I'd been holding my breath until I let it out. Jason was going to be able to live with the hand he'd been dealt. He was going to be okay.

The relief was incredible, like I'd removed something jammed painfully between my teeth or shaken a sharp rock out of my shoe. For days, weeks even, I'd been worried, and now that anxiety was gone. That didn't mean Jason's life as a shape-shifter would be worry-free, at least from my point of view. If he married a regular human woman, their kids would be normal. But if he married into the shifter community at Hotshot, I'd have nieces or nephews who turned into animals once a month. At least, they would after puberty; that would give them, and their auntie Sook, some preparation time.

Luckily for Jason, he had plenty of vacation days, so he wasn't due at the parish road department. But I had to work tonight. As soon as Jason left in his flashy pickup truck, I crawled back into bed, jeans and all, and in about five minutes I was fast asleep. The relief acted as a kind of sedative.

When I woke up, it was nearly three o'clock and time for me to get ready for my shift at Merlotte's. The sun outside was bright and clear, and the temperature was fifty-two, said my indoor-outdoor thermometer. This isn't too unusual in north Louisiana in January. The temperature would drop after the sun went down, and Jason would shift. But he'd have some fur—not a full coat, since he turned into half-man, half-cat—and he'd be with other panthers. They'd go hunting. The woods around Hotshot, which lay in a remote corner of Renard Parish, would be dangerous again tonight.

As I went about eating, showering, folding laundry, I thought of a dozen things I'd like to know. I wondered if the shifters would kill a human being if they came upon one in the woods. I wondered how much of their human consciousness they retained in their animal form. If they mated in panther form, would they have a kitten or a baby? What happened when a pregnant werepanther saw the full moon? I wondered if Jason knew the answer to all these questions yet, if Calvin had given him some kind of briefing.

But I was glad I hadn't questioned Jason this morning while everything was still so new to him. I'd have plenty of chances to ask him later.

For the first time since New Year's Day, I was thinking about the future. The full moon symbol on my calendar no longer seemed to be a period marking the end of something, but just another way of counting time. As I pulled on my waitress outfit (black pants and a white boat-neck T-shirt and black Reeboks), I felt almost giddy with cheer. For once, I left my hair down instead of pulling it back and up into a ponytail. I put in some bright red dot earrings and matched my lipstick to the color. A little eye makeup and some blush, and I was good to go.

I'd parked at the rear of the house last night, and I checked the back porch carefully to make sure there weren't any lurking vampires before I shut and locked the back door behind me. I'd been surprised before, and it wasn't a pleasant feeling. Though it was barely dark, there might be some early risers around. Probably the last thing the Japanese had expected when they'd developed synthetic blood was that its availability would bring vampires out of the realm of legend and into the light of fact. The Japanese had just been trying to make a few bucks hawking the blood substitute to ambulance companies and hospital emergency rooms. Instead, the way we looked at the world had changed forever.

Speaking of vampires (if only to myself), I wondered if Bill Compton was home. Vampire Bill had been my first love, and he lived right across the cemetery from me. Our houses lay on a parish road outside the little town of Bon Temps and south of the bar where I worked. Lately, Bill had been traveling a lot. I only found out he was home if he happened to come into Merlotte's, which he did every now and then to mix with the natives and have some warm O-positive. He preferred TrueBlood, the most expensive Japanese synthetic. He'd told me it almost completely satisfied his cravings for blood fresh from the source. Since I'd witnessed Bill going into a bloodlust fit, I could only thank God for TrueBlood. Sometimes I missed Bill an awful lot.

I gave myself a mental shake. Snapping out of a slump, that was what today was all about. No more worry! No more fear! Free and twenty-six! Working! House paid for! Money in the bank! These were all good, positive things.

The parking lot was full when I got to the bar. I could see I'd be busy tonight. I drove around back to the employees' entrance. Sam Merlotte, the owner and my boss, lived back there in a very nice double-wide that even had a little yard surrounded by a hedge, Sam's equivalent of a white picket fence. I locked my car and went in the employees' back door, which opened into the hallway off of which lay the men's and the ladies', a large stock room, and Sam's office. I stowed my purse and coat in an empty desk drawer, pulled up my red socks, shook my head to make my hair hang right, and went through the doorway (this door was almost always propped open) that led to the big room of the bar/restaurant. Not that the kitchen produced anything but the most basic stuff: hamburgers, chicken strips, fries and onion rings, salads in the summer and chili in the winter.

Sam was the bartender, the bouncer, and on occasion the cook, but lately we'd been lucky in getting our positions filled: Sam's seasonal allergies had hit hard, making him less than ideal as a food handler. The new cook had shown up in answer to Sam's ad just the week before. Cooks didn't seem to stay long at Merlotte's, but I was hoping that Sweetie Des Arts would stick around a while. She showed up on time, did her job well, and never gave the rest of the staff any trouble. Really, that was all you could ask for. Our last cook, a guy, had given my friend Arlene a big rush of hope that he was The One—in this case, he'd have been her fourth or fifth One—before he'd decamped overnight with her plates and forks and a CD player. Her kids had been devastated; not because they'd loved the guy, but because they missed their CD player.

I walked into a wall of noise and cigarette smoke that made it seem like I was passing into another universe. Smokers all sit on the west side of the room, but the smoke doesn't seem to know it should stay there. I put a smile on my face and stepped behind the bar to give Sam a pat on the arm. After he expertly filled a glass with beer and slid it to a patron, he put another glass under the tap and began the process all over again.

"How are things?" Sam asked carefully. He knew all about Jason's problems, since he'd been with me the night I'd found Jason being held prisoner in a toolshed in Hotshot. But we had to be roundabout in our speech; vampires had gone public, but shape-shifters and Weres were still cloaked in secrecy. The underground world of supernatural beings was waiting to see how vampires fared before they followed the vampire example by going public.

"Better than I expected." I smiled up at him, though not too far up, since Sam's not a big man. He's built lean, but he's much stronger than he looks. Sam is in his thirties—at least, I think he is—and he has reddish gold hair that halos his head. He's a good man, and a great boss. He's also a shape-shifter, so he can change into any animal. Most often, Sam turns into a very cute collie with a gorgeous coat. Sometimes he comes over to my place and I let him sleep on the rug in the living room. "He's gonna be fine."

"I'm glad," he said. I can't read shifter minds as easily as I read human minds, but I can tell if a mood is true or not. Sam was happy because I was happy.

"When are you taking off?" I asked. He had that faraway look in his eyes, the look that said he was mentally running through the woods, tracking possums.

"As soon as Terry gets here." He smiled at me again, but this time the smile was a bit strained. Sam was getting antsy.

The door to the kitchen was just outside the bar area at the west end, and I stuck my head in the door to say hi to Sweetie. Sweetie was bony and brunette and fortyish, and she wore a lot of makeup for someone who was going to be out of sight in the kitchen all evening. She also seemed a little sharper, perhaps better educated, than any of Merlotte's previous short-order cooks.

"You doing okay, Sookie?" she called, flipping a hamburger as she spoke. Sweetie was in constant motion in the kitchen, and she didn't like anyone getting in her way. The teenager who assisted her and bussed tables was terrified of Sweetie, and he took care to dodge her as she moved from griddle to fryer. This teenage boy got the plates ready, made the salads, and went to the window to tell the barmaids which order was up. Out on the floor, Holly Cleary and her best friend, Danielle, were working hard. They'd both looked relieved when they'd seen me come in. Danielle worked the smoking section to the west, Holly usually worked the middle area in front of the bar, and I worked the east when three of us were on duty.

"It looks like I better get moving," I told Sweetie.

She gave me a quick smile and turned back to the griddle. The cowed teenager, whose name I had yet to catch, gave me a ducked-head nod and went back to loading the dishwasher.

I wished Sam had called me before things had gotten so busy; I wouldn't have minded coming in a little earlier. Of course, he wasn't exactly himself tonight. I began checking the tables in my section, getting fresh drinks and clearing off food baskets, collecting money and bringing change.

"Barmaid! Bring me a Red Stuff!" The voice was unfamiliar, and the order was unusual. Red Stuff was the cheapest artificial blood, and only the newest vampires would be caught dead asking for it. I got a bottle from the clear-fronted refrigerator and stuck it in the microwave. While it warmed, I scanned the crowd for the vamp. He was sitting with my friend Tara Thornton. I'd never seen him before, which was worrisome. Tara'd been dating an older vampire (much older: Franklin Mott had been older than Tara in human years before he died, and he'd been a vampire for over three hundred years), and he'd been giving her lavish gifts—like a Camaro. What was she doing with this new guy? At least Franklin had nice manners.

I put the warm bottle on a tray and carried it over to the couple. The lighting in Merlotte's at night isn't particularly bright, which is how patrons like it, and it wasn't until I'd gotten quite near that I could appreciate Tara's companion. He was slim and narrow shouldered with slicked-back hair. He had long fingernails and a sharp face. I supposed that, in a way, he was attractive—if you like a liberal dose of danger with your sex.

I put the bottle down in front of him and glanced uncertainly at Tara. She looked great, as usual. Tara is tall, slim, and dark haired, and she has a wardrobe of wonderful clothes. She'd overcome a truly horrible childhood to own her own business and actually join the chamber of commerce. Then she started dating the wealthy vampire, Franklin Mott, and she quit sharing her life with me.

"Sookie," she said, "I want you to meet Franklin's friend Mickey." She didn't sound like she wanted us to meet. She sounded like she wished I'd never come over with Mickey's drink. Her own glass was almost empty, but she said, "No," when I asked her if she was ready for another.

I exchanged a nod with the vampire; they don't shake hands, not normally. He was watching me as he took a gulp from the bottled blood, his eyes as cold and hostile as a snake's. If he was a friend of the ultra-urbane Franklin, I was a silk purse. Hired hand, more like. Maybe a bodyguard? Why would Franklin give Tara a bodyguard?

She obviously wasn't going to talk openly in front of this slimeball, so I said, "Catch you later," and took Mickey's money to the till.

I was busy all night, but in the spare moments I had, I thought about my brother. For a second night, he was out frolicking under the moon with the other beasties. Sam had taken off like a shot the moment Terry Bellefleur arrived, though his office wastebasket was full of crumpled tissues. His face had been tense with anticipation.

It was one of those nights that made me wonder how the humans around me could be so oblivious to the other world operating right beside ours. Only willful ignorance could ignore the charge of magic in the air. Only a group lack of imagination could account for people not wondering what went on in the dark around them.

But not too long ago, I reminded myself, I'd been as willfully blind as any of the crowd in Merlotte's. Even when the vampires had made their carefully coordinated worldwide announcement that their existence was fact, few authorities or citizens seemed to take the next mental step: *If vampires exist, what else could be lurking just outside the edge of the light?*

Out of curiosity, I began to dip into the brains around me, testing to see their fears. Most of the people in the bar were thinking about Mickey. The women, and some of the men, were wondering what it would be like to be with him. Even stick-in-the-mud lawyer Portia Bellefleur was peeking around her conservative beau to study Mickey. I could only wonder at these speculations. Mickey was terrifying. That negated any physical attraction I might have felt toward him. But I had lots of evidence that the other humans in the bar didn't feel the same way.

I've been able to read minds all my life. The ability is no great gift. Most peoples' minds don't bear reading. Their thoughts are boring, disgusting, disillusioning, but very seldom amusing. At least Bill had helped me learn how to cut out some of the buzz. Before he'd given me some clues, it had been like tuning in to a hundred radio stations simultaneously. Some of them had come in crystal clear, some had been remote, and some, like the thoughts of shape-shifters, had been full of static and obscurity. But they'd all added up to cacophony. No wonder lots of people had treated me as a half-wit.

Vampires were silent. That was the great thing about vamps, at least from my point of view: They were dead. Their minds were dead, too. Only once in a coon's age did I get any kind of flash from a vampire mind.

Shirley Hunter, my brother's boss at his parish roadwork job, asked me where Jason was when I brought a pitcher of beer to his table. Shirley was universally known as "Catfish."

"Your guess is as good as mine," I said mendaciously, and he winked at me. The first guess as to where Jason was always involved a woman, and the second guess usually included another woman. The tableful of men, still in their working clothes, laughed more than the answer warranted, but then they'd had a lot of beer.

I raced back to the bar to get three bourbon-and-Cokes from Terry Bellefleur, Portia's cousin, who was working under pressure. Terry, a Vietnam vet with a lot of physical and emotional scars, appeared to be holding up well on this busy night. He liked simple jobs that required concentration. His graying auburn hair was pulled back in a ponytail and his face was intent as he plied the bottles. The drinks were ready in no time, and Terry smiled at me as I put them on my tray. A smile from Terry was a rare thing, and it warmed me.

Just as I was turning with my tray resting on my right hand, trouble erupted. A Louisiana Tech student from Ruston got into a one-on-one class war with Jeff LaBeff, a redneck who had many children and made a kind of living driving a garbage truck. Maybe it was just a case of two stubborn guys colliding and really didn't have much to do with town vs. gown (not that we were that close to Ruston). Whatever the reason for the original quarrel, it took me a few seconds to realize the fight was going to be more than a shouting match.

In those few seconds, Terry tried to intervene. Moving quickly, he got between Jeff and the student and caught firm hold of both their wrists. I thought for a minute it would work, but Terry wasn't as young or as active as he had been, and all hell broke loose.

"You could stop this," I said furiously to Mickey as I hurried past his and Tara's table on my way to try to make peace.

He sat back in his chair and sipped his drink. "Not my job," he said calmly.

I got that, but it didn't endear the vampire to me, especially when the student whirled and took a swing at me as I approached him from behind. He missed, and I hit him over the head with my tray. He staggered to one side, maybe bleeding a little, and Terry was able to subdue Jeff LaBeff, who was looking for an excuse to quit.

Incidents like this had been happening with more frequency, especially when Sam was gone. It was evident to me that we needed a bouncer, at least on weekend nights . . . and full-moon nights.

The student threatened to sue.

"What's your name?" I asked.

"Mark Duffy," the young man said, clutching his head.

"Mark, where you from?"

"Minden."

I did a quick evaluation of his clothes, his demeanor, and the contents of his head. "I'm gonna enjoy calling your mama and telling her you took a swing at a woman," I said. He blanched and said no more about suing, and he and his buds left soon after. It always helps to know the most effective threat.

We made Jeff leave, too.

Terry resumed his place behind the bar and began dispensing drinks, but he was limping slightly and had a strained look in his face, which worried me. Terry's war experiences hadn't left him real stable. I'd had enough trouble for one night.

But of course the night wasn't over yet.

About an hour after the fight, a woman came into Merlotte's. She was plain and plainly dressed in old jeans and a camo coat. She had on boots that had been wonderful when they'd been new, but that had been a long time ago. She didn't carry a purse, and she had her hands thrust into her pockets.

There were several indicators that made my mental antennae twitch. First of all, this gal didn't look right. A local woman might dress like that if she were going hunting or doing farm work, but not to come to Merlotte's. For an evening out at the bar, most women fixed themselves up. So this woman was in a working mode; but she wasn't a whore by the same reasoning.

That meant drugs.

To protect the bar in Sam's absence, I tuned in to her thoughts. People don't think in complete sentences, of course, and I'm smoothing it out, but what was running through her head was along the order of: *Three vials left getting old losing power gotta sell it tonight so I can get back to Baton Rouge and buy some more. Vampire in the bar if he catches me with vamp blood I'm dead. This town is a dump. Back to the city first chance I get.*

She was a Drainer, or maybe she was just a distributor. Vampire blood was the most intoxicating drug on the market, but of course vamps didn't give it up willingly. Draining a vampire was a hazardous occupation, boosting prices of the tiny vials of blood to amazing sums.

What did the drug user get for parting with a lot of money? Depending on the age of the blood—that is, the time since it'd been removed from its owner—and the age of the vampire from whom the blood had been removed, and the individual chemistry of the drug user, it could be quite a lot. There was the feeling of omnipotence, the increased strength, acute vision, and hearing. And most important of all for Americans, an enhanced physical appearance.

Still, only an idiot would drink black-market vampire blood. For one thing, the results were notoriously unpredictable. Not only did the effects vary, but those effects could last anywhere from two weeks to two months. For another thing, some people simply went mad when the blood hit their system—sometimes homicidally mad. I'd heard of dealers who sold gullible users pig's blood or contaminated human blood. But the most important reason to avoid the black market in vamp blood was this: Vampires hated Drainers, and they hated the users of the drained blood (commonly known as bloodheads). You just don't want a vampire pissed off at you.

There weren't any off-duty police officers in Merlotte's that night. Sam was out wagging his tail somewhere. I hated to tip off Terry, because I didn't know how he'd react. I had to do something about this woman.

Truly, I try not to intervene in events when my only connection comes through my telepathy. If I stuck my oar in every time I learned something that would affect the lives around me (like knowing the parish clerk was embezzling, or that one of the local detectives took bribes), I wouldn't be able to live in Bon Temps, and it was my home. But I couldn't permit this scraggy woman to sell her poison in Sam's bar.

She perched on an empty barstool and ordered a beer

from Terry. His gaze lingered on her. Terry, too, realized something was wrong about the stranger.

I came to pick up my next order and stood by her. She needed a bath, and she'd been in a house heated by a wood fireplace. I made myself touch her, which always improved my reception. Where was the blood? It was in her coat pocket. Good.

Without further ado, I dumped a glass of wine down her front.

"Dammit!" she said, jumping off the stool and patting ineffectually at her chest. "You are the clumsiest-ass woman I ever saw!"

" 'Scuse me," I said abjectly, putting my tray on the bar and meeting Terry's eyes briefly. "Let me put some soda on that." Without waiting for her permission, I pulled her coat down her arms. By the time she understood what I was doing and began to struggle, I had taken charge of the coat. I tossed it over the bar to Terry. "Put some soda on that, please," I said. "Make sure the stuff in her pockets didn't get wet, too." I'd used this ploy before. I was lucky it was cold weather and she'd had the stuff in her coat, not in her jeans pocket. That would have taxed my inventiveness.

Under the coat, the woman was wearing a very old Dallas Cowboys T-shirt. She began shivering, and I wondered if she'd been sampling more conventional drugs. Terry made a show of patting soda on the wine stain. Following my hint, he delved into the pockets. He looked down at his hand with disgust, and I heard a clink as he threw the vials in the trash can behind the bar. He returned everything else to her pockets.

She'd opened her mouth to shriek at Terry when she realized she really couldn't. Terry stared directly at her, daring her to mention the blood. The people around us watched with interest. They knew something was up, but not what, because the whole thing had gone down very quickly. When Terry was sure she wasn't going to start yelling, he handed me the coat. As I held it so she could slide her arms in, Terry told her, "Don't you come back here no more."

If we kept throwing people out at this rate, we wouldn't have many customers.

"You redneck son of a bitch," she said. The crowd around us drew in a collective breath. (Terry was almost as unpredictable as a bloodhead.)

"Doesn't matter to me what you call me," he said. "I guess an insult from you is no insult at all. You just stay away." I expelled a long breath of relief.

She shoved her way through the crowd. Everyone in the room marked her progress toward the door, even Mickey the vampire. In fact, he was doing something with a device in his hands. It looked like one of those cell phones that can take a picture. I wondered to whom he was sending it. I wondered if she'd make it home.

Terry pointedly didn't ask how I'd known the scruffy woman had something illegal in her pockets. That was another weird thing about the people of Bon Temps. The rumors about me had been floating around as long as I could remember, from when I was little and my folks put me through the mental health battery. And yet, despite the evidence at their disposal, almost everyone I knew would much rather regard me as a dim and peculiar young woman than acknowledge my strange ability. Of course, I was careful not to stick it in their faces. And I kept my mouth shut.

Anyway, Terry had his own demons to fight. Terry subsisted on some kind of government pension, and he cleaned Merlotte's early in the morning, along with a couple of other businesses. He stood in for Sam three or four times a month. The rest of his time was his own, and no one seemed to know what he did with it. Dealing with people exhausted Terry, and nights like tonight were simply not good for him.

It was lucky he wasn't in Merlotte's the next night, when all hell broke loose.

AT FIRST, I THOUGHT EVERYTHING HAD RETURNED TO normal. The bar seemed a little calmer the next night. Sam was back in place, relaxed and cheerful. Nothing seemed to rile him, and when I told him what had happened with the dealer the night before, he complimented me on my finesse.

Tara didn't come in, so I couldn't ask her about Mickey. But was it really any of my business? Probably not my business—but my concern, definitely.

Jeff LaBeff was back and sheepish about getting riled by the college kid the night before. Sam had learned about the incident through a phone call from Terry, and he gave Jeff a word of warning.

Andy Bellefleur, a detective on the Renard parish force and Portia's brother, came in with the young woman he was dating, Halleigh Robinson. Andy was older than me, and I'm twenty-six. Halleigh was twenty-one—just old enough to be in Merlotte's. Halleigh taught at the elementary school, she was right out of college, and she was real attractive, with short earlobe-length brown hair and huge brown eyes and a nicely rounded figure. Andy had been dating Halleigh for about two months, and from the little I saw of the couple, they seemed to be progressing in their relationship at a predictable rate.

Andy's true thoughts were that he liked Halleigh very much (though she was a tad boring), and he was really ready for her to give it up. Halleigh thought Andy was sexy and a real man of the world, and she really loved the newly restored Bellefleur family mansion, but she didn't believe he'd hang around long after she slept with him. I hate knowing more about relationships than the people in them know—but no matter how battened down I am, I pick up a trickle of stuff.

Claudine came in the bar that night, toward closing time. Claudine is six feet tall, with black hair that ripples down her back and bruised-looking white skin that looks thin and glossy like a plum's. Claudine dresses for attention. Tonight she was wearing a terra-cotta pants suit, cut very snug on her Amazonian body. She works in the complaint department of a big store at the mall in Ruston during the day. I wished she'd brought her brother, Claude, with her. He doesn't swing in my direction, but he's a treat for the eyes.

He's a fairy. I mean, literally. So's Claudine, of course.

She waved at me across the heads of the crowd. I waved back smiling. Everyone's happy around Claudine, who is always cheerful when there are no vampires in her vicinity. Claudine is unpredictable and a lot of fun, though like all fairies, she's as dangerous as a tiger when she's angry. Fortunately, that doesn't happen often.

Fairies occupy a special place in the hierarchy of magical

creatures. I haven't figured out exactly what it is yet, but sooner or later I'll piece it together.

Every man in the bar was drooling over Claudine, and she was eating it up. She gave Andy Bellefleur a long, big-eyed look, and Halleigh Robinson glared, mad enough to spit, until she remembered she was a sweet southern girl. But Claudine abandoned all interest in Andy when she saw he was drinking ice tea with lemon. Fairies are even more violently allergic to lemon than vampires are to garlic.

Claudine worked her way over to me, and she gave me a big hug, to the envy of every male in the bar. She took my hand to pull me into Sam's office. I went with her out of sheer curiosity.

"Dear friend," Claudine said, "I have bad news for you."

"What?" I'd gone from bemused to scared in a heartbeat.

"There was a shooting early this morning. One of the werepanthers was hit."

"Oh, no! Jason!" But surely one of his friends would've called if he hadn't gone into work today?

"No, your brother is fine, Sookie. But Calvin Norris was shot."

I was stunned. Jason hadn't called to tell me this? I had to find out from someone else?

"Shot dead?" I asked, hearing my voice shake. Not that Calvin and I were close—far from it—but I was shocked. Heather Kinman, a teenager, had been fatally shot the week before. What was happening in Bon Temps?

"Shot in the chest. He's alive, but he's bad hurt."

"Is he in the hospital?"

"Yes, his nieces took him to Grainger Memorial."

Grainger was a town farther southeast than Hotshot, and a shorter drive from there than the parish hospital in Clarice.

"Who did it?"

"No one knows. Someone shot him early this morning, when Calvin was on his way to work. He'd come home from his, um, time of the month, changed, and started into town for his shift." Calvin worked at Norcross.

"How'd you come to know all this?"

"One of his cousins came into the store to buy some pajamas, since Calvin didn't have any. Guess he sleeps in the buff," Claudette said. "I don't know how they think they're going to get a pajama top on over the bandages. Maybe they just needed the pants? Calvin wouldn't like to be shuffling around the hospital with only one of those nasty gowns between him and the world."

Claudine often took long side trails in her conversation.

"Thanks for telling me," I said. I wondered how the cousin had known Claudine, but I wasn't going to ask.

"That's okay. I knew you'd want to know. Heather Kinman was a shape-shifter, too. Bet you didn't know that. Think about it."

Claudine gave me a kiss on the forehead—fairies are very touchy-feely—and we went back into the bar area. She'd stunned me into silence. Claudine herself was back to business as usual. The fairy ordered a 7-and-7 and was surrounded by suitors in about two minutes flat. She never left with anyone, but the men seemed to enjoy trying. I'd decided that Claudine fed off this admiration and attention.

Even Sam was beaming at her, and she didn't tip.

By the time we were closing the bar, Claudine had left to go back to Monroe, and I'd passed along her news to Sam. He was as appalled by the story as I was. Though Calvin Norris was the leader of the small shifter community of Hotshot, the rest of the world knew him as a steady, quiet bachelor who owned his own home and had a good job as crew foreman at the local lumber mill. It was hard to imagine either of his personas leading to an assassination attempt. Sam decided to send some flowers from the bar's staff.

I pulled on my coat and went out the bar's back door just ahead of Sam. I heard him locking the door behind me. Suddenly I remembered that we were getting low on bottled blood, and I turned to tell Sam this. He caught my movement and stopped, waiting for me to speak, his face expectant. In the length of time it takes to blink, his expression changed from expectant to shocked, dark red began to spread on his left leg, and I heard the sound of a shot.

Then blood was everywhere, Sam crumpled to the ground, and I began to scream.

I'D NEVER HAD TO PAY THE COVER CHARGE AT FANG-tasia before. The few times I'd come through the public entrance, I'd been with a vampire. But now I was by myself and feeling mighty conspicuous. I was exhausted from an especially long night. I'd been at the hospital until six in the morning, and I'd had only a few hours' fitful sleep after I'd gotten home.

Pam was taking the cover charge and showing the customers to tables. She was wearing the long filmy black outfit she usually wore when she was on door duty. Pam never looked happy when she was dressed like a fictional vampire. She was the real thing and proud of it. Her personal taste leaned more toward slack sets in pastel colors and penny loafers. She looked as surprised as a vampire can look when she saw me.

"Sookie," she said, "do you have an appointment with Eric?" She took my money without a blink.

I was actually happy to see her: pathetic, huh? I don't have a lot of friends, and I value the ones I have, even if I suspect they dream about catching me in a dark alley and having their bloody way with me. "No, but I do need to talk to him. Business," I added hastily. I didn't want anyone thinking I was courting the romantic attention of the undead head honcho of Shreveport, a position called "sheriff" by the vamps. I shrugged off my new cranberry-colored coat and folded it carefully over my arm. WDED, the Baton Rouge–based all-vampire radio station, was being piped over the sound system. The smooth voice of the early night deejay, Connie the Corpse, said, "And here's a song for all you lowlifes who were outside howling earlier this week . . . 'Bad Moon Rising,' an old hit from Creedence Clearwater Revival." Connie the Corpse was giving a private tip of the hat to the shape-shifters.

"Wait at the bar while I tell him you're here," Pam said. "You'll enjoy the new bartender."

Bartenders at Fangtasia didn't tend to last long. Eric and Pam always tried to hire someone colorful—an exotic bartender drew in the human tourists who came by the busloads to take a walk on the wild side—and in this they were successful. But somehow the job had acquired a high attrition rate.

The new man gave me a white-toothed smile when I perched on one of the high stools. He was quite an eyeful. He had a head full of long, intensely curly hair, chestnut brown in color. It clustered thickly on his shoulders. He also sported a mustache and a Vandyke. Covering his left eye was a black eye patch. Since his face was narrow and the features on it sizable, his face was crowded. He was about my height, five foot six, and he was wearing a black poet shirt and black pants and high black boots. All he needed was a bandanna tied around his head and a pistol.

"Maybe a parrot on your shoulder?" I said.

"Aaargh, dear lady, you are not the first to suggest such a thing." He had a wonderful rich baritone voice. "But I understand there are health department regulations against having an uncaged bird in an establishment serving drinks." He bowed to me as deeply as the narrow area behind the bar permitted. "May I get you a drink and have the honor of your name?"

I had to smile. "Certainly, sir. I'm Sookie Stackhouse." He'd caught the whiff of otherness about me. Vampires almost always pick up on it. The undead usually note me; humans don't. It's kind of ironic that my mind reading doesn't work on the very creatures who believe it distinguishes me from the rest of the human race, while humans would rather believe I was mentally ill than credit me with an unusual ability.

The woman on the barstool next to me (credit cards maxed out, son with ADD) half turned to listen in. She was jealous, having been trying to entice the bartender into showing her some attention for the past thirty minutes. She eyed me, trying to figure out what had caused the vamp to choose to open a conversation with me. She wasn't impressed at all with what she saw.

"I am delighted to meet you, fair maiden," the new vampire said smoothly, and I grinned. Well, at least I was fair— in the blond-and-blue-eyed sense. His eyes took me in; of course, if you're a woman who works in a bar, you're used to that. At least he didn't look at me offensively; and believe me, if you're a woman who works in a bar, you can tell the difference between an evaluation and an eye fuck.

"I bet good money she's no maiden," said the woman next to me.

She was right, but that was beside the point.

"You must be polite to other guests," the vampire told her, with an altered version of his smile. Not only were his fangs slightly extended, but I also noticed he had crooked (though beautifully white) teeth. American standards of tooth straightness are very modern.

"No one tells me how to act," the woman said combatively. She was sullen because the evening wasn't going as she'd planned. She'd thought it would be easy to attract a vampire, that any vamp would think he was lucky to have her. She'd planned to let one bite her neck, if he'd just settle her credit card bills.

She was overestimating herself and underestimating vampires.

"I beg your pardon, madam, but while you are in Fangtasia, most definitely I shall tell you how to act," the bartender said.

She subsided after he fixed her with his quelling gaze, and I wondered if he hadn't given her a dose of glamour.

"My name," he said, returning his attention to me, "is Charles Twining."

"Pleased to meet you," I said.

"And the drink?"

"Yes, please. A ginger ale." I had to drive back to Bon Temps after I'd seen Eric.

He raised his arched brows but poured me the drink and placed it on a napkin in front of me. I paid him and deposited a good tip in the jar. The little white napkin had some fangs outlined in black, with a single drop of red falling from the right fang—custom-made napkins for the vampire bar. "Fangtasia" was printed in jazzy red script on the opposite corner of the napkin, duplicating the sign outside. Cute. There were T-shirts for sale in a case over in a corner, too, along with glasses decorated with the same logo. The legend underneath read, "Fangtasia—The Bar with a Bite." Eric's merchandising expertise had made great strides in the past few months.

As I waited my turn for Eric's attention, I watched Charles Twining work. He was polite to everyone, served the drinks swiftly, and never got rattled. I liked his technique much better than that of Chow, the previous bartender, who'd always made patrons feel like he was doing them a favor by bringing them drinks at all. Long Shadow, the bartender before Chow, had had too much of an eye for the female customers. That'll cause a lot of strife in a bar.

Lost in my own thoughts, I didn't realize Charles Twining was right across the bar from me until he said, "Miss Stackhouse, may I tell you how lovely you look tonight?"

"Thank you, Mr. Twining," I said, entering into the spirit of the encounter. The look in Charles Twining's one visible brown eye let me know that he was a first-class rogue, and I didn't trust him any farther than I could throw him, which was maybe two feet. (The effects of my last infusion of vampire blood had worn off, and I was my regular human self. Hey, I'm no junkie; it had been an emergency situation calling for extra strength.)

Not only was I back at average stamina for a fit woman in her twenties, my looks were back to normal; no vampire-blood enhancement. I hadn't dressed up, since I didn't want Eric to think I was dressing up for him, but I hadn't wanted to look like a slob, either. So I was wearing low-riding blue jeans and a fuzzy white long-sleeved sweater with a boat-neck. It stopped just at my waist, so some tummy showed when I walked. That tummy wasn't fish-belly white, either, thanks to the tanning bed at the video rental place.

"Please, dear lady, call me Charles," the bartender said, pressing his hand to his heart.

I laughed out loud, despite my weariness. The gesture's theatricality wasn't diminished by the fact that Charles's heart wasn't beating.

"Of course," I said agreeably. "If you'll call me Sookie."

He rolled his eyes up as if the excitement was too much for him, and I laughed again. Pam tapped me on the shoulder.

"If you can tear yourself away from your new buddy, Eric's free."

I nodded to Charles and eased off the stool to follow Pam. To my surprise, she didn't lead me back to Eric's office, but to one of the booths. Evidently, tonight Eric was on bar duty. All the Shreveport-area vampires had to agree to show themselves at Fangtasia for a certain number of hours each week so the tourists would keep coming; a vampire bar without any actual vampires is a money-losing establishment. Eric set a good example for his underlings by sitting out in the bar at regular intervals.

Usually the sheriff of Area Five sat in the center of the room, but tonight he was in the corner booth. He watched me approach. I knew he was taking in my jeans, which were on the tight side, and my tummy, which was on the flat side, and my soft fuzzy white sweater, which was filled with natural bounty. I should have worn my frumpiest clothes. (Believe me, I have plenty in my closet.) I shouldn't have carried the cranberry coat, which Eric had given me. I should have done *anything* but look good for Eric—and I had to admit to myself that that had been my goal. I'd blindsided myself.

Eric slid out of the booth and rose to his considerable height—around six foot four. His mane of blond hair rippled down his back, and his blue eyes sparkled from his white, white face. Eric has bold features, high cheekbones, and a square jaw. He looks like a lawless Viking, the kind that could pillage a village in no time at all; and that's exactly what he had been.

Vampires don't shake hands except under extraordinary circumstances, so I didn't expect any salutation from Eric. But he bent to give me a kiss on the cheek, and he gave it lingeringly, as if he wanted me to know he'd like to seduce me.

He didn't realize he'd already kissed just about every inch of Sookie Stackhouse. We'd been as up close and personal as a man and a woman could be.

Eric just couldn't remember anything about it. I wanted it to stay that way. Well, not exactly *wanted*; but I knew it was better all the way around if Eric didn't recall our little fling.

"What pretty nail polish," Eric said, smiling. He had a slight accent. English was not his second language, of course; it was maybe his twenty-fifth.

I tried not to smile back, but I was pleased at his compliment. Trust Eric to pick out the one thing that was new and different about me. I'd never had long nails until recently, and they were painted a wonderful deep red—cranberry, in fact, to match the coat.

"Thank you," I murmured. "How you been doing?"

"Just fine." He raised a blond eyebrow. Vampires didn't have variable health. He waved a hand at the empty side of the booth, and I slid into it.

"Had any trouble picking up the reins?" I asked, to clarify.

A few weeks previously, a witch had given Eric amnesia, and it had taken several days to restore his sense of identity. During that time, Pam had parked him with me to keep him concealed from the witch who'd cursed him. Lust had taken its course. Many times.

"Like riding a bicycle," Eric said, and I told myself to focus. (Though I wondered when bicycles had been invented, and if Eric had had anything to do with it.) "I did receive a call from Long Shadow's sire, an American Indian whose name seems to be Hot Rain. I'm sure you remember Long Shadow."

"I was just thinking of him," I said.

Long Shadow had been the first bartender of Fangtasia. He'd been embezzling from Eric, who had coerced me into interrogating the barmaids and other human employees until I discovered the culprit. About two seconds before Long Shadow would have ripped out my throat, Eric had executed the bartender with the traditional wooden stake. Killing another vampire is a very serious thing, I gathered, and Eric had had to pay a stiff fine—to whom, I hadn't known, though now I was sure the money had gone to Hot Rain. If Eric had killed Long Shadow without any justification, other penalties would have come into play. I was content to let those remain a mystery.

"What did Hot Rain want?" I said.

"To let me know that though I had paid him the price set by the arbitrator, he didn't consider himself satisfied."

"Did he want more money?"

"I don't think so. He seemed to think financial recompense was not all he required." Eric shrugged. "As far as I'm concerned, the matter is settled." Eric took a swallow of synthetic blood, leaned back in his chair, and looked at me with unreadable blue eyes. "And so is my little amnesia episode. The crisis is over, the witches are dead, and order is restored in my little piece of Louisiana. How have things been for you?"

"Well, I'm here on business," I said, and I put my business face on.

"What can I do for you, my Sookie?" he asked.

"Sam wants to ask you for something," I said.

"And he sends you to ask for it. Is he very clever or very stupid?" Eric asked himself out loud.

"Neither," I said, trying not to sound snippy. "He's very leg-broken. That is to say, he got his leg broken last night. He got shot."

"How did this come about?" Eric's attention sharpened.

I explained. I shivered a little when I told him Sam and I had been alone, how silent the night had been.

"Arlene was just out of the parking lot. She went on home without knowing a thing. The new cook, Sweetie— she'd just left, too. Someone shot him from the trees north of the parking lot." I shivered again, this time with fear.

"How close were you?"

"Oh," I said, and my voice shook. "I was real close. I'd just turned to . . . then he was . . . There was blood all over."

Eric's face looked hard as marble. "What did you do?"

"Sam had his cell phone in his pocket, thank God, and I held one hand over the hole in his leg and I dialed nine-one-one with the other."

"How is he?"

"Well." I took a deep breath and tried to make myself still. "He's pretty good, all things considered." I'd put that quite calmly. I was proud. "But of course, he's down for a while, and so much . . . so many odd things have been happening at the bar lately. . . . Our substitute bartender, he just can't handle it for more than a couple of nights. Terry's kind of damaged."

"So what's Sam's request?"

"Sam wants to borrow a bartender from you until his leg heals."

"Why's he making this request of me, instead of the packmaster of Shreveport?" Shifters seldom got organized, but the city werewolves had. Eric was right: It would have been far more logical for Sam to make the request of Colonel Flood.

I looked down at my hands wrapped around the ginger ale glass. "Someone's gunning for the shifters and Weres in

Bon Temps," I said. I kept my voice very low. I knew he would hear me through the music and the talk of the bar.

Just then a man lurched up to the booth, a young serviceman from Barksdale Air Force Base, which is a part of the Shreveport area. (I pigeonholed him instantly from his haircut, fitness, and his running buddies, who were more or less clones.) He rocked on his heels for a long moment, looking from me to Eric.

"Hey, you," the young man said to me, poking my shoulder. I looked up at him, resigned to the inevitable. Some people court their own disaster, especially when they drink. This young man, with his buzz haircut and sturdy build, was far from home and determined to prove himself.

There's not much I dislike more than being addressed as "Hey, you" and being poked with a finger. But I tried to present a pleasant face to the young man. He had a round face and round dark eyes, a small mouth and thick brown brows. He was wearing a clean knit shirt and pressed khakis. He was also primed for a confrontation.

"I don't believe I know you," I said gently, trying to defuse the situation.

"You shouldn't be sitting with a vamp," he said. "Human girls shouldn't go with dead guys."

How often had I heard that? I'd gotten an earful of this kind of crap when I'd been dating Bill Compton.

"You should go back over there to your friends, Dave. You don't want your mama to get a phone call about you being killed in a bar fight in Louisiana. Especially not in a vampire bar, right?"

"How'd you know my name?" he asked slowly.

"Doesn't make any difference, does it?"

From the corner of my eye, I could see that Eric was shaking his head. Mild deflection was not his way of dealing with intrusion.

Abruptly, Dave began to simmer down.

"How'd you know about me?" he asked in a calmer voice.

"I have x-ray vision," I said solemnly. "I can read your driver's license in your pants."

He began to smile. "Hey, can you see other stuff through my pants?"

I smiled back at him. "You're a lucky man, Dave," I said ambiguously. "Now, I'm actually here to talk business with this guy, so if you'd excuse us . . ."

"Okay. Sorry, I . . ."

"No problem at all," I assured him. He went back to his friends, walking cocky. I was sure he'd give them a highly embellished account of the conversation.

Though everyone in the bar had tried to pretend they weren't watching the incident, which had so much potential for some juicy violence, they had to scramble to look busy when Eric's eyes swept the surrounding tables.

"You were starting to tell me something when we were so rudely interrupted," he said. Without my asking, a barmaid came up and deposited a fresh drink in front of me, whisking my old glass away. Anyone sitting with Eric got the deluxe treatment.

"Yes. Sam isn't the only shape-shifter who's been shot in Bon Temps lately. Calvin Norris was shot in the chest a few days ago. He's a werepanther. And Heather Kinman was shot before that. Heather was just nineteen, a werefox."

Eric said, "I still don't see why this is interesting."

"Eric, she was killed."

He still looked inquiring.

I clenched my teeth together so I wouldn't try to tell him what a nice girl Heather Kinman had been: She'd just graduated from high school and she was working at her first job as a clerk at Bon Temps Office Supplies. She'd been drinking a milkshake at the Sonic when she'd been shot. Today, the crime lab would be comparing the bullet that had shot Sam with the bullet that had killed Heather, and both of those with the bullet from Calvin's chest. I assumed the bullets would match.

"I'm trying to explain to you why Sam doesn't want to ask another shape-shifter or Were to step in to help," I said through clenched teeth. "He thinks that might be putting him or her in danger. And there's just not a local human who's got the qualifications for the job. So he asked me to come to you."

"When I stayed at your house, Sookie . . ."

I groaned. "Oh, Eric, give it a *rest*."

It griped Eric's butt that he couldn't remember what had happened while he was cursed. "Someday I'll remember," he said almost sullenly.

When he remembered everything, he wouldn't just recall the sex.

He'd also recall the woman who'd been waiting in my kitchen with a gun. He'd remember that he'd saved my life by taking the bullet meant for me. He'd remember that I'd shot her. He'd remember disposing of the body.

He'd realize that he had power over me forever.

He might also recall that he'd humbled himself enough to offer to abandon all his businesses and come to live with me.

The sex, he'd enjoy remembering. The power, he'd enjoy remembering. But somehow I didn't think Eric would enjoy remembering that last bit.

"Yes," I said quietly, looking down at my hands. "Someday, I expect you will remember." WDED was playing an old Bob Seger song, "Night Moves." I noticed Pam was twirling unself-consciously in her own dance, her unnaturally strong and limber body bending and twisting in ways human bodies couldn't.

I'd like to see her dance to live vampire music. You ought

to hear a vampire band. You'll never forget that. They mostly play New Orleans and San Francisco, sometimes Savannah or Miami. But when I'd been dating Bill, he'd taken me to hear a group playing in Fangtasia for one night while making their way south to New Orleans. The lead singer of the vampire band—Renfield's Masters, they'd called themselves—had wept tears of blood as he sang a ballad.

"Sam was clever to send you to ask me," Eric said after a long pause. I had nothing to say to that. "I'll spare someone." I could feel my shoulders relax with relief. I focused on my hands and took a deep breath. When I glanced over at him, Eric was looking around the bar, considering the vampires present.

I'd met most of them in passing. Thalia had long black ringlets down her back and a profile that could best be described as classical. She had a heavy accent—Greek, I thought—and she also had a hasty temper. Indira was a tiny Indian vamp, complete with doe eyes and tikal; no one would take her seriously until things got out of hand. Maxwell Lee was an African-American investment banker. Though strong as any vampire, Maxwell tended to enjoy more cerebral pastimes than acting as a bouncer.

"What if I send Charles?" Eric sounded casual, but I knew him well enough to suspect he wasn't.

"Or Pam," I said. "Or anyone else who can keep their temper." I watched Thalia crush a metal mug with her fingers to impress a human male who was trying to put the moves on her. He blanched and scurried back to his table. Some vampires enjoy human company, but Thalia was not one of them.

"Charles is the least temperamental vampire I've ever met, though I confess I don't know him well. He's been working here only two weeks."

"You seem to be keeping him busy here."

"I can spare him." Eric gave me a haughty look that said quite clearly it was up to him to decide how busy he wanted to keep his employee.

"Um . . . okeydokey." The patrons of Merlotte's would like the pirate just fine, and Sam's revenue would jump in consequence.

"Here are the terms," Eric said, fixing me with his gaze. "Sam supplies unlimited blood for Charles and a secure place to stay. You might want to keep him in your house, as you did me."

"And I might not," I said indignantly. "I'm not running any hostel for traveling vampires." Frank Sinatra began to croon "Strangers in the Night" in the background.

"Oh, of course, I forgot. But you were generously paid for my board."

He'd touched on a sore spot. In fact, he'd poked it with a sharp stick. I flinched. "That was my brother's idea," I said. I saw Eric's eyes flash, and I flushed all over. I'd just confirmed a suspicion he'd had. "But he was absolutely right," I said with conviction. "Why should I have put a vampire up in my house without getting paid? After all, I needed the money."

"Is the fifty thousand already gone?" Eric said very quietly. "Did Jason ask for a share of it?"

"None of your business," I said, my voice exactly as sharp and indignant as I'd intended it to be. I'd given Jason only a fifth of it. He hadn't exactly asked, either, though I had to admit to myself he'd clearly expected me to give him some. Since I needed it a lot worse, I'd kept more of it than I'd initially planned.

I had no health insurance. Jason, of course, was covered through the parish plan. I'd begun thinking, *What if I was disabled? What if I broke my arm or had to have my appendix out?* Not only would I not put in my hours at work, but I'd have hospital bills. And any stay in a hospital, in this day and age, is an expensive one. I'd incurred a few medical bills during the past year, and it had taken me a long, painful time to pay them off.

Now I was profoundly glad I'd had that twinge of caution. In the normal course of things, I don't look real far ahead, because I'm used to living day to day. But Sam's injury had opened my eyes. I'd been thinking of how badly I needed a new car—well, a newer secondhand one. I'd been thinking of how dingy the living room drapes were, how pleasant it would be to order new ones from JCPenney. It had even crossed my mind that it would be a lot of fun to buy a dress that wasn't on sale. But I'd been shocked out of such frivolity when Sam had his leg broken.

As Connie the Corpse introduced the next song ("One of These Nights"), Eric examined my face. "I wish that I could read your mind as you can read the minds of others," he said. "I wish very much that I could know what was going on in your head. I wish I knew why I cared what's going on in that head."

I gave him a lopsided smile. "I agree to the terms: free blood and lodging, though the lodging won't necessarily be with me. What about the money?"

Eric smiled. "I'll take my payment in kind. I like Sam owing me a favor."

I called Sam with the cell phone he'd lent me. I explained.

Sam sounded resigned. "There's a place in the bar the vamp can sleep. All right. Room and board, and a favor. When can he come?"

I relayed the question to Eric.

"Right now." Eric beckoned to a human waitress, who was wearing the low-cut long black dress all the female human employees wore. (I'll tell you something about vampires: They don't like to wait tables. And they're pretty poor at it, too. You won't catch a vamp bussing tables, either. The vamps almost always hire humans to do the grubbier work at their establishments.) Eric told her to fetch Charles from behind the bar. She bowed, fist to her opposite shoulder, and said, "Yes, Master."

Honestly, it just about made you sick.

Anyway, Charles leapt over the bar theatrically, and while patrons applauded, he made his way to Eric's booth.

Bowing to me, he turned to Eric with an air of attentiveness that should have seemed subservient but instead seemed simply matter-of-fact.

"This woman will tell you what to do. As long as she needs you, she is your master." I just couldn't decipher Charles Twining's expression as he heard Eric's directive. Lots of vampires simply wouldn't agree to being at a human's beck and call, no matter what their head honcho said.

"No, Eric!" I was shocked. "If you make him answerable to anyone, it should be Sam."

"Sam sent you. I'm entrusting Charles's direction to you." Eric's face closed down. I knew from experience that once Eric got that expression, there was no arguing with him.

I couldn't see where this was going, but I knew it wasn't good.

"Let me get my coat, and I'll be ready anytime it pleases you to leave," Charles Twining said, bowing in a courtly and gracious way that made me feel like an idiot. I made a strangled noise in acknowledgment, and though he was still in the down position, his patch-free eye rolled up to give me a wink. I smiled involuntarily and felt much better.

Over the music system, Connie the Corpse said, "Hey, you night listeners. Continuing ten in a row for us genuine deadheads, here's a favorite." Connie began playing "Here Comes the Night," and Eric said, "Will you dance?"

I looked over at the little dance floor. It was empty.

However, Eric had arranged for a bartender and bouncer for Sam as Sam had asked. I should be gracious. "Thank you," I said politely, and slid out of the booth. Eric offered me his hand, I took it, and he put his other hand on my waist.

Despite the difference in our heights, we managed quite well. I pretended I didn't know everyone in the bar was looking at us, and we glided along as if we knew what we were doing. I focused on Eric's throat so I wouldn't be looking up into his eyes.

When the dance was over, he said, "Holding you seems very familiar, Sookie."

With a tremendous effort, I kept my eyes fixed on his Adam's apple. I had a dreadful impulse to say, "You told me you loved me and would stay with me forever."

"You wish," I said briskly instead. I let go of his hand as quickly as I could and stepped away from his embrace. "By the way, have you ever run across a kind of mean-looking vampire named Mickey?"

Eric grabbed my hand again and squeezed it. I said, "Ow!" and he eased up.

"He was in here last week. Where have you seen Mickey?" he demanded.

"In Merlotte's." I was astonished at the effect my last-minute question had had on Eric. "What's the deal?"

"What was he doing?"

"Drinking Red Stuff and sitting at a table with my friend Tara. You know, you saw her? At Club Dead, in Jackson?"

"When I saw her she was under the protection of Franklin Mott."

"Well, they were dating. I can't understand why he'd let her go out with Mickey. I hoped maybe Mickey was just there as her bodyguard or something." I retrieved my coat from the booth. "So, what's the bottom line on this guy?" I asked.

"Stay away from him. Don't talk to him, don't cross him, and don't try to help your friend Tara. When he was here, Mickey talked mostly to Charles. Charles tells me he is a rogue. He's capable of . . . things that are barbarous. Don't go around Tara."

I opened my hands, asking Eric to explain.

"He'll do things the rest of us won't," Eric said.

I stared up at Eric, shocked and deeply worried. "I can't just ignore her situation. I don't have so many friends that I can afford to let one go down the drain."

"If she's involved with Mickey, she's just meat on the hoof," Eric said with a brutal simplicity. He took my coat from me and held it while I slid into it. His hands massaged my shoulders after I'd buttoned it.

"It fits well," he said. It didn't take a mind reader to guess that he didn't want to say any more about Mickey.

"You got my thank-you note?"

"Of course. Very, ah, seemly."

I nodded, hoping to indicate this was the end of the subject. But, of course, it wasn't.

"I still wonder why your old coat had bloodstains on it," Eric murmured, and my eyes flashed up to his. I cursed my carelessness once again. When he'd come back to thank me for keeping him, he'd roamed the house while I was busy until he'd come across the coat. "What did we do, Sookie? And to whom?"

"It was chicken blood. I killed a chicken and cooked it," I lied. I'd seen my grandmother do that when I was little, many a time, but I'd never done it myself.

"Sookie, Sookie. My bullshit meter is reading that as a 'false,'" Eric said, shaking his head in a chiding way.

I was so startled I laughed. It was a good note on which to leave. I could see Charles Twining standing by the front door, thoroughly modern padded jacket at the ready. "Good-bye,

Eric, and thanks for the bartender," I said, as if Eric had loaned me some AA batteries or a cup of rice. He bent and brushed my cheek with his cool lips.

"Drive safely," he said. "And stay away from Mickey. I need to find out why he's in my territory. Call me if you have any problems with Charles." (If the batteries are defective, or if the rice is full of worms.) Beyond him I could see the same woman was still sitting at the bar, the one who'd remarked that I was no maiden. She was obviously wondering what I had done to secure the attention of a vampire as ancient and attractive as Eric.

I often wondered the same thing.

4

THE DRIVE BACK TO BON TEMPS WAS PLEASANT. Vampires don't smell like humans or act like humans, but they're sure relaxing to my brain. Being with a vampire is almost as tension-free as being alone, except, of course, for the blood-sucking possibilities.

Charles Twining asked a few questions about the work for which he'd been hired and about the bar. My driving seemed to make him a little uneasy—though possibly his unease was due to simply being in a car. Some of the pre–Industrial Revolution vamps loathe modern transportation. His eye patch was on his left eye, on my side, which gave me the curious feeling I was invisible.

I'd run him by the vampire hostel where he'd been living so he could gather a few things. He had a sports bag with him, one large enough to hold maybe three days' worth of clothes. He'd just moved into Shreveport, he told me, and hadn't had time to decide where he would settle.

After we'd been on our way for about forty minutes, the vampire said, "And you, Miss Sookie? Do you live with your father and mother?"

"No, they've been gone since I was seven," I said. Out of the corner of my eye, I caught a hand gesture inviting me to continue. "There was a whole lot of rain in a real short time one night that spring, and my dad tried to cross a little bridge that had water already over it. They got swept away."

I glanced to my right to see that he was nodding. People died, sometimes suddenly and unexpectedly, and sometimes for very little reason. A vampire knew that better than anyone. "My brother and I grew up with my grandmother," I said. "She died last year. My brother has my parents' old house, and I have my grandmother's."

"Lucky to have a place to live," he commented.

In profile, his hooked nose was an elegant miniature. I wondered if he cared that the human race had gotten larger, while he had stayed the same.

"Oh, yes," I agreed. "I'm major lucky. I've got a job, I've got my brother, I've got a house, I've got friends. And I'm healthy."

He turned to look at me full-face, I think, but I was passing a battered Ford pickup, so I couldn't return his gaze. "That's interesting. Forgive me, but I was under the impression from Pam that you have some kind of disability."

"Oh, well, yeah."

"And that would be . . . ? You look very, ah, robust."

"I'm a telepath."

He mulled that over. "And that would mean?"

"I can read other humans' minds."

"But not vampires."

"No, not vampires."

"Very good."

"Yes, I think so." If I could read vampire minds, I'd have been dead long ago. Vampires value their privacy.

"Did you know Chow?" he asked.

"Yes." It was my turn to be terse.

"And Long Shadow?"

"Yes."

"As the newest bartender at Fangtasia, I have a definite interest in their deaths."

Understandable, but I had no idea how to respond. "Okay," I said cautiously.

"Were you there when Chow died again?" This was the way some vamps referred to the final death.

"Um . . . yes."

"And Long Shadow?"

"Well . . . yes."

"I would be interested in hearing what you had to say."

"Chow died in what they're calling the Witch War. Long Shadow was trying to kill me when Eric staked him because he'd been embezzling."

"You're sure that's why Eric staked him? For embezzling?"

"I was there. I oughta know. End of subject."

"I suppose your life has been complicated," Charles said after a pause.

"Yes."

"Where will I be spending the sunlight hours?"

"My boss has a place for you."

"There is a lot of trouble at this bar?"

"Not until recently." I hesitated.

"Your regular bouncer can't handle shifters?"

"Our regular bouncer is the owner, Sam Merlotte. He is a shifter. Right now, he's a shifter with a broken leg. He got shot. And he's not the only one."

This didn't seem to astonish the vampire. "How many?"

"Three that I know of. A werepanther named Calvin

Norris, who wasn't mortally wounded, and then a shifter girl named Heather Kinman, who's dead. She was shot at the Sonic. Do you know what Sonic is?" Vampires didn't always pay attention to fast-food restaurants, because they didn't eat. (Hey, how many blood banks can you locate off the top of your head?)

Charles nodded, his curly chestnut hair bouncing on his shoulders. "That's the one where you eat in your car?"

"Yes, right," I said. "Heather had been in a friend's car, talking, and she got out to walk back to her car a few slots down. The shot came from across the street. She had a milk-shake in her hand." The melting chocolate ice cream had blended with blood on the pavement. I'd seen it in Andy Bellefleur's mind. "It was late at night, and all the businesses on the other side of the street had been closed for hours. So the shooter got away."

"All three shootings were at night?"

"Yes."

"I wonder if that's significant."

"Could be; but maybe it's just that there's better conceal-ment at night."

Charles nodded.

"Since Sam got hurt, there's been a lot of anxiety among the shifters because it's hard to believe three shootings could be a coincidence. And regular humans are worried because in their view three people have been shot at random, people with nothing in common and few enemies. Since everyone's tense, there are more fights in the bar."

"I've never been a bouncer before," Charles said conversa-tionally. "I was the youngest son of a minor baronet, so I've had to make my own way, and I've done many things. I've worked as a bartender before, and many years ago I was shill for a whorehouse. Stood outside, trumpeted the wares of the strumpets—that's a neat phrase, isn't it?—threw out men who got too rough with the whores. I suppose that's the same as being a bouncer."

I was speechless at this unexpected confidence.

"Of course, that was after I lost my eye, but before I became a vampire," the vampire said.

"Of course," I echoed weakly.

"Which was while I was a pirate," he continued. He was smiling. I checked with a sideways glance.

"What did you, um, pirate?" I didn't know if that was a verb or not, but he got my meaning clearly.

"Oh, we'd try to catch almost anyone unawares," he said blithely. "Off and on I lived on the coast of America, down close to New Orleans, where we'd take small cargo ships and the like. I sailed aboard a small hoy, so we couldn't take on too large or well defended a ship. But when we caught up with some bark, then there was fighting!" He sighed— recalling the happiness of whacking at people with a sword, I guess.

"And what happened to you?" I asked politely, meaning how did he come to depart his wonderful warm-blooded life of rapine and slaughter for the vampire edition of the same thing.

"One evening, we boarded a galleon that had no living crew," he said. I noticed that his hands had curled into fists. His voice chilled. "We had sailed to the Tortugas. It was dusk. I was first man to go down into the hold. What was in the hold got me first."

After that little tale, we fell silent by mutual consent.

Sam was on the couch in the living room of his trailer. Sam had had the double-wide anchored so it was at a right angle to the back of the bar. That way, at least he opened his front door to a view of the parking lot, which was better than looking at the back of the bar, with its large garbage bin between the kitchen door and the employees' entrance.

"Well, there you are," Sam said, and his tone was grumpy. Sam was never one for sitting still. Now that his leg was in a cast, he was fretting from the inactivity. What would he do during the next full moon? Would the leg be healed enough by then for him to change? If he changed, what would happen to the cast? I'd known other injured shape-shifters before, but I hadn't been around for their recuperation, so this was new territory for me. "I was beginning to think you'd gotten lost on the way back." Sam's voice returned me to the here and now. It had a distinct edge.

" 'Gee, thanks, Sookie, I see you returned with a bouncer,' " I said. " 'I'm so sorry you had to go through the humiliating experience of asking Eric for a favor on my behalf.' " At that moment, I didn't care if he was my boss or not.

Sam looked embarrassed.

"Eric agreed, then," he said. He nodded at the pirate.

"Charles Twining, at your service," said the vampire.

Sam's eyes widened. "Okay. I'm Sam Merlotte, owner of the bar. I appreciate your coming to help us out here."

"I was ordered to do so," the vampire said coolly.

"So the deal you struck was room, board, and favor," Sam said to me. "I owe Eric a favor." This was said in a tone that a kind person would describe as grudging.

"Yes." I was mad now. "You sent me to make a deal. I checked the terms with you! That's the deal I made. You asked Eric for a favor; now he gets a favor in return. No matter what you told yourself, that's what it boils down to."

Sam nodded, though he didn't look happy. "Also, I changed my mind. I think Mr. Twining, here, should stay with you."

"And why would you think that?"

"The closet looked a little cramped. You have a light-tight place for vampires, right?"

"You didn't ask me if that was okay."

"You're refusing to do it?"

"Yes! I'm not the vampire hotel keeper!"

"But you work for me, and he works for me . . ."

"Uh-huh. And would you ask Arlene or Holly to put him up?"

Sam looked even more amazed. "Well, no, but that's because—" He stopped then.

"Can't think of how to finish the sentence, can you?" I snarled. "Okay, buddy, I'm out of here. I spent a whole evening putting myself in an embarrassing situation for you. And what do I get? *No effing thanks!*"

I stomped out of the double-wide. I didn't slam the door because I didn't want to be childish. Door slamming just isn't adult. Neither is whining. Okay, maybe stomping out isn't, either. But it was a choice between making an emphatic verbal exit or slapping Sam. Normally Sam was one of my favorite people in the world, but tonight . . . not.

I was working the early shift for the next three days—not that I was sure I had a job anymore. When I got into Merlotte's at eleven the next morning, dashing to the employees' door through the pouring rain in my ugly but useful rain slicker, I was nearly sure that Sam would tell me to collect my last paycheck and hit the door. But he wasn't there. I had a moment of what I recognized as disappointment. Maybe I'd been spoiling for another fight, which was odd.

Terry Bellefleur was standing in for Sam again, and Terry was having a bad day. It wasn't a good idea to ask him questions or even to talk to him beyond the necessary relay of orders.

Terry particularly hated rainy weather, I'd noticed, and he also didn't like Sheriff Bud Dearborn. I didn't know the reason for either prejudice. Today, gray sheets of rain battered at the walls and roof, and Bud Dearborn was pontificating to five of his cronies over on the smoking side. Arlene caught my eye and widened her eyes to give me a warning.

Though Terry was pale, and perspiring, he'd zipped up the light jacket he often wore over his Merlotte's T-shirt. I noticed his hands shaking as he pulled a draft beer. I wondered if he could last until dark.

At least there weren't many customers, if something did go wrong. Arlene drifted over to catch up with a married couple who'd come in, friends of hers. My section was almost empty, with the exception of my brother, Jason, and his friend Hoyt.

Hoyt was Jason's sidekick. If they weren't both definitely heterosexual, I would have recommended they marry, they complemented each other so well. Hoyt enjoyed jokes, and Jason enjoyed telling them. Hoyt was at a loss to fill his free time, and Jason was always up to something. Hoyt's mother was a little overwhelming, and Jason was parent-free. Hoyt was firmly anchored in the here and now, and had an iron sense of what the community would tolerate and what it would not. Jason didn't.

I thought of what a huge secret Jason now had, and I wondered if he was tempted to share it with Hoyt.

"How you doing, Sis?" Jason asked. He held up his glass, indicating he'd like a refill on his Dr Pepper. Jason didn't drink until after his workday was over, a large point in his favor.

"Fine, Brother. You want some more, Hoyt?" I asked.

"Please, Sookie. Ice tea," Hoyt said.

In a second I was back with their drinks. Terry glared at me when I went behind the bar, but he didn't speak. I can ignore a glare.

"Sook, you want to go with me to the hospital in Grainger this afternoon after you get off?" Jason asked.

"Oh," I said. "Yeah, sure." Calvin had always been good to me.

Hoyt said, "Sure is crazy, Sam and Calvin and Heather getting shot. What do you make of it, Sookie?" Hoyt has decided I am an oracle.

"Hoyt, you know as much about it as I do," I told him. "I think we all should be careful." I hoped the significance of this wasn't lost on my brother. He shrugged.

When I looked up, I saw a stranger waiting to be seated and hurried over to him. His dark hair, turned black by the rain, was pulled back in a ponytail. His face was scarred with one long thin white line that ran along one cheek. When he pulled off his jacket, I could see that he was a bodybuilder.

"Smoking or non?" I asked, with a menu already in my hand.

"Non," he said, and followed me to a table. He carefully hung his wet jacket on the back of a chair and took the menu after he was seated. "My wife will be along in a few minutes," he said. "She's meeting me here."

I put another menu at the adjacent place. "Do you want to order now or wait for her?"

"I'd like some hot tea," he asked. "I'll wait until she comes to order food. Kind of a limited menu here, huh?" He glanced over at Arlene and then back at me. I began to feel uneasy. I knew he wasn't here because this place was convenient for lunch.

"That's all we can handle," I said, taking care to sound relaxed. "What we've got, it's good."

When I assembled the hot water and a tea bag, I put a saucer with a couple of lemon slices on the tray, too. No fairies around to offend.

"Are you Sookie Stackhouse?" he asked when I returned with his tea.

"Yes, I am." I put the saucer gently on the table, right beside the cup. "Why do you want to know?" I already knew why, but with regular people, you had to ask.

"I'm Jack Leeds, a private investigator," he said. He laid a business card on the table, turned so I could read it. He waited for a beat, as if he usually got a dramatic reaction to that statement. "I've been hired by a family in Jackson, Mississippi—the Pelt family," he continued, when he saw I wasn't going to speak.

My heart sank to my shoes before it began pounding at an accelerated rate. This man believed that Debbie was dead. And he thought there was a good chance I might know something about it.

He was absolutely right.

I'd shot Debbie Pelt dead a few weeks before, in self-defense. Hers was the body Eric had hidden. Hers was the bullet Eric had taken for me.

Debbie's disappearance after leaving a "party" in Shreveport, Louisiana (in fact a life-and-death brawl between witches, vamps, and Weres), had been a nine days' wonder. I'd hoped I'd heard the end of it.

"So the Pelts aren't satisfied with the police investigation?" I asked. It was a stupid question, one I picked out of the air at random. I had to say something to break up the gathering silence.

"There really wasn't an investigation," Jack Leeds said. "The police in Jackson decided she probably vanished voluntarily." He didn't believe that, though.

His face changed then; it was like someone had switched on a light behind his eyes. I turned to look where he was looking, and I saw a blond woman of medium height shaking her umbrella out at the door. She had short hair and pale skin, and when she turned, I saw that she was very pretty; at least, she would have been if she had been more animated.

But that wasn't a factor to Jack Leeds. He was looking at the woman he loved, and when she saw him, the same light switched on behind her eyes, too. She came across the floor to his table as smoothly as if she were dancing, and when she shed her own wet jacket, I saw her arms were as muscular as his. They didn't kiss, but his hand slid over hers and squeezed just briefly. After she'd taken her chair and asked for some diet Coke, her eyes went to the menu. She was thinking that all the food Merlotte's offered was unhealthy. She was right.

"Salad?" Jack Leeds asked.

"I have to have something hot," she said. "Chili?"

"Okay. Two chilis," he told me. "Lily, this is Sookie Stackhouse. Ms. Stackhouse, this is Lily Bard Leeds."

"Hello," she said. "I've just been out to your house."

Her eyes were light blue, and she had a stare like a laser. "You saw Debbie Pelt the night she disappeared." Her mind added, *You're the one she hated so much.*

They didn't know Debbie Pelt's true nature, and I was relieved that the Pelts hadn't been able to find a Were investigator. They wouldn't out their daughter to regular detectives. The longer the two-natured could keep the fact of their existence a secret, the better, as far as they were concerned.

"Yes," I said. "I saw her that night."

"Can we come talk to you about that? After you get off work?"

"I have to go see a friend in the hospital after work," I said.

"Sick?" Jack Leeds asked.

"Shot," I said.

Their interest quickened. "By someone local?" the blond woman asked.

Then I saw how it might all work. "By a sniper," I said. "Someone's been shooting people at random in this area."

"Have any of them vanished?" Jack Leeds asked.

"No," I admitted. "They've all been left lying. Of course, there were witnesses to all of the shootings. Maybe that's why." I hadn't heard of anyone actually seeing Calvin get shot, but someone had come along right afterward and called 911.

Lily Leeds asked me if they could talk to me the next day before I went to work. I gave them directions to my house and told them to come at ten. I didn't think talking to them was a very good idea, but I didn't think I had much of a choice, either. I would become more of an object of suspicion if I refused to talk about Debbie.

I found myself wishing I could call Eric tonight and tell him about Jack and Lily Leeds; worries shared are worries halved. But Eric didn't remember any of it. I wished that I could forget Debbie's death, too. It was awful to know something so heavy and terrible, to be unable to share it with a soul.

I knew so many secrets, but almost none of them were my own. This secret of mine was a dark and bloody burden.

Charles Twining was due to relieve Terry at full dark. Arlene was working late, since Danielle was attending her daughter's dance recital, and I was able to lighten my mood a little by briefing Arlene on the new bartender/bouncer. She was intrigued. We'd never had an Englishman visit the bar, much less an Englishman with an eye patch.

"Tell Charles I said hi," I called as I began to put on my rain gear. After a couple of hours of sprinkling, the drops were beginning to come faster again.

I splashed out to my car, the hood pulled well forward over my face. Just as I unlocked the driver's door and pulled it open, I heard a voice call my name. Sam was standing on crutches in the door of his trailer. He'd added a roofed porch a couple of years before, so he wasn't getting wet, but he didn't need to be standing there, either. Slamming the car door shut, I leaped over puddles and across the stepping-stones. In a second or two, I was standing on his porch and dripping all over it.

"I'm sorry," he said.

I stared at him. "You should be," I said gruffly.

"Well, I am."

"Okay. Good." I resolutely didn't ask him what he'd done with the vampire.

"Anything happen over at the bar today?"

I hesitated. "Well, the crowd was thin, to put it mildly. But . . ." I started to tell him about the private detectives, but then I knew he'd ask questions. And I might end up telling him the whole sorry story just for the relief of confessing to someone. "I have to go, Sam. Jason's taking me to visit Calvin Norris in the hospital in Grainger."

He looked at me. His eyes narrowed. The lashes were the same red-gold as his hair, so they showed up only when you were close to him. And I had no business at all thinking about Sam's eyelashes, or any other part of him, for that matter.

"I was a shit yesterday," he said. "I don't have to tell you why."

"Well, I guess you do," I said, bewildered. "Because I sure don't understand."

"The point is, you know you can count on me."

To get mad at me for no reason? To apologize afterward? "You've really confused me a lot lately," I said. "But you've been my friend for years, and I have a very high opinion of you." That sounded way too stilted, so I tried smiling. He smiled back, and a drop of rain fell off my hood and splashed on my nose, and the moment was over. I said, "When do you think you'll get back to the bar?"

"I'll try to come in tomorrow for a while," he said. "At least I can sit in the office and work on the books, get some filing done."

"See you."

"Sure."

And I dashed back to my car, feeling that my heart was much lighter than it had been before. Being at odds with Sam had felt wrong. I didn't realize how that wrongness had colored my thoughts until I was right with him again.

5

THE RAIN PELTED DOWN AS WE PULLED IN TO THE parking lot of the Grainger hospital. It was as small as the one in Clarice, the one most Renard Parish people were carried to. But the Grainger hospital was newer and had more of the diagnostic machines modern hospitals seemed to require.

I'd changed into jeans and a sweater, but I'd resumed wearing my lined slicker. As Jason and I hurried to the sliding glass doors, I was patting myself on the back for wearing boots. Weather-wise, the evening was proving as nasty as the morning had been.

The hospital was roiling with shifters. I could feel their anger as soon as I was inside. Two of the werepanthers from Hotshot were in the lobby; I figured they were acting as guards. Jason went to them and took their hands firmly. Maybe he exchanged some kind of secret shake or something;

I don't know. At least they didn't rub against one another's legs. They didn't seem quite as happy to see Jason as he was to see them, and I noticed that Jason stepped back from them with a little frown between his eyes. The two looked at me intently. The man was of medium height and stocky, and he had thick brownish-blond hair. His eyes were full of curiosity.

"Sook, this is Dixon Mayhew," Jason said. "And this is Dixie Mayhew, his twin sister." Dixie wore her hair, the same color as her brother's, almost as short as Dixon's, but she had dark, almost black, eyes. The twins were certainly not identical.

"Has it been quiet here?" I asked carefully.

"No problems so far," Dixie said, keeping her voice low. Dixon's gaze was fixed on Jason. "How's your boss?"

"He's in a cast, but he'll heal."

"Calvin was shot bad." Dixie eyed me for a minute. "He's up in 214."

Having been given the seal of approval, Jason and I went to the stairs. The twins watched us all the way. We passed the hospital auxiliary "pink lady" on duty at the visitors' desk. I felt kind of worried about her: white-haired, heavy glasses, sweet face with a full complement of wrinkles. I hoped nothing would happen during her watch to upset her worldview.

It was easy to pick which room was Calvin's. A slab of muscle was leaning against the wall outside, a barrel-shaped man I'd never seen. He was a werewolf. Werewolves make good bodyguards, according to the common wisdom of the two-natured, because they are ruthless and tenacious. From what I've seen, that's just the bad-boy image Weres have. But it's true that as a rule, they're the roughest element of the two-natured community. You won't find too many Were doctors, for example, but you will find a lot of Weres in construction work. Jobs relating to motorcycles are heavily dominated by Weres, too. Some of those gangs do more than drink beer on the full-moon nights.

Seeing a Were disturbed me. I was surprised the panthers of Hotshot had brought in an outsider. Jason murmured, "That's Dawson. He owns the small engine repair shop between Hotshot and Grainger."

Dawson was on the alert as we came down the hall.

"Jason Stackhouse," he said, identifying my brother after a minute. Dawson was wearing a denim shirt and jeans, but his biceps were about to burst through the material. His black leather boots were battle scarred.

"We've come to see how Calvin is doing," Jason said. "This here's my sister, Sookie."

"Ma'am," Dawson rumbled. He eyeballed me slowly, and there wasn't anything lascivious about it. I was glad I'd left my purse in the locked truck. He would've gone through it, I was sure. "You want to take off that coat and turn around for me?"

I didn't take offense; Dawson was doing his job. I didn't want Calvin to get hurt again, either. I took off my slicker, handed it to Jason, and rotated. A nurse who'd been entering something in a chart watched this procedure with open curiosity. I held Jason's jacket as he took his turn. Satisfied, Dawson knocked on the door. Though I didn't hear a response, he must have, because he opened the door and said, "The Stackhouses."

Just a whisper of a voice came from the room. Dawson nodded.

"Miss Stackhouse, you can go in," he said. Jason started to follow me, but Dawson put a massive arm in front of him. "Only your sister," he said.

Jason and I began to protest at the same moment, but then Jason shrugged. "Go ahead, Sook," he said. There was obviously no budging Dawson, and there was no point to upsetting a wounded man, for that matter. I pushed the heavy door wide open.

Calvin was by himself, though there was another bed in the room. The panther leader looked awful. He was pale and drawn. His hair was dirty, though his cheeks above his trim beard had been shaved. He was wearing a hospital gown, and he was hooked up to lots of things.

"I'm so sorry," I blurted. I was horrified. Though many brains had indicated as much, I could see that if Calvin hadn't been two-natured, the wound would have killed him instantly. Whoever had shot him had wanted his death.

Calvin turned his head to me, slowly and with effort. "It's not as bad as it looks," he said dryly, his voice a thread. "They're going to take me off some of this stuff tomorrow."

"Where were you hit?" I asked.

Calvin moved one hand to touch his upper left chest. His golden brown eyes captured mine. I went closer to him and covered his hand with mine. "I'm so sorry," I said again. His fingers curled under mine until he was holding my hand.

"There've been others," he said in a whisper of a voice.

"Yes."

"Your boss."

I nodded.

"That poor girl."

I nodded again.

"Whoever's doing this, they've got to be stopped."

"Yes."

"It's got to be someone who hates shifters. The police will never find out who's doing this. We can't tell them what to look for."

Well, that was part of the problem of keeping your condition a secret. "It'll be harder for them to find the person," I conceded. "But maybe they will."

"Some of my people wonder if the shooter is someone

who's a shifter," Calvin said. His fingers tightened around mine. "Someone who didn't want to become a shifter in the first place. Someone who was bitten."

It took a second for the light to click on in my head. I am such an idiot.

"Oh, no, Calvin, no, no," I said, my words stumbling over each other in my haste. "Oh, Calvin, please don't let them go after Jason. Please, he's all I've got." Tears began to run down my cheeks as if someone had turned on a faucet in my head. "He was telling me how much he enjoyed being one of you, even if he couldn't be exactly like a born panther. He's so new, he hasn't had time to figure out who all else is two-natured. I don't think he even realized Sam and Heather were. . . ."

"No one's gonna take him out until we know the truth," Calvin said. "Though I might be in this bed, I'm still the leader." But I could tell he'd had to argue against it, and I also knew (from hearing it right out of Calvin's brain) that some of the panthers were still in favor of executing Jason. Calvin couldn't prevent that. He might be angry afterward, but if Jason were dead, that wouldn't make one little bit of difference. Calvin's fingers released mine, and his hand rose with an effort to wipe the tears off my cheek.

"You're a sweet woman," he said. "I wish you could love me."

"I wish I could, too," I said. So many of my problems would be solved if I loved Calvin Norris. I'd move out to Hotshot, become a member of the secretive little community. Two or three nights a month, I'd have to be sure to stay inside, but other than that, I'd be safe. Not only would Calvin defend me to the death, but so would the other members of the Hotshot clan.

But the thought of it just made me shudder. The wind-swept open fields, the powerful and ancient crossroads around which the little houses clustered . . . I didn't think I could handle the perpetual isolation from the rest of the world. My Gran would have urged me to accept Calvin's offer. He was a steady man, was a shift leader at Norcross, a job that came with good benefits. You might think that's laughable, but wait until you have to pay for your insurance all by yourself; then laugh.

It occurred to me (as it should have right away) that Calvin was in a perfect position to force my compliance—Jason's life for my companionship—and he hadn't taken advantage of it.

I leaned over and gave Calvin a kiss on the cheek. "I'll pray for your recovery," I said. "Thank you for giving Jason a chance." Maybe Calvin's nobility was partly due to the fact that he was in no shape to take advantage of me, but it was nobility, and I noted and appreciated it. "You're a good man," I said, and touched his face. The hair of his neat beard felt soft.

His eyes were steady as he said good-bye. "Watch out for that brother of yours, Sookie," he said. "Oh, and tell Dawson I don't want no more company tonight."

"He won't take my word for it," I said.

Calvin managed to smile. "Wouldn't be much of a bodyguard if he did, I guess."

I relayed the message to the Were. But sure enough, as Jason and I walked back to the stairs, Dawson was going into the room to check with Calvin.

I debated for a couple of minutes before I decided it would be better if Jason knew what he was up against. In the truck, as he drove home, I relayed my conversation with Calvin to my brother.

He was horrified that his new buddies in the werepanther world could believe such a thing of him. "If I'd thought of that before I changed for the first time, I can't say it wouldn't have been tempting," Jason said as we drove back to Bon Temps through the rain. "I was mad. Not just mad, furious. But now that I've changed, I see it different." He went on and on while my thoughts ran around inside my head in a circle, trying to think of a way out of this mess.

The sniping case had to be solved by the next full moon. If it wasn't, the others might tear Jason up when they changed. Maybe he could just roam the woods around his house when he turned into his panther-man form, or maybe he could hunt the woods around my place—but he wouldn't be safe out at Hotshot. And they might come looking for him. I couldn't defend him against them all.

By the next full moon, the shooter had to be in custody.

Until I was washing my few dishes that night, it didn't strike me as odd that though Jason was being accused by the werepanther community of being an assassin, I was the one who'd actually shot a shifter. I'd been thinking of the private detectives' appointment to meet me here the next morning. And, as I found myself doing out of habit, I'd been scanning the kitchen for signs of the death of Debbie Pelt. From watching the Discovery Channel and the Learning Channel, I knew that there was no way I could completely eradicate the traces of blood and tissue that had spattered my kitchen, but I'd scrubbed and cleaned over and over. I was certain that no casual glance—in fact, no careful inspection by the naked eye—could reveal anything amiss in this room.

I had done the only thing I could, short of standing there to be murdered. Was that what Jesus had meant by turning the other cheek? I hoped not, because every instinct in me had urged me to defend myself, and the means at hand had been a shotgun.

Of course, I should immediately have reported it. But by

then, Eric's wound had healed, the one made when Debbie'd hit him while trying to shoot me. Aside from the testimony of a vampire and myself, there was no proof that she'd fired first, and Debbie's body would have been a powerful statement of our guilt. My first instinct had been to cover up her visit to my house. Eric hadn't given me any other advice, which also might have changed things.

No, I wasn't blaming my predicament on Eric. He hadn't even been in his right mind at the time. It was my own fault that I hadn't sat down to think things through. There would have been gunshot residue on Debbie's hand. Her gun had been fired. Some of Eric's dried blood would have been on the floor. She'd broken in through my front door, and the door had shown clear signs of her trespass. Her car was hidden across the road, and only her fingerprints would've been in it.

I'd panicked, and blown it.

I just had to live with that.

But I was very sorry about the uncertainty her family was suffering. I owed them certainty—which I couldn't deliver.

I wrung out the washcloth and hung it neatly over the sink divider. I dried off my hands and folded the dish towel. Okay, now I'd gotten my guilt straight. That was so much better! *Not.* Angry with myself, I stomped out to the living room and turned on the television: another mistake. There was a story about Heather's funeral; a news crew from Shreveport had come to cover the modest service this afternoon. Just think of the sensation it would cause if the media realized how the sniper was selecting his victims. The news anchor, a solemn African-American man, was saying that police in Renard Parish had discovered other clusters of apparently random shootings in small towns in Tennessee and Mississippi. I was startled. A serial shooter, here?

The phone rang. "Hello," I said, not expecting anything good.

"Sookie, hi, it's Alcide."

I found myself smiling. Alcide Herveaux, who worked in his father's surveying business in Shreveport, was one of my favorite people. He was a Were, he was both sexy and hardworking, and I liked him very much. He'd also been Debbie Pelt's fiancé. But Alcide had abjured her before she vanished, in a rite that made her invisible and inaudible to him—not literally, but in effect.

"Sookie, I'm at Merlotte's. I'd thought you might be working tonight, so I drove over. Can I come to the house? I need to talk to you."

"You know you're in danger, coming to Bon Temps."

"No, why?"

"Because of the sniper." I could hear the bar sounds in the background. There was no mistaking Arlene's laugh. I was betting the new bartender was charming one and all.

"Why would I worry about that?" Alcide hadn't been thinking about the news too hard, I decided.

"All the people who got shot? They were two-natured," I said. "Now they're saying on the news there've been a lot more across the south. Random shootings in small towns. Bullets that match the one recovered from Heather Kinman here. And I'm betting all the other victims were shapeshifters, too."

There was a thoughtful silence on the end of the line, if silence can be characterized.

"I hadn't realized," Alcide said. His deep, rumbly voice was even more deliberate than normal.

"Oh, and have you talked to the private detectives?"

"What? What are you talking about?"

"If they see us talking together, it'll look very suspicious to Debbie's family."

"Debbie's family has hired private eyes to look for her?"

"That's what I'm saying."

"Listen, I'm coming to your house." He hung up the phone.

I didn't know why on earth the detectives would be watching my house, or where they'd watch it from, but if they saw Debbie's former fiancé tootling down my driveway, it would be easy to connect the dots and come up with a totally erroneous picture. They'd think Alcide killed Debbie to clear the way for me, and nothing could be more wrong. I hoped like hell that Jack Leeds and Lily Bard Leeds were sound asleep rather than staked out in the woods somewhere with a pair of binoculars.

Alcide hugged me. He always did. And once again I was overwhelmed by the size of him, the masculinity, the familiar smell. Despite the warning bell ringing in my head, I hugged him back.

We sat on the couch and half turned to face each other. Alcide was wearing work clothes, which in this weather consisted of a flannel shirt worn open over a T-shirt, heavy jeans, and thick socks under his work boots. His tangle of black hair had a crease in it from his hard hat, and he was beginning to look a little bristly.

"Tell me about the detectives," he said, and I described the couple and told him what they'd said.

"Debbie's family didn't say anything to me about it," Alcide said. He turned it over in his head for a minute. I could follow his thinking. "I think that means they're sure I made her vanish."

"Maybe not. Maybe they just think you're so grieved they don't want to bring it up."

"Grieved." Alcide mulled that over for a minute. "No. I spent all the . . ." He paused, grappling for words. "I used up all the energy I had to spare for her," he said finally. "I was so blind, I almost think she used some kind of magic on me. Her mother's a spellcaster and half shifter. Her dad's a full-blooded shifter."

"You think that's possible? Magic?" I wasn't questioning that magic existed, but that Debbie had used it.

"Why else would I stick with her for so long? Ever since she's gone missing, it's been like someone took a pair of dark glasses off my eyes. I was willing to forgive her so much, like when she pushed you into the trunk."

Debbie had taken an opportunity to push me in a car trunk with my vampire boyfriend, Bill, who'd been starved for blood for days. And she'd walked off and left me in the trunk with Bill, who was about to awake.

I looked down at my feet, pushing away the recollection of the desperation, the pain.

"She let you get raped," Alcide said harshly.

Him saying it like that, flat out, shocked me. "Hey, Bill didn't know it was me," I said. "He hadn't had anything to eat for days and days, and the impulses are so closely related. I mean, he stopped, you know? He stopped, when he knew it was me." I couldn't put it like that to myself; I couldn't say that word. I knew beyond a doubt that Bill would rather have chewed off his own hand than done that to me if he'd been in his right mind. At that time, he'd been the only sex partner I'd ever had. My feelings about the incident were so confused that I couldn't even bear to try to pick through them. When I'd thought of rape before, when other girls had told me what had happened to them or I'd read it in their brains, I hadn't had the ambiguity I felt over my own short, awful time in the trunk.

"He did something you didn't want him to do," Alcide said simply.

"He wasn't himself," I said.

"But he did it."

"Yes, he did, and I was awful scared." My voice began to shake. "But he came to his senses, and he *stopped,* and I was okay, and he was really, really sorry. He's never laid a finger on me since then, never asked me if we could have sex, never . . ." My voice trailed off. I stared down at my hands. "Yes, Debbie was responsible for that." Somehow, saying that out loud made me feel better. "She knew what would happen, or at least she didn't care what would happen."

"And even then," Alcide said, returning to his main point, "she kept coming back and I kept trying to rationalize her behavior. I can't believe I would do that if I wasn't under some kind of magical influence."

I wasn't about to try to make Alcide feel guiltier. I had my own load of guilt to carry. "Hey, it's over."

"You sound sure."

I looked Alcide directly in the eyes. His were narrow and green. "Do you think there's the slightest chance that Debbie's alive?" I asked.

"Her family . . ." Alcide stopped. "No, I don't."

I couldn't get rid of Debbie Pelt, dead or alive.

"Why'd you need to talk to me in the first place?" I asked. "You said over the phone you needed to tell me something."

"Colonel Flood died yesterday."

"Oh, I'm so sorry! What happened?"

"He was driving to the store when another driver hit him broadside."

"That's awful. Was anyone in the car with him?"

"No, he was by himself. His kids are coming back to Shreveport for the funeral, of course. I wondered if you'd come to the funeral with me."

"Of course. It's not private?"

"No. He knew so many people still stationed at the Air Force base, and he was head of his Neighborhood Watch group and the treasurer of his church, and of course he was the packmaster."

"He had a big life," I said. "Lots of responsibility."

"It's tomorrow at one. What's your work schedule?"

"If I can swap shifts with someone, I'd need to be back here at four thirty to change and go to work."

"That shouldn't be a problem."

"Who'll be packmaster now?"

"I don't know," Alcide said, but his voice wasn't as neutral as I'd expected.

"Do you want the job?"

"No." He seemed a little hesitant, I thought, and I felt the conflict in his head. "But my father does." He wasn't finished. I waited.

"Were funerals are pretty ceremonial," he said, and I realized he was trying to tell me something. I just wasn't sure what it was.

"Spit it out." Straightforward is always good, as far as I'm concerned.

"If you think you can overdress for this, you can't," he said. "I know the rest of the shifter world thinks Weres only go for leather and chains, but that's not true. For funerals, we go all out." He wanted to give me even more fashion tips, but he stopped there. I could see the thoughts crowding right behind his eyes, wanting to be let out.

"Every woman wants to know what's appropriate to wear," I said. "Thanks. I won't wear pants."

He shook his head. "I know you can do that, but I'm always taken by surprise." I could hear that he was disconcerted. "I'll pick you up at eleven thirty," he said.

"Let me see about swapping shifts."

I called Holly and found it suited her to switch shifts with me. "I can just drive over there and meet you," I offered.

"No," he said. "I'll come get you and bring you back."

Okay, if he wanted to go to the trouble of fetching me, I could live with it. I'd save mileage on my car, I figured. My old Nova was none too reliable.

"All right. I'll be ready."

"I better go," he said. The silence drew out. I knew Alcide was thinking of kissing me. He leaned over and kissed me lightly on the lips. We regarded each other from a few inches apart.

"Well, I have some things I need to be doing, and you should be going back to Shreveport. I'll be ready at eleven thirty tomorrow."

After Alcide left, I got my library book, Carolyn Haines's latest, and tried to forget my worries. But for once, a book just couldn't do the trick. I tried a hot soak in the bathtub, and I shaved my legs until they were perfectly smooth. I painted my toenails and fingernails a deep pink and then I plucked my eyebrows. Finally, I felt relaxed, and when I crawled into my bed I had achieved peace through pampering. Sleep came upon me in such a rush that I didn't finish my prayers.

YOU HAVE TO FIGURE OUT WHAT TO WEAR TO A FU-
neral, just like any other social occasion, even if it seems
your clothes should be the last thing on your mind. I had
liked and admired Colonel Flood during our brief acquaintance, so I wanted to look appropriate at his burial service,
especially after Alcide's comments.

I just couldn't find anything in my closet that seemed
right. About eight the next morning, I phoned Tara, who
told me where her emergency key was. "Get whatever you
need out of my closet," Tara said. "Just be sure you don't go
into any other rooms, okay? Go straight from the back door
to my room and back out again."

"That's what I'd be doing anyway," I said, trying not to
sound offended. Did Tara think I'd rummage around her
house just to pry?

"Of course you would, but I just feel responsible."

Suddenly, I understood that Tara was telling me that there was a vampire sleeping in her house. Maybe it was the bodyguard Mickey, maybe Franklin Mott. After Eric's warning, I wanted to stay far away from Mickey. Only the very oldest vampires could rise before dark, but coming across a sleeping vampire would give me a nasty start in and of itself.

"Okay, I get you," I said hastily. The idea of being alone with Mickey made me shiver, and not with happy anticipation. "Straight in, straight out." Since I didn't have any time to waste, I jumped in my car and drove into town to Tara's little house. It was a modest place in a modest part of town, but Tara's owning her own home was a miracle, when I recalled the place where she'd grown up.

Some people should never breed; if their children have the misfortune to be born, those children should be taken away immediately. That's not allowed in our country, or any country that I know of, and I'm sure in my brainier moments that's a good thing. But the Thorntons, both alcoholics, had been vicious people who should have died years earlier than they did. (I forget my religion when I think of them.) I remember Myrna Thornton tearing my grandmother's house up looking for Tara, ignoring my grandmother's protests, until Gran had to call the sheriff's department to come drag Myrna out. Tara had run out our back door to hide in the woods behind our house when she had seen the set of her mother's shoulders as Mrs. Thornton staggered to our door, thank God. Tara and I had been thirteen at the time.

I can still see the look on my grandmother's face while she talked to the deputy who'd just put Myrna Thornton in the back of the patrol car, handcuffed and screaming.

"Too bad I can't drop her off in the bayou on the way back to town," the deputy had said. I couldn't recall his name, but his words had impressed me. It had taken me a minute to be sure what he meant, but once I was, I realized that other people knew what Tara and her siblings were going through. These other people were all-powerful adults. If they knew, why didn't they solve the problem?

I sort of understood now that it hadn't been so simple; but I still thought the Thornton kids could have been spared a few years of their misery.

At least Tara had this neat little house with all-new appliances, and a closet full of clothes, and a rich boyfriend. I had an uneasy feeling that I didn't know everything that was happening in Tara's life, but on the surface of it, she was still way ahead of the predictions.

As she'd directed, I went through the spanky-clean kitchen, turned right, and crossed a corner of the living room to pass through the doorway to Tara's bedroom. Tara hadn't had a chance to make her bed that morning. I pulled the sheets straight in a flash and made it look nice. (I couldn't help it.) I couldn't decide if that was a favor to her or not, since now she'd know I minded it not being made, but for the life of me I couldn't mess it up again.

I opened her walk-in closet. I spotted exactly what I needed right away. Hanging in the middle of the rear rack was a knit suit. The jacket was black with creamy pink facings on the lapels, meant to be worn over the matching pink shell on the hanger beneath it. The black skirt was pleated. Tara had had it hemmed up; the alteration tag was still on the plastic bag covering the garment. I held the skirt up to me and looked in Tara's full-length mirror. Tara was two or three inches taller than I, so the skirt fell just an inch above my knees, a fine length for a funeral. The sleeves of the jacket were a little long, but that wasn't so obvious. I had some black pumps and a purse, and even some black gloves that I'd tried to save for nice.

Mission accomplished, in record time.

I slid the jacket and shell into the plastic bag with the skirt and walked straight out of the house. I'd been in Tara's place less than ten minutes. In a hurry, because of my ten o'clock appointment, I began getting ready. I French braided my hair and rolled the remaining tail under, securing everything with some antique hairpins my grandmother had stashed away; they'd been her grandmother's. I had some black hose, fortunately, and a black slip, and the pink of my fingernails at least coordinated with the pink of the jacket and shell. When I heard a knock on the front door at ten, I was ready except for my shoes. I stepped into my pumps on the way to the door.

Jack Leeds looked openly astonished at my transformation, while Lily's eyebrows twitched.

"Please come in," I said. "I'm dressed for a funeral."

"I hope you're not burying a friend," Jack Leeds said. His companion's face might have been sculpted from marble. Had the woman never heard of a tanning bed?

"Not a close one. Won't you sit down? Can I get you anything? Coffee?"

"No, thank you," he said, his smile transforming his face.

The detectives sat on the couch while I perched on the edge of the La-Z-Boy. Somehow, my unaccustomed finery made me feel braver.

"About the evening Ms. Pelt vanished," Leeds began. "You saw her in Shreveport?"

"Yes, I was invited to the same party she was. At Pam's place." All of us who'd lived through the Witch War—Pam, Eric, Clancy, the three Wiccans, and the Weres who had survived—had agreed on our story: Instead of telling the police that Debbie had left from the dilapidated and abandoned store where the witches had established their hideout, we'd said that we'd stayed the whole evening at Pam's house, and Debbie had left in her car from that address. The neighbors might have testified that everyone had left earlier en masse if the Wiccans hadn't done a little magic to haze their memories of the evening.

"Colonel Flood was there," I said. "Actually, it's his funeral I'm going to."

Lily looked inquiring, which was probably the equivalent of someone else exclaiming, "Oh, you've got to be kidding!"

"Colonel Flood died in a car accident two days ago," I told them.

They glanced at each other. "So, were there quite a few people at this party?" Jack Leeds said. I was sure he had a complete list of the people who'd been sitting in Pam's living room for what had been essentially a war council.

"Oh, yes. Quite a few. I didn't know them all. Shreveport people." I'd met the three Wiccans that evening for the first time. I'd known the werewolves slightly. The vampires, I'd known.

"But you'd met Debbie Pelt before?"

"Yes."

"When you were dating Alcide Herveaux?"

Well. They'd certainly done their homework.

"Yes," I said. "When I was dating Alcide." My face was as smooth and impassive as Lily's. I'd had lots of practice in keeping secrets.

"You stayed with him once at the Herveaux apartment in Jackson?"

I started to blurt out that we'd stayed in separate bedrooms, but it really wasn't their business. "Yes," I said with a certain edge to my voice.

"You two ran into Ms. Pelt one night in Jackson at a club called Josephine's?"

"Yes, she was celebrating her engagement to some guy named Clausen," I said.

"Did something happen between you that night?"

"Yes." I wondered whom they'd been talking to; someone had given the detectives a lot of information that they shouldn't have. "She came over to the table, made a few remarks to us."

"And you also went to see Alcide at the Herveaux office a few weeks ago? You two were at a crime scene that afternoon?"

They'd done *way* too much homework. "Yes," I said.

"And you told the officers at that crime scene that you and Alcide Herveaux were engaged?"

Lies will come back to bite you in the butt. "I think it was Alcide who said that," I said, trying to look thoughtful.

"And was his statement true?"

Jack Leeds was thinking that I was the most erratic woman he'd ever met, and he couldn't understand how someone who could get engaged and unengaged so adeptly could be the sensible hardworking waitress he'd seen the day before.

She was thinking my house was very clean. (Strange, huh?) She also thought I was quite capable of killing Debbie Pelt, because she'd found people were capable of the most horrible things. She and I shared more than she'd ever know. I had the same sad knowledge, since I'd heard it directly from their brains.

"Yes," I said. "At the time, it was true. We were engaged for, like, ten minutes. Just call me Britney." I hated lying. I almost always knew when someone else was lying, so I felt I had LIAR printed in big letters on my forehead.

Jack Leeds's mouth quirked, but my reference to the pop singer's fifty-five-hour marriage didn't make a dent in Lily Bard Leeds.

"Ms. Pelt object to your seeing Alcide?"

"Oh, yes." I was glad I'd had years of practice of hiding my feelings. "But Alcide didn't want to marry her."

"Was she angry with you?"

"Yes," I said, since undoubtedly they knew the truth of that. "Yes, you could say that. She called me some names. You've probably heard that Debbie didn't believe in hiding her emotions."

"So when did you last see her?"

"I last saw her . . ." *(with half her head gone, sprawled on my kitchen floor, her legs tangled up in the legs of a chair)* "Let me think. . . . As she left the party that night. She walked off into the dark by herself." Not from Pam's, but from another location altogether; one full of dead bodies, with blood splashed on the walls. "I just assumed she was starting back to Jackson." I shrugged.

"She didn't come by Bon Temps? It's right off the interstate on her return route."

"I can't imagine why she would. She didn't knock on my door." She'd broken in.

"You didn't see her after the party?"

"I have not seen her since that night." Now, *that* was the absolute truth.

"You've seen Mr. Herveaux?"

"Yes, I have."

"Are you engaged now?"

I smiled. "Not that I know of," I said.

I wasn't surprised when the woman asked if she could use my bathroom. I'd let down my guard to find out how suspicious the detectives were, so I knew she wanted to have a more extensive look at my house. I showed her to the bathroom in the hall, not the one in my bedroom; not that she'd find anything suspicious in either of them.

"What about her car?" Jack Leeds asked me suddenly. I'd been trying to steal a glimpse of the clock on the mantel over the fireplace, because I wanted to be sure the duo were gone before Alcide picked me up for the funeral.

"Hmm?" I'd lost track of the conversation.

"Debbie Pelt's car."

"What about it?"

"Do you have any idea where it is?"

"Not an idea in the world," I said with complete honesty.

As Lily came back into the living room, he asked, "Ms. Stackhouse, just out of curiosity, what do you think happened to Debbie Pelt?"

I thought, *I think she got what was coming to her*. I was a little shocked at myself. Sometimes I'm not a very nice person, and I don't seem to be getting any nicer. "I don't know, Mr. Leeds," I said. "I guess I have to tell you that except for her family's worry, I don't really care. We didn't like each other. She burned a hole in my shawl, she called me a whore, and she was awful to Alcide; though since he's a grown-up, that's his problem. She liked to jerk people around. She liked to make them dance to her tune." Jack Leeds was looking a little dazed at this flow of information. "So," I concluded, "that's the way I feel."

"Thanks for your honesty," he said, while his wife fixed me with her pale blue eyes. If I'd had any doubt, I understood clearly now that she was the more formidable of the two. Considering the depth of the investigation Jack Leeds had performed, that was saying something.

"Your collar is crooked," she said quietly. "Let me fix it." I held still while her deft fingers reached behind me and twitched the jacket until the collar lay down correctly.

They left after that. After I watched their car go down the driveway, I took my jacket off and examined it very carefully. Though I hadn't picked up any such intention from her brain, maybe she'd put a bug on me? The Leeds might be more suspicious than they'd sounded. No, I discovered: she really was the neat freak she'd seemed, and she really had been unable to withstand my turned-up collar. As long as I was being suspicious, I inspected the hall bathroom. I hadn't been in it since the last time I'd cleaned it a week ago, so it looked quite straight and as fresh and as sparkly as a very old bathroom in a very old house can look. The sink was damp, and the towel had been used and refolded, but that was all. Nothing extra was there, and nothing was missing, and if the detective had opened the bathroom cabinet to check its contents, I just didn't care.

My heel caught on a hole where the flooring had worn through. For about the hundredth time, I wondered if I could teach myself how to lay linoleum, because the floor could sure use a new layer. I also wondered how I could conceal the fact that I'd killed a woman in one minute, and worry about the cracked linoleum in the bathroom the next.

"She was bad," I said out loud. "She was mean and bad, and she wanted me to die for no very good reason at all."

That was how I could do it. I'd been living in a shell of guilt, but it had just cracked and fallen apart. I was tired of being all angst-y over someone who would have killed me in a New York minute, someone who'd tried her best to cause my death. I would never have lain in wait to ambush Debbie, but I hadn't been prepared to let her kill me just because it suited her to have me dead.

To hell with the whole subject. They'd find her, or they wouldn't. No point in worrying about it either way.

Suddenly, I felt a lot better.

I heard a vehicle coming through the woods. Alcide was right on time. I expected to see his Dodge Ram, but to my surprise he was in a dark blue Lincoln. His hair was as smooth as it could be, which wasn't very, and he was wearing a sober charcoal gray suit and a burgundy tie. I gaped at him through the window as he came up the stepping-stones to the front porch. He looked good enough to eat, and I tried not to giggle like an idiot at the mental image.

When I opened the door, he seemed equally stunned. "You look wonderful," he said after a long stare.

"You, too," I said, feeling almost shy.

"I guess we need to get going."

"Sure, if we want to be there on time."

"We need to be there ten minutes early," he said.

"Why that, exactly?" I picked up my black clutch purse, glanced in the mirror to make sure my lipstick was still fresh, and locked the front door behind me. Fortunately, the day was just warm enough for me to leave my coat at home. I didn't want to cover up my outfit.

"This is a Were funeral," he said in a tone of significance.

"That's different from a regular funeral how?"

"It's a packmaster's funeral, and that makes it more . . . formal."

Okay, he'd told me that the day before. "How do you keep regular people from realizing?"

"You'll see."

I felt misgivings about the whole thing. "Are you sure I should be going to this?"

"He made you a friend of the pack."

I remembered that, though at the time I hadn't realized it was a title, the way Alcide made it sound now: Friend of the Pack.

I had an uneasy feeling that there was a lot more to know

about Colonel Flood's funeral ceremony. Usually I had more information than I could handle about any given subject, since I could read minds; but there weren't any Weres in Bon Temps, and the other shifters weren't organized like the wolves were. Though Alcide's mind was hard to read, I could tell he was preoccupied with what was going to happen in the church, and I could tell he was worried about a Were named Patrick.

The service was being held at Grace Episcopal, a church in an older, affluent suburb of Shreveport. The church edifice was very traditional, built of gray stone, and topped with a steeple. There wasn't an Episcopal church in Bon Temps, but I knew that the services were similar to those of the Catholic church. Alcide had told me that his father was attending the funeral, too, and that we'd come over from Bon Temps in his father's car. "My truck didn't look dignified enough for the day, my father thought," Alcide said. I could tell that his father was foremost in Alcide's thoughts.

"Then how's your dad getting here?" I asked.

"His other car," Alcide said absently, as if he weren't really listening to what I was saying. I was a little shocked at the idea of one man owning two cars: In my experience, men might have a family car and a pickup, or a pickup and a four-wheeler. My little shocks for the day were just beginning. By the time we had reached I-20 and turned west, Alcide's mood had filled up the car. I wasn't sure what it was, but it involved silence.

"Sookie," Alcide said abruptly, his hands tightening on the wheel until his knuckles were white.

"Yes?" The fact that bad stuff was coming into the conversation might as well have been written in blinking letters above Alcide's head. Mr. Inner Conflict.

"I need to talk to you about something."

"What? Is there something suspicious about Colonel

Flood's death?" *I should have wondered!* I chided myself. But the other shifters had been shot. A traffic accident was such a contrast.

"No," Alcide said, looking surprised. "As far as I know, the accident was just an accident. The other guy ran a red light."

I settled back into the leather seat. "So what's the deal?"

"Is there anything you want to tell me?"

I froze. "Tell you? About what?"

"About that night. The night of the Witch War."

Years of controlling my face came to my rescue. "Not a thing," I said calmly enough, though I may have been clenching my hands as I said it.

Alcide said nothing more. He parked the car and came around to help me out, which was unnecessary but nice. I'd decided I wouldn't need to take my purse inside, so I stuck it under the seat and Alcide locked the car. We started toward the front of the church. Alcide took my hand, somewhat to my surprise. I might be a friend of the pack, but I was apparently supposed to be friendlier with one member of the pack than the others.

"There's Dad," Alcide said as we approached a knot of mourners. Alcide's father was a little shorter than Alcide, but he was a husky man like his son. Jackson Herveaux had iron-gray hair instead of black, and a bolder nose. He had the same olive skin as Alcide. Jackson looked all the darker because he was standing by a pale, delicate woman with gleaming white hair.

"Father," Alcide said formally, "this is Sookie Stackhouse."

"A pleasure to meet you, Sookie," Jackson Herveaux said. "This is Christine Larrabee." Christine, who might have been anything from fifty-seven to sixty-seven, looked like a painting done in pastels. Her eyes were a washed-out blue, her smooth skin was magnolia pale with the faintest tinge of pink, her white hair was immaculately groomed. She was wearing a light blue suit, which I personally wouldn't have worn until the winter was completely over, but she looked great in it, for sure.

"Nice to meet you," I said, wondering if I should curtsy. I'd shaken hands with Alcide's father, but Christine didn't extend hers. She gave me a nod and a sweet smile. Probably didn't want to bruise me with her diamond rings, I decided after a squint at her fingers. Of course, they matched her earrings. I was outclassed, no doubt about it. *Eff it,* I thought. It seemed to be my day for shrugging off unpleasant things.

"Such a sad occasion," Christine said.

If she wanted to do polite chitchat, I was up to it. "Yes, Colonel Flood was a wonderful man," I said.

"Oh, you knew him, dear?"

"Yes," I said. As a matter of fact, I'd seen him naked, but in decidedly unerotic circumstances.

My brief answer didn't leave her much of anywhere to go. I saw genuine amusement lurking in her pale eyes. Alcide and his dad were exchanging low-voiced comments, which we were obviously supposed to be ignoring. "You and I are strictly decorations today," Christine said.

"Then you know more than I do."

"I expect so. You're not one of the two-natured?"

"No." Christine was, of course. She was a full-blooded Were, like Jackson and Alcide. I couldn't picture this elegant woman changing into a wolf, especially with the down-and-dirty reputation the Weres had in the shifter community, but the impressions I got from her mind were unmistakable.

"The funeral of the packmaster marks the opening of the campaign to replace him," Christine said. Since that was more solid information than I'd gotten in two hours from Alcide, immediately I felt kindly disposed toward the older woman.

"You must be something extraordinary, for Alcide to choose you as his companion today," Christine continued.

"I don't know about *extra*ordinary. In the literal sense, I guess I am. I have extras that aren't ordinary."

"Witch?" Christine guessed. "Fairy? Part goblin?"

Gosh. I shook my head. "None of the above. So what's going to happen in there?"

"There are more roped-off pews than usual. The whole pack will sit at the front of the church, the mated ones with their mates, of course, and their children. The candidates for packmaster will come in last."

"How are they chosen?"

"They announce themselves," she said. "But they'll be put to the test, and then the membership votes."

"Why is Alcide's dad bringing you, or is that a real personal question?"

"I'm the widow of the packmaster prior to Colonel Flood," Christine Larrabee said quietly. "That gives me a certain influence."

I nodded. "Is the packmaster always a man?"

"No. But since strength is part of the test, males usually win."

"How many candidates are there?"

"Two. Jackson, of course, and Patrick Furnan." She inclined her patrician head slightly to her right, and I gave a closer look at the couple that had been on the periphery of my attention.

Patrick Furnan was in his mid-forties, somewhere between Alcide and his father. He was a thick-bodied man with a light brown crew cut and a very short beard shaved into a fancy shape. His suit was brown, too, and he'd had trouble buttoning the jacket. His companion was a pretty woman who believed in a lot of lipstick and jewelry. She had short brown hair, too, but it was highlighted with blond streaks and elaborately styled. Her heels were at least three inches high. I eyed the shoes with awe. I would break my neck if I tried to walk in them. But this woman maintained a smile and offered a good word to everyone who approached. Patrick Furnan was colder. His narrow eyes measured and assessed every Were in the gathering crowd.

"Tammy Faye, there, is his wife?" I asked Christine in a discreetly low tone.

Christine made a sound that I would have called snigger if it had issued from someone less patrician. "She does wear a lot of makeup," Christine said. "Her name is Libby, actually. Yes, she's his wife and a full-blooded Were, and they have two children. So he's added to the pack."

Only the oldest child would become a Were at puberty.

"What does he do for a living?" I asked.

"He owns a Harley-Davidson dealership," Christine said.

"That's a natural." Weres tended to like motorcycles a lot.

Christine smiled, probably as close as she came to laughing out loud.

"Who's the front-runner?" I'd been dumped into the middle of a game, and I needed to learn the rules. Later, I was going to let Alcide have it right between the eyes; but right now, I was going to get through the funeral, since that's what I'd come for.

"Hard to say," Christine murmured. "I wouldn't have thrown in with either one, given a choice, but Jackson called on our old friendship, and I had to come down on his side."

"That's not nice."

"No, but it's practical," she said, amused. "He needs all the support he can get. Did Alcide ask you to endorse his father?"

"No. I'd be completely ignorant of the situation if you hadn't been kind enough to fill me in." I gave her a nod of thanks.

"Since you're not a Were—excuse me, honey, but I'm just trying to figure this out—what can you do for Alcide, I wonder? Why'd he drag you into this?"

"He'll have to tell me that real soon," I said, and if my voice was cold and ominous, I just didn't care.

"His last girlfriend disappeared," Christine said thoughtfully. "They were pretty on-again, off-again, Jackson tells me. If his enemies had something to do with it, you might watch your step."

"I don't think I'm in danger," I said.

"Oh?"

But I'd said enough.

"Hmmmm," Christine said after a long, thoughtful look at my face. "Well, she was too much of a diva for someone who isn't even a Were." Christine's voice expressed the contempt the Weres feel for the other shifters. ("Why bother to change, if you can't change into a wolf?" I'd heard a Were say once.)

My attention was caught by the dull gleam of a shaved head, and I stepped a bit to my left to have a better view. I'd never seen this man before. I would certainly have remembered him; he was very tall, taller than Alcide or even Eric, I thought. He had big shoulders and arms roped with muscle. His head and arms were the brown of a Caucasian with a real tan. I could tell, because he was wearing a sleeveless black silk tee tucked into black pants and shiny dress shoes. It was a nippy day at the end of January, but the cold didn't seem to affect him at all. There was a definite space between him and the people around him.

As I looked at him, wondering, he turned and looked at me, as if he could feel my attention. He had a proud nose, and his face was as smooth as his shaved head. At this distance, his eyes looked black.

"Who is that?" I asked Christine, my voice a thread in the wind that had sprung up, tossing the leaves of the holly bushes planted around the church.

Christine darted a look at the man, and she must have known whom I meant, but she didn't answer.

Regular people had gradually been filtering through the Weres, going up the steps and into the church. Now two men in black suits appeared at the doors. They crossed their hands in front of them, and the one on the right nodded at Jackson Herveaux and Patrick Furnan.

The two men, with their female companions, came to stand facing each other at the bottom of the steps. The assembled Weres passed between them to enter the church. Some nodded at one, some at the other, some at both. Fence-sitters. Even after their ranks had been reduced by the recent war with the witches, I counted twenty-five full-blooded adult Weres in Shreveport, a very large pack for such a small city. Its size was attributable to the Air Force base, I figured.

Everyone who walked between the two candidates was a full Were. I saw only two children. Of course, some parents might have left their kids in school rather than bring them to the funeral. But I was pretty sure I was seeing the truth of what Alcide had told me: Infertility and a high infant mortality rate plagued the Weres.

Alcide's younger sister, Janice, had married a human. She herself would never change shape, since she was not the firstborn child. Her son's recessive Were traits, Alcide had told me, might show as increased vigor and a great healing ability. Many professional athletes came from couples whose genetic pool contained a percentage of Were blood.

"We go in a second," Alcide murmured. He was standing beside me, scanning the faces as they went by.

"I'm going to kill you later," I told him, keeping my face calm for the Weres passing by. "Why didn't you explain this?"

The tall man walked up the steps, his arms swinging as he walked, his large body moving with purpose and grace. His head swung toward me as he went by, and I met his eyes. They were very dark, but still I couldn't distinguish the color. He smiled at me.

Alcide touched my hand, as if he knew my attention had wandered. He leaned over to whisper in my ear, "I need your help. I need you to find a chance after the funeral to read Patrick's mind. He's going to do something to sabotage my father."

"Why didn't you just ask me?" I was confused, and mostly I was hurt.

"I thought you might feel like you owed me anyway!"

"How do you figure that?"

"I know you killed Debbie."

If he'd slapped me, it couldn't have shocked me more. I have no idea what my face looked like. After the impact of the shock and the reflexive guilt wore off, I said, "You'd abjured her. What's it to you?"

"Nothing," he said. "Nothing. She was already dead to me." I didn't believe that for a minute. "But you thought it would be a big deal to me, and you concealed it. I figure you'd guess you owed me."

If I'd had a gun in my purse, I would've been tempted to pull it out then. "I don't owe you squat," I said. "I think you came to get me in your dad's car because you knew I'd drive away once you said that."

"No," he said. We were still keeping our voices down, but I could see from the sideways glances we were getting that our intense colloquy was attracting attention. "Well, maybe. Please, forget what I said about you owing me. The fact is, my dad's in trouble and I'd do just about anything to help him out. And you can help."

"Next time you need help, just *ask*. Don't trying blackmailing me into it or maneuvering me into it. I like to help people. But I hate to be pushed and tricked." He'd lowered his eyes, so I grabbed his chin and made him look into mine. "*I hate it.*"

I glanced up at the top of the steps to gauge how much interest our quarrel was attracting. The tall man had reappeared. He was looking down at us without perceptible expression. But I knew we had his attention.

Alcide glanced up, too. His face reddened. "We need to go in now. Will you go with me?"

"What is the meaning of me going in with you?"

"It means you're on my father's side in his bid for the pack."

"What does that oblige me to do?"

"Nothing."

"Then why is it important for me to do it?"

"Though choosing a packmaster is pack business, it may influence those who know how much you helped us during the Witch War."

Witch Skirmish would have been more accurate, because though it had certainly been them vs. us, the total number of people involved had been fairly small—say, forty or fifty. But in the history of the Shreveport pack, it was an epic episode, I gathered.

I glared down at my black pumps. I struggled with my

warring instincts. They seemed about equally strong. One said, "You're at a funeral. Don't make a scene. Alcide has been good to you, and it wouldn't hurt you to do this for him." The other said, "Alcide helped you in Jackson because he was trying to get his dad out of trouble with the vampires. Now, again, he's willing to involve you in something dangerous to help his dad out." The first voice chipped in, "He knew Debbie was bad. He tried to pull away from her, and then he abjured her." The second said, "Why'd he love a bitch like Debbie in the first place? Why'd he even consider sticking with her when he had clear evidence she was evil? No one else has suggested she had spellcasting power. This 'spellcasting' thing is a cheap excuse." I felt like Linda Blair in the *The Exorcist,* with her head whirling around on her neck.

Voice number one won out. I put my hand on Alcide's crooked elbow and we went up the stairs and into the church.

The pews were full of regular people. The front three rows on both sides had been saved for the pack. But the tall man, who would stand out anywhere, sat in the back row. I caught a glimpse of his big shoulders before I had to pay strict attention to the pack ceremony. The two Furnan children, cute as the dickens, went solemnly down to the front pew on the right of the church. Then Alcide and I entered, preceding the two candidates for packmaster. This seating ceremony was oddly like a wedding, with Alcide and me being the best man and maid of honor. Jackson and Christine and Patrick and Libby Furnan would enter like the parents of the bride and groom.

What the civilians made of this I don't know.

I knew they were all staring, but I'm used to that. If being a barmaid will get you used to anything, it's being looked over. I was dressed appropriately and I looked as good as I could make myself look, and Alcide had done the same, so let them stare. Alcide and I sat on the front row on the left side of the church, and moved in. I saw Patrick Furnan and his wife, Libby, enter the pew across the aisle. Then I looked back to see Jackson and Christine coming in slowly, looking fittingly grave. There was a slight flutter of heads and hands, a tiny buzz of whispers, and then Christine sidled into the pew, Jackson beside her.

The coffin, draped with an elaborately embroidered cloth, was wheeled up the aisle as we all stood, and then the somber service began.

After going through the litany, which Alcide showed me in the Prayer Book, the priest asked if anyone would like to say a few words about Colonel Flood. One of his Air Force friends went first and spoke of the colonel's devotion to duty and his sense of pride in his command. One of his fellow church members took the next turn, praising the colonel's generosity and applauding the time he'd spent balancing the church's books.

Patrick Furnan left his pew and strode to the lectern. He didn't do a good stride; he was too stout for that. But his speech was certainly a change from the elegies the two previous men had given. "John Flood was a remarkable man and a great leader," Furnan began. He was a much better speaker than I'd expected. Though I didn't know who'd written his remarks, it was someone educated. "In the fraternal order we shared, he was always the one who told us the direction we should take, the goal we should achieve. As he grew older, he remarked often that this was a job for the young."

A right turn from eulogy to campaign speech. I wasn't the only one who'd noticed this; all around me there were little movements, whispered comments.

Though taken aback by the reaction he'd aroused, Patrick Furnan plowed ahead. "I told John that he was the finest man for the job we'd ever had, and I still believe that. No matter who follows in his footsteps, John Flood will never be forgotten or replaced. The next leader can only hope to work as hard as John. I'll always be proud that John put his trust in me more than once, that he even called me his right hand." With those sentences, the Harley dealer underscored his bid to take Colonel's Flood's job as packmaster (or, as I referred to it internally, Leader of the Pack).

Alcide, to my right, was rigid with anger. If he hadn't been sitting in the front row of a funeral, he would have loved to address a few remarks to me on the subject of Patrick Furnan. On the other side of Alcide, I could just barely see Christine, whose face looked carved out of ivory. She was suppressing quite a few things herself.

Alcide's dad waited a moment to begin his trip to the lectern. Clearly, he wanted us to cleanse our mental palate before he gave his address.

Jackson Herveaux, wealthy surveyor and werewolf, gave us the chance to examine his maturely handsome face. He began, "We will not soon see the likes of John Flood. A man whose wisdom had been tempered and tested by the years . . ." Oh, ouch. This wasn't going to be pointed or anything, no sirree.

I tuned out for the rest of the service to think my own thoughts. I had plenty of food for thought. We stood as John Flood, Air Force colonel and packmaster, exited this church for the last time. I remained silent during the ride to the cemetery, stood by Alcide's side during the graveside service, and got back in the car when it was over and all the post-funeral handshaking was done.

I looked for the tall man, but he wasn't at the cemetery.

On the drive back to Bon Temps, Alcide obviously wanted to keep our silence nice and clean, but it was time to answer some questions.

"How did you know?" I asked.

He didn't even try to pretend to misunderstand what I was talking about. "When I came to your house yesterday, I could smell a very, very faint trace of her at your front door," he said. "It took me a while to think it through."

I'd never considered the possibility.

"I don't think I would've picked up on it if I hadn't known her so well," he offered. "I certainly didn't pick up a whiff anywhere else in the house."

So all my scrubbing had been to some avail. I was just lucky Jack and Lily Leeds weren't two-natured. "Do you want to know what happened?"

"I don't think so," he said after an appreciable pause. "Knowing Debbie, I'm guessing you only did what you had to do. After all, it was her scent at your house. She had no business there."

This was far from a ringing endorsement.

"And Eric was still at your house then, wasn't he? Maybe it was Eric?" Alcide sounded almost hopeful.

"No," I said.

"Maybe I do want the whole story."

"Maybe I've changed my mind about telling it to you. You either believe in me, or you don't. Either you think I'm the kind of person who'd kill a woman for no good reason, or you know I'm not." Truly, I was hurt more than I thought I'd be. I was very careful not to slip into Alcide's head, because I was afraid I might pick up on something that would have been even more painful.

Alcide tried several times to open another conversation, but the drive couldn't end soon enough for me. When he pulled into the clearing and I knew I was yards away from being in my own house, the relief was overwhelming. I couldn't scramble out of that fancy car fast enough.

But Alcide was right behind me.

"I don't care," he said in a voice that was almost a growl.

"What?" I'd gotten to my front door, and the key was in the lock.

"I don't care."

"I don't believe that for one minute."

"What?"

"You're harder to read than a plain human, Alcide, but I can see the pockets of reservation in your mind. Since you wanted me to help you out with your dad, I'll tell you: Patrick Whatsisname plans to bring up your dad's gambling problems to show he's unsuitable as packleader." Nothing more underhanded and supernatural than the truth. "I'd read his mind before you asked me to. I don't want to see you for a long, long, long time."

"What?" Alcide said again. He looked like I'd hit him in the head with an iron.

"Seeing you . . . listening to your head . . . makes me feel bad." Of course, there were several different reasons they did, but I didn't want to enumerate them. "So, thanks for the ride to the funeral." (I may have sounded a bit sarcastic.) "I appreciate your thinking of me." (Even a higher probability of sarcasm here.) I entered the house, shut the door on his startled face, and locked it just to be on the safe side. I marched across the living room so he could hear my steps, but then I stopped in the hall and waited to listen while he got back in the Lincoln. I listened to the big car rocket down the driveway, probably putting ruts in my beautiful gravel.

As I shed Tara's suit and bundled it up to drop at the dry

cleaner's, I confess I was mopey. They say when one door shuts, another one opens. But they haven't been living at my house.

Most of the doors I open seem to have something scary crouched behind them, anyway.

7~

SAM WAS IN THE BAR THAT NIGHT, SEATED AT A COR-
ner table like a visiting king, his leg propped up on another
chair cushioned with pillows. He was keeping one eye on
Charles, one eye on the clientele's reaction to a vampire bartender.

People would stop by, drop down in the chair across from
him, visit for a few minutes, and then vacate the chair. I
knew Sam was in pain. I can always read the preoccupation of
people who are hurting. But he was glad to be seeing other
people, glad to be back in the bar, pleased with Charles's
work.

All this I could tell, and yet when it came to the question
of who had shot him, I didn't have a clue. Someone was gunning for the two-natured, someone who'd killed quite a few
and wounded even more. Discovering the identity of the
shooter was imperative. The police didn't suspect Jason, but

his own people did. If Calvin Norris's people decided to take matters into their own hands, they could easily find a chance to take out Jason. They didn't know there were more victims than those in Bon Temps.

I probed into minds, I tried to catch people in unguarded moments, I even tried to think of the most promising candidates for the role of assassin so I wouldn't waste time listening to (for example) Liz Baldwin's worries about her oldest granddaughter.

I assumed the shooter was almost certainly a guy. I knew plenty of women who went hunting and plenty more with access to rifles. But weren't snipers always men? The police were baffled by this sniper's selection of targets, because they didn't know the true nature of all the victims. The two-natured were hampered in their search because they were looking only at local suspects.

"Sookie," Sam said as I passed close to him. "Kneel down here a minute."

I sank to one knee right by his chair so he could speak in a low voice.

"Sookie, I hate to ask you again, but the closet in the storeroom isn't working out for Charles." The cleaning supplies closet in the storeroom was not exactly built to be light tight, but it was inaccessible to daylight, which was good enough. After all, the closet had no windows, and it was inside a room with no windows.

It took me a minute to switch my train of thought to another track. "You can't tell me he's not able to sleep," I said incredulously. Vampires could sleep in the daytime under any circumstances. "And I'm sure you put a lock on the inside of the door, too."

"Yes, but he has to kind of huddle on the floor, and he says it smells like old mops."

"Well, we did keep the cleaning stuff in there."

"What I'm saying is, would it be so bad for him to stay at your place?"

"Why do you really want me to have him at the house?" I asked. "There's got to be a reason more than a strange vampire's comfort during the day, when he's dead, anyway."

"Haven't we been friends a long time, Sookie?"

I smelled something big and rotten.

"Yes," I admitted, standing so that he would have to look up at me. "And?"

"I hear through the grapevine that the Hotshot community has hired a Were bodyguard for Calvin's hospital room."

"Yeah, I think that's kind of strange, too." I acknowledged his unspoken concern. "So I guess you heard what they suspect."

Sam nodded. His bright blue eyes caught mine. "You have to take this seriously, Sookie."

"What makes you think I don't?"

"You refused Charles."

"I don't see what telling him he couldn't sleep in my house has to do with worrying about Jason."

"I think he'd help you protect Jason, if it came to that. I'm down with this leg, or I'd . . . I don't believe it was Jason who shot me."

A knot of tension within me relaxed when Sam said that. I hadn't realized I'd been worried about what he thought, but I had.

My heart softened a little. "Oh, all right," I said with poor grace. "He can come stay with me." I stomped off grumpily, still not certain why I'd agreed.

Sam beckoned Charles over, conferred with him briefly. Later in the evening Charles borrowed my keys to stow his bag in the car. After a few minutes, he was back at the bar and signaled he'd returned my keys to my purse. I nodded, maybe a little curtly. I wasn't happy, but if I had to be sad-dled with a houseguest, at least he was a polite houseguest.

Mickey and Tara came into Merlotte's that night. As before, the dark intensity of the vampire made everyone in the bar a little excited, a little louder. Tara's eyes followed me with a kind of sad passivity. I was hoping to catch her alone, but I didn't see her leave the table for any reason. I found that was another cause for alarm. When she'd come into the bar with Franklin Mott, she'd always taken a minute to give me a hug, chat with me about family and work.

I caught a glimpse of Claudine the fairy across the room, and though I planned to work my way over to have a word with her, I was too preoccupied with Tara's situation. As usual, Claudine was surrounded by admirers.

Finally, I got so anxious that I took the vampire by the fangs and went over to Tara's table. The snakelike Mickey was staring at our flamboyant bartender, and he scarcely flicked a gaze at me as I approached. Tara looked both hope-ful and frightened, and I stood by her and laid my hand on her shoulder to get a clearer picture of her head. Tara has done so well for herself I seldom worry over her one weak-ness: She picks the wrong men. I was remembering when she dated "Eggs" Benedict, who'd apparently died in a fire the previous fall. Eggs had been a heavy drinker and a weak personality. Franklin Mott had at least treated Tara with re-spect and had showered her with presents, though the na-ture of the presents had said, "I'm a mistress," rather than "I'm an honored girlfriend." But how had it come to pass that she was in Mickey's company—Mickey, whose name made even Eric hesitate?

I felt like I'd been reading a book only to discover that someone had ripped a few pages from the middle.

"Tara," I said quietly. She looked up at me, her big brown eyes dull and dead: past fear, past shame.

To the outer eye she looked almost normal. She was well groomed and made up, and her clothing was fashionable and attractive. But inside, Tara was in torment. What was wrong with my friend? Why hadn't I noticed before that something was eating her up from the inside out?

I wondered what to do next. Tara and I were just staring at each other, and though she knew what I was seeing inside her, she wasn't responding. "Wake up," I said, not even knowing where the words were coming from. "Wake up, Tara!"

A white hand grabbed my arm and removed my hand from Tara's shoulder forcibly. "I'm not paying you to touch my date," Mickey said. He had the coldest eyes I'd ever seen—mud colored, reptilian. "I'm paying you to bring our drinks."

"Tara is my friend," I said. He was still squeezing my arm, and if a vampire squeezes you, you know about it. "You're doing something to her. Or you're letting someone else hurt her."

"It's none of your concern."

"It is my concern," I said. I knew my eyes were tearing up from the pain, and I had a moment of sheer cowardice. Looking into his face, I knew he could kill me and be out of the bar before anyone there could stop him. He could take Tara with him, like a pet dog or his livestock. Before the fear could get a grip, I said, "Let go of me." I made each word clear and distinct, even though I knew he could hear a pin drop in a storm.

"You're shaking like a sick dog," he said scornfully.

"Let go of me," I repeated.

"Or you'll do—what?"

"You can't stay awake forever. If it's not me, it'll be someone else."

Mickey seemed to be reconsidering. I don't think it was my threat, though I meant it from the tips of my toes to the roots of my hair.

He looked down at Tara, and she spoke, as though he'd pulled a string. "Sookie, don't make such a big deal out of nothing. Mickey is my man now. Don't embarrass me in front of him."

My hand dropped back to her shoulder and I risked taking my eyes off Mickey to look down at her. She definitely wanted me to back off; she was completely sincere about that. But her thinking about her motivation was curiously murky.

"Okay, Tara. Do you need another drink?" I asked slowly. I was feeling my way through her head, and I was meeting a wall of ice, slippery and nearly opaque.

"No, thank you," Tara said politely. "Mickey and I need to be going now."

That surprised Mickey, I could tell. I felt a little better; Tara was in charge of herself, at least to some extent.

"I'll return your suit. I took it by the cleaner's, already," I said.

"No hurry."

"All right. I'll see you later." Mickey had a firm grip on my friend's arm as the two made their way through the crowd.

I got the empty glasses off the table, swabbed it down, and turned back to the bar. Charles Twining and Sam were on alert. They'd been observing the whole small incident. I shrugged, and they relaxed.

When we closed the bar that night, the new bouncer was waiting at the back door for me when I pulled on my coat and got my keys out of my purse.

I unlocked my car doors and he climbed in.

"Thanks for agreeing to have me in your home," he said.

I made myself say the polite thing back. No point in being rude.

"Do you think Eric will mind my being here?" Charles asked as we drove down the narrow parish road.

"It's not his say-so," I said curtly. It irked me that he automatically wondered about Eric.

"He doesn't come to see you often?" enquired Charles with unusual persistence.

I didn't answer until we'd parked behind my house. "Listen," I said, "I don't know what you heard, but he's not . . . we're not . . . like that." Charles looked at my face and wisely said nothing as I unlocked my back door.

"Feel free to explore," I said after I'd invited him over the threshold. Vampires like to know entrances and exits. "Then I'll show you your sleeping place." While the bouncer looked curiously around the humble house where my family had lived for so many years, I hung up my coat and put my purse in my room. I made myself a sandwich after asking Charles if he wanted some blood. I keep some type O in the refrigerator, and he seemed glad to sit down and drink after he'd studied the house. Charles Twining was a peaceful sort of guy to be around, especially for a vampire. He didn't letch after me, and he didn't seem to want anything from me.

I showed him the lift-up floor panel in the guest bedroom closet. I told him how the television remote worked, showed him my little collection of movies, and pointed out the books on the shelves in the guest bedroom and living room.

"Is there anything else you can think of you might need?" I asked. My grandmother brought me up right, though I don't think she ever imagined I'd have to be hostess to a bunch of vampires.

"No, thank you, Miss Sookie," Charles said politely. His

long white fingers tapped his eye patch, an odd habit of his that gave me the cold gruesomes.

"Then, if you'll excuse me, I'll say good night." I was tired, and it was exhausting work making conversation with a near stranger.

"Of course. Rest easy, Sookie. If I want to roam in the woods . . . ?"

"Feel free," I said immediately. I had an extra key to the back door, and I got it out of the drawer in the kitchen where I kept all the keys. This had been the odds and ends drawer for perhaps eighty years, since the kitchen had been added onto the house. There were at least a hundred keys in it. Some, those that were old when the kitchen was added, were mighty strange looking. I'd labeled the ones from my generation, and I'd put the back door key on a bright pink plastic key ring from my State Farm insurance agent. "Once you're in for the night—well, for good—shoot the dead bolt, please."

He nodded and took the key.

It was usually a mistake to feel sympathy for a vampire, but I couldn't help but think there was something sad about Charles. He struck me as lonely, and there's always something pathetic about loneliness. I'd experienced it myself. I would ferociously deny I was pathetic, but when I viewed loneliness in someone else, I could feel the tug of pity.

I scrubbed my face and pulled on some pink nylon pajamas. I was already half-asleep as I brushed my teeth and crawled into the high old bed my grandmother had slept in until she died. My great-grandmother had made the quilt I pulled over me, and my great-aunt Julia had embroidered the pattern on the edges of the bedspread. Though I might actually be alone in the world—with the exception of my brother, Jason—I went to sleep surrounded by my family.

My deepest sleep is around three a.m., and sometime

during that period I was awakened by the grip of a hand on my shoulder.

I was shocked into total awareness, like a person being thrown into a cold pool. To fight off the shock that was close to paralyzing me, I swung my fist. It was caught in a chilly grip.

"No, no, no, ssshhh" came a piercing whisper out of the darkness. English accent. Charles. "Someone's creeping around outside your house, Sookie."

My breath was as wheezy as an accordion. I wondered if I was going to have a heart attack. I put a hand over my heart, as if I could hold it in when it seemed determined to pound its way out of my chest.

"Lie down!" he said right into my ear, and then I felt him crouch beside my bed in the shadows. I lay down and closed my eyes almost all the way. The headboard of the bed was situated between the two windows in the room, so whoever was creeping around my house couldn't really get a good look at my face. I made sure I was lying still and as relaxed as I could get. I tried to think, but I was just too scared. If the creeper was a vampire, he or she couldn't come in—unless it was Eric. Had I rescinded Eric's invitation to enter? I couldn't remember. *That's the kind of thing I need to keep track of,* I babbled to myself.

"He's passed on," Charles said in a voice so faint it was almost the ghost of a voice.

"What is it?" I asked in a voice I hoped was nearly as soundless.

"It's too dark outside to tell." If a vampire couldn't see what was out there, it must be really dark. "I'll slip outside and find out."

"No," I said urgently, but it was too late.

Jesus Christ, shepherd of Judea! What if the prowler was Mickey? He'd kill Charles—I just knew it.

"Sookie!" The last thing I expected—though frankly, I was way beyond consciously expecting anything—was for Charles to call to me. "Come out here, if you please!"

I slid my feet into my pink fuzzy slippers and hurried down the hall to the back door; that was where the voice had been coming from, I thought.

"I'm turning on the outside light," I yelled. Didn't want anyone to be blinded by the sudden electricity. "You sure it's safe out there?"

"Yes," said two voices almost simultaneously.

I flipped the switch with my eyes shut. After a second, I opened them and stepped to the door of the screened-in back porch, in my pink jammies and slippers. I crossed my arms over my chest. Though it wasn't cold tonight, it was cool.

I absorbed the scene in front of me. "Okay," I said slowly. Charles was in the graveled area where I parked, and he had an elbow around the neck of Bill Compton, my neighbor. Bill is a vampire, has been since right after the Civil War. We have a history. It's probably just a pebble of a history in Bill's long life, but in mine, it's a boulder.

"Sookie," Bill said between clenched teeth. "I don't want to cause this foreigner harm. Tell him to get his hands off me."

I mulled that over at an accelerated rate. "Charles, I think you can let him go," I said, and as fast as I could snap my fingers, Charles was standing beside me.

"You know this man?" Charles's voice was steely.

Just as coldly, Bill said, "She does know me, intimately."

Oh, *gack*.

"Now, is that polite?" I may have had a little cold steel in my own voice. "I don't go around telling everyone the details of our former relationship. I would expect the same of any gentleman."

To my gratification, Charles glared at Bill, raising one eyebrow in a very superior and irritating way.

"So this one is sharing your bed now?" Bill jerked his head toward the smaller vampire.

If he'd said anything else, I could've held on to my temper. I don't lose it a lot, but when I do, it's well and truly lost. "Is that any of your business?" I asked, biting off each word. "If I sleep with a hundred men, or a hundred sheep, it's not any of your business! Why are you creeping around my house in the middle of the night? You scared me halfway to death."

Bill didn't look remotely repentant. "I'm sorry you wakened and were frightened," he said insincerely. "I was checking on your safety."

"You were roaming around the woods and smelled another vampire," I said. He'd always had an extremely acute sense of smell. "So you came over here to see who it was."

"I wanted to be sure you weren't being attacked," Bill said. "I thought I caught a sniff of human, too. Did you have a human visitor today?"

I didn't believe for a minute Bill was only concerned with my safety, but I didn't want to believe jealousy brought him to my window, or some kind of prurient curiosity. I just breathed in and out for a minute, calming down and considering.

"Charles is not attacking me," I said, proud I was speaking so levelly.

Bill sneered. "Charles," he repeated in tones of great scorn.

"Charles Twining," said my companion, bowing—if you could call a slight inclination of his curly brown head a bow.

"Where did you come up with this one?" Bill's voice had regained its calm.

"Actually, he works for Eric, like you do."

"Eric's provided you with a bodyguard? You need a bodyguard?"

"Listen, bozo," I said through clenched jaws, "my life goes on while you're gone. So does the town. People are getting shot around here, among them Sam. We needed a substitute bartender, and Charles was volunteered to help us out." That may not have been entirely accurate, but I was not in the accuracy business at the moment. I was in the Make My Point business.

At least Bill was appropriately taken aback by the information.

"Sam. Who else?"

I was shivering, since it wasn't nylon pajama weather. But I didn't want Bill in the house. "Calvin Norris and Heather Kinman."

"Shot dead?"

"Heather was. Calvin was pretty badly wounded."

"Have the police arrested anyone?"

"No."

"Do you know who did it?"

"No."

"You're worried about your brother."

"Yes."

"He turned at the full moon."

"Yes."

Bill looked at me with what might have been pity. "I'm sorry, Sookie," he said, and he meant it.

"No point telling me about it," I snapped. "Tell Jason—it's him who turns fuzzy."

Bill's face went cold and stiff. "Excuse my intrusion," he said. "I'll go." He melted into the woods.

I don't know how Charles reacted to the episode, because I turned and stalked back into the house, turning off the outside light as I went. I threw myself back in bed and lay there, fuming and fussing silently. I pulled the covers up over my head so the vampire would take the hint that I didn't want to discuss the incident. He moved so quietly, I couldn't be sure where he was in the house; I think he paused in the doorway for a second, and then moved on.

I lay awake for at least forty-five minutes, and then I found myself settling back into sleep.

Then someone shook me by the shoulder. I smelled sweet perfume, and I smelled something else, something awful. I was terribly groggy.

"Sookie, your house is on fire," a voice said.

"Couldn't be," I said. "I didn't leave anything on."

"You have to get out now," the voice insisted. A persistent shriek reminded me of fire drills at the elementary school.

"Okay," I said, my head thick with sleep and (I saw when I opened my eyes) smoke. The shriek in the background, I slowly realized, was my smoke detector. Thick gray plumes were drifting through my yellow and white bedroom like evil genies. I wasn't moving fast enough for Claudine, who yanked me out of bed and carried me out the front door. A woman had never lifted me, but, of course, Claudine was no ordinary woman. She set me on my feet in the chilly grass of the front yard. The cold feel of it suddenly woke me up. This was not a nightmare.

"My house caught on fire?" I was still struggling to be alert.

"The vampire says it was that human, there," she said, pointing to the left of the house. But for a long minute my eyes were fixed on the terrible sight of flames, and the red glow of fire lighting the night. The back porch and part of the kitchen were blazing.

I made myself look at a huddled form on the ground, close to a forsythia in bud. Charles was kneeling by it.

"Have you called the fire department?" I asked them both as I picked my way around the house in my bare feet to have a look at the recumbent figure. I peered at the dead man's slack face in the poor light. He was white, clean-shaven, and probably in his thirties. Though conditions were hardly ideal, I didn't recognize him.

"Oh, no, I didn't think of it." Charles looked up from the body. He came from a time before fire departments.

"And I forgot my cell phone," said Claudine, who was thoroughly modern.

"Then I have to go back in and do it, if the phones still work," I said, turning on my heel. Charles rose to his inconsiderable height and stared at me.

"You will not go back in there." This was definitely an order from Claudine. "New man, you run fast enough to do that."

"Fire," Charles said, "is very quickly fatal to vampires."

It was true; they went up like a torch once they caught. Selfishly, for a second I almost insisted; I wanted my coat and my slippers and my purse.

"Go call from Bill's phone," I said, pointing in the right direction, and off he took like a jackrabbit. The minute he was out of sight and before Claudine could stop me, I dashed back in the front door and made my way to my room. The smoke was much thicker, and I could see the flames a few feet down the hall in the kitchen. As soon as I saw the flames I knew I'd made a huge mistake by reentering the house, and it was hard not to panic. My purse was right where I'd left it, and my coat was tossed over the slipper chair in a corner of my room. I couldn't find my slippers, and I knew I couldn't stay. I fumbled in a drawer for a pair of socks, since I knew for sure they were there, and then I ran out of my room, coughing and choking. Acting through sheer instinct, I turned briefly to my left to shut the door to the kitchen, and then whirled to hurry out the front door. I fell over a chair in the living room.

"That was stupid," said Claudine the fairy, and I shrieked. She grabbed me around the waist and ran out of the house again, with me under her arm like a rolled-up carpet.

The combination of shrieking and coughing tied my respiratory system in knots for a minute or two, during which time Claudine moved me farther away from my house. She sat me down on the grass and put the socks on my feet. Then she helped me stand up and get my arms into the coat. I buttoned it around me gratefully.

This was the second time Claudine had appeared out of nowhere when I was about to get into serious trouble. The first time, I'd fallen asleep at the wheel after a very long day.

"You're making it awfully hard on me," she said. She still sounded cheerful, but maybe not quite as sweet.

Something changed about the house, and I realized the night-light in the hall had gone out. Either the electricity was out, or the line had been shut down in town by the fire department.

"I'm sorry," I said, feeling that was appropriate, though I had no idea why Claudine felt put upon when it was my house that was burning. I wanted to hurry to the backyard to get a better view, but Claudine caught hold of my arm.

"No closer," she said simply, and I could not break her hold. "Listen, the trucks are coming."

Now I could hear the fire engines, and I blessed every person who was coming to help. I knew the pagers had gone off all over the area, and the volunteers had rushed to the firehouse straight from their beds.

Catfish Hunter, my brother's boss, pulled up in his car. He leaped out and ran right to me. "Anyone left inside?" he asked urgently. The town's fire truck pulled in after him, scattering my new gravel all to hell.

"No," I said.

"Is there a propane tank?"

"Yes."

"Where?"

"Backyard."

"Where's your car, Sookie?"

"In the back," I said, and my voice was starting to shake.

"Propane tank in the back!" Catfish bellowed over his shoulder.

There was an answering yell, followed by a lot of purposeful activity. I recognized Hoyt Fortenberry and Ralph Tooten, plus four or five other men and a couple of women.

Catfish, after a quick conversation with Hoyt and Ralph, called over a smallish woman who seemed swamped by her gear. He pointed to the still figure in the grass, and she threw off her helmet and knelt beside him. After some peering and touching, she shook her head. I barely recognized her as Dr. Robert Meredith's nurse, Jan something.

"Who's the dead man?" asked Catfish. He didn't seem too upset by the corpse.

"I have no idea," I said. I only discovered how shocked I was by the way my voice came out—quavery, small. Claudine put her arm around me.

A police car pulled in to the side of the fire truck, and Sheriff Bud Dearborn got out of the driver's seat. Andy Bellefleur was his passenger.

Claudine said, "Ah-oh."

"Yeah," I said.

Then Charles was with me again, and Bill was right on his heels. The vampires took in the frantic but purposeful activity. They noticed Claudine.

The small woman, who'd stood to resume her gear, called, "Sheriff, do me a favor and call an ambulance to take this body away."

Bud Dearborn glanced at Andy, who turned away to speak into the car radio.

"Having one dead beau ain't enough, Sookie?" Bud Dearborn asked me.

Bill snarled, the firefighters broke out the window by my great-great-grandmother's dining table, and a visible rush of heat and sparks gushed into the night. The pumper truck made a lot of noise, and the tin roof that covered the kitchen and porch separated from the house.

My home was going up in flames and smoke.

8

CLAUDINE WAS ON MY LEFT. BILL CAME TO STAND TO my right and took my hand. Together, we watched the firefighters aim the hose through the broken window. A sound of shattering glass from the other side of the house indicated they were breaking the window over the sink, too. While the firefighters concentrated on the fire, the police concentrated on the body. Charles stepped up to bat right away.

"I killed him," he said calmly. "I caught him setting fire to the house. He was armed, and he attacked me."

Sheriff Bud Dearborn looked more like a Pekinese than any human should look. His face was practically concave. His eyes were round and bright, and at the moment extremely curious. His brown hair, liberally streaked with gray, was combed back from his face all around, and I expected him to snuffle when he spoke. "And you would be?" he asked the vampire.

"Charles Twining," Charles answered gracefully. "At your service."

I wasn't imagining the snort the sheriff gave or Andy Bellefleur's eye roll.

"And you'd be on the spot because . . . ?"

"He's staying with me," Bill said smoothly, "while he works at Merlotte's."

Presumably the sheriff had already heard about the new bartender, because he just nodded. I was relieved at not having to confess that Charles was supposed to be sleeping in my closet, and I blessed Bill for having lied about that. Our eyes met for a moment.

"So you admit you killed this man?" Andy asked Charles. Charles nodded curtly.

Andy beckoned to the woman in hospital scrubs who'd been waiting by her car—which made maybe five cars in my front yard, plus the fire truck. This new arrival glanced at me curiously as she walked past to the huddled form in the bushes. Pulling a stethoscope from a pocket, she knelt by the man and listened to various parts of his body. "Yep, dead as a doornail," she called.

Andy had gotten a Polaroid out of the police car to take pictures of the body. Since the only light was the flash of the camera and the flicker of flame from my burning house, I didn't think the pictures would turn out too well. I was numb with shock, and I watched Andy as if this were an important activity.

"What a pity. It would have been a good thing to find out why he torched Sookie's house," Bill said as he watched Andy work. His voice rivaled a refrigerator for coldness.

"In my fear for Sookie's safety, I suppose I struck too hard." Charles tried to look regretful.

"Since his neck seems to be broken, I suppose you did," said the doctor, studying Charles's white face with the same careful attention she'd given mine. The doctor was in her thirties, I thought; a woman slim to the point of skinny, with very short red hair. She was about five foot three, and she had elfin features, or at least the kind I'd always thought of as elfin: a short, turned-up nose, wide eyes, large mouth. Her words were both dry and bold, and she didn't seem at all disconcerted by or excited at being called out in the middle of the night for something like this. She must be the parish coroner, so I must have voted for her, but I couldn't recall her name.

"Who are you?" Claudine asked in her sweetest voice.

The doctor blinked at the vision of Claudine. Claudine, at this ungodly hour of the morning, was in full makeup and a fuchsia knit top with black knit leggings. Her shoes were fuchsia and black striped, and her jacket was, too. Claudine's black rippling hair was held off her face with fuchsia combs.

"I'm Dr. Tonnesen. Linda. Who are you?"

"Claudine Crane," the fairy said. I'd never known the last name Claudine used.

"And why were you here on the spot, Ms. Crane?" Andy Bellefleur asked.

"I'm Sookie's fairy godmother," Claudine said, laughing. Though the scene was grim, everyone else laughed, too. It was like we just couldn't stop being cheerful around Claudine. But I wondered very much about Claudine's explanation.

"No, really," Bud Dearborn said. "Why are you here, Ms. Crane?"

Claudine smiled impishly. "I was spending the night with Sookie," she said, winking.

In a second, we were the objects of fascinated scrutiny from every male within hearing, and I had to lock down my head as if it were a maximum-security prison to block the mental images the guys were broadcasting.

Andy shook himself, closed his mouth, and squatted by

the dead man. "Bud, I'm going to roll him," he said a little hoarsely, and turned the corpse so he could feel inside the dead man's pockets. The man's wallet proved to be in his jacket, which seemed a little unusual to me. Andy straightened and stepped away from the body to examine the billfold's contents.

"You want to have a look, see if you recognize him?" Sheriff Dearborn asked me. Of course I didn't, but I also saw that I really didn't have a choice. Nervously, I inched a little closer and looked again at the face of the dead man. He still looked ordinary. He still looked dead. He might be in his thirties. "I don't know him," I said, my voice small in the din of the firefighters and the water pouring onto the house.

"What?" Bud Dearborn was having trouble hearing me. His round brown eyes were locked onto my face.

"Don't know him!" I said, almost yelling. "I've never seen him, that I remember. Claudine?"

I don't know why I asked Claudine.

"Oh, yes, I've seen him," she said cheerfully.

That attracted the undivided attention of the two vampires, the two lawmen, the doctor, and me.

"Where?"

Claudine threw her arm around my shoulders. "Why, he was in Merlotte's tonight. You were too worried about your friend to notice, I guess. He was over in the side of the room where I was sitting." Arlene had been working that side.

It wasn't too amazing that I'd missed one male face in a crowded bar. But it did bother me that I'd been listening in to people's thoughts and I'd missed out on thoughts that must have been relevant to me. After all, he was in the bar with me, and a few hours later he'd set fire to my house. He must have been mulling me over, right?

"This driver's license says he's from Little Rock, Arkansas," Andy said.

"That wasn't what he told me," Claudine said. "He said he was from Georgia." She looked just as radiant when she realized he'd lied to her, but she wasn't smiling. "He said his name was Marlon."

"Did he tell you why he was in town, Ms. Crane?"

"He said he was just passing through, had a motel room up on the interstate."

"Did he explain any further?"

"Nope."

"Did you go to his motel, Ms. Crane?" Bud Dearborn asked in his best nonjudgmental voice.

Dr. Tonnesen was looking from speaker to speaker as if she was at a verbal tennis match.

"Gosh, no, I don't do things like that." Claudine smiled all around.

Bill looked as if someone had just waved a bottle of blood in front of his face. His fangs extended, and his eyes fixed on Claudine. Vampires can only hold out so long when fairies are around. Charles had stepped closer to Claudine, too.

She had to leave before the lawmen observed how the vampires were reacting. Linda Tonnesen had already noticed; she herself was pretty interested in Claudine. I hoped she'd just attribute the vamps' fascination to Claudine's excellent looks, rather than the overwhelming allure fairies held for vamps.

"Fellowship of the Sun," Andy said. "He has an honest-to-God membership card in here. There's no name written on the card; that's strange. His license is issued to Jeff Marriot." He looked at me questioningly.

I shook my head. The name meant nothing to me.

It was just like a Fellowship member to think that he could do something as nasty as torching my house—with me in it—and no one would question him. It wasn't the first time the Fellowship of the Sun, an anti-vampire hate group, had tried to burn me alive.

"He must have known you've had, ah, an association with vampires," Andy said into the silence.

"I'm losing my home, and I could have died, because I know vampires?"

Even Bud Dearborn looked a little embarrassed.

"Someone must have heard you used to date Mr. Compton, here," Bud muttered. "I'm sorry, Sookie."

I said, "Claudine needs to leave."

The abrupt change of subject startled both Andy and Bud, as well as Claudine. She looked at the two vampires, who were perceptibly closer to her, and hastily said, "Yes, I'm sorry, I have to get back home. I have to work tomorrow."

"Where's your car, Ms. Crane?" Bud Dearborn looked around elaborately. "I didn't see any car but Sookie's, and it's parked in the back."

"I'm parked over at Bill's," Claudine lied smoothly, having had years of practice. Without waiting for further discussion, she disappeared into the woods, and only my hands gripping their arms prevented Charles and Bill from gliding into the darkness after her. They were staring into the blackness of the trees when I pinched them, hard.

"What?" asked Bill, almost dreamily.

"Snap out of it," I muttered, hoping Bud and Andy and the new doctor wouldn't overhear. They didn't need to know that Claudine was supernatural.

"That's quite a woman," Dr. Tonnesen said, almost as dazed as the vampires. She shook herself. "The ambulance will come get, uh, Jeff Marriot. I'm just here because I had my scanner turned on as I was driving back from my shift at the Clarice hospital. I need to get home and get some sleep. Sorry about your fire, Ms. Stackhouse, but at least you didn't end up like this guy here." She nodded down at the corpse.

As she got into her Ranger, the fire chief trudged up to us. I'd known Catfish Hunter for years—he'd been a friend of my dad's—but I'd never seen him in his capacity as volunteer fire chief. Catfish was sweating despite the cold, and his face was smudged with smoke.

"Sookie, we done got it out," he said wearily. "It's not as bad as you might think."

"It's not?" I asked in a small voice.

"No, honey. You lost your back porch and your kitchen and your car, I'm afraid. He splashed some gas in that, too. But most of the house should be okay."

The kitchen . . . where the only traces of the death I'd caused could have been found. Now not even the technicians featured on the Discovery Channel could find any blood traces in the scorched room. Without meaning to, I began to laugh. "The kitchen," I said between giggles. "The kitchen's all gone?"

"Yes," said Catfish uneasily. "I hope you got you some homeowners insurance."

"Oh," I said, trying hard not to giggle any more. "I do. It was hard for me to keep up the payments, but I kept the policy Grandmother had on the house." Thank God my grandmother had been a great believer in insurance. She'd seen too many people drop policy payments to cut their monthly expenses and then suffer losses they were unable to recoup.

"Who's it with? I'll call right now." Catfish was so anxious to stop me laughing, he was ready to make clown faces and bark if I asked him to.

"Greg Aubert," I said.

The whole night suddenly rose up and whalloped me one. My house had burned, at least partially. I'd had more than one prowler. I had a vampire in residence for whom daytime cover had to be provided. My car was gone. There was a dead man named Jeff Marriot in my yard, and he'd set fire to my house and car out of sheer prejudice. I was overwhelmed.

"Jason isn't at home," Catfish said from a distance. "I tried him. He'd want her to come over to his house."

"She and Charles—that is, Charles and I will take her over to my house," Bill said. He seemed to be equally far away.

"I don't know about that," Bud Dearborn said doubtfully. "Sookie, is that okay with you?"

I could barely make my mind shuffle through a few options. I couldn't call Tara because Mickey was there. Arlene's trailer was as crowded as it needed to be already.

"Yes, that would be all right," I said, and my voice sounded remote and empty, even to my own ears.

"All right, long's we know where to reach you."

"I called Greg, Sookie, and left a message on his office answering machine. You better call him yourself in the morning," Catfish said.

"Fine," I said.

And all the firefighters shuffled by, and they all told me how sorry they were. I knew every one of them: friends of my father's, friends of Jason's, regulars at the bar, high school acquaintances.

"You all did the best you could," I said over and over. "Thanks for saving most of it."

And the ambulance came to cart away the arsonist.

By then, Andy had found a gasoline can in the bushes, and the corpse's hands reeked of gasoline, Dr. Tonnesen said.

I could hardly believe that a stranger had decided I should lose my home and my life because of my dating preference. Thinking at that moment of how close I'd come to death, I didn't feel it was unjust that he'd lost his own life in the process. I admitted to myself that I thought Charles had done a good thing. I might owe my life to Sam's insistence that the vampire be billeted at my house. If Sam had been

there at the moment, I would have given him a very enthu-
siastic thank-you.

Finally Bill and Charles and I started over to Bill's house.
Catfish had advised me not to go back into my house until
the morning, and then only after the insurance agent and
the arson investigator had checked it over. Dr. Tonnesen had
told me that if I felt wheezy, to come in to her office in the
morning. She'd said some other stuff, but I hadn't quite absorbed it.

It was dark in the woods, of course, and by then it was
maybe five in the morning. After a few paces into the trees,
Bill picked me up and carried me. I didn't protest, because I
was so tired I'd been wondering how I was going to manage
stumbling through the cemetery.

He put me down when we reached his house. "Can you
make it up the stairs?" he asked.

"I'll take you," offered Charles.

"No, I can do it," I said, and started up before they
could say anything more. To tell the truth, I was not so sure
I could, but slowly I made my way up to the bedroom I'd
used when Bill had been my boyfriend. He had a snug
light-tight place somewhere on the ground floor of the
house, but I'd never asked him exactly where. (I had a
pretty good idea it was in the space the builders had lopped
off the kitchen to create the hot tub/plant room.) Though
the water table is too high in Louisiana for houses to have
basements, I was almost as sure there was another dark hole
concealed somewhere. He had room for Charles without
them bunking together, anyway—not that that was too
high on my list of concerns. One of my nightgowns still lay
in the drawer in the old-fashioned bedroom, and there was
still a toothbrush of mine in the hall bathroom. Bill hadn't
put my things in the trash; he'd left them, like he'd expected me to return.

Or maybe he just hadn't had much reason to go upstairs since we'd broken up.

Promising myself a long shower in the morning, I took off my smelly, stained pajamas and ruined socks. I washed my face and pulled on the clean nightgown before I crawled in the high bed, using the antique stool still positioned where I'd left it. As the incidents of the day and night buzzed in my head like bees, I thanked God for the fact that my life had been spared, and that was all I had time to say to Him before sleep swallowed me up.

I slept only three hours. Then worry woke me up. I was up in plenty of time to meet Greg Aubert, the insurance agent. I dressed in a pair of Bill's jeans and a shirt of his. They'd been left outside my door, along with heavy socks. His shoes were out of the question, but to my delight I found an old pair of rubber-soled slippers I'd left at the very back of the closet. Bill still had some coffee and a coffeemaker in his kitchen from our courtship, and I was grateful to have a mug to carry with me as I made my way carefully across the cemetery and through the belt of woods surrounding what was left of my house.

Greg was pulling into the front yard as I stepped from the trees. He got out of his truck, scanned my oddly fitting ensemble, and politely ignored it. He and I stood side by side, regarding the old house. Greg had sandy hair and rimless glasses, and he was an elder in the Presbyterian Church. I'd always liked him, at least in part because whenever I'd taken my grandmother by to pay her premiums, he'd come out of his office to shake her hand and make her feel like a valued client. His business acumen was matched only by his luck. People had said for years that his personal good fortune extended to his policyholders, though of course they said this in a joking kind of way.

"If only I could have foreseen this," Greg said. "Sookie, I am so sorry this happened."

"What do you mean, Greg?"

"Oh, I'm just . . . I wish I'd thought of you needing more coverage," he said absently. He began walking around to the back of the house, and I trailed behind him. Curious, I began to listen in to his head, and I was startled out of my gloom by what I heard there.

"So casting spells to back up your insurance really works?" I asked.

He yelped. There's no other word for it. "It's true about you," he gasped. "I—I don't—it's just . . ." He stood outside my blackened kitchen and gaped at me.

"It's okay," I said reassuringly. "You can pretend I don't know if it'll help you feel better."

"My wife would just die if she knew," he said soberly. "And the kids, too. I just want them kept separate from this part of my life. My mother was . . . she was . . ."

"A witch?" I supplied helpfully.

"Well, yes." Greg's glasses glinted in the early morning sun as he looked at what was left of my kitchen. "But my dad always pretended he didn't know, and though she kept training me to take her place, I wanted to be a normal man more than anything in the world." Greg nodded, as if to say he'd achieved his goal.

I looked down into my mug of coffee, glad I had something to hold in my hands. Greg was lying to himself in a major way, but it wasn't up to me to point that out to him. It was something he'd have to square with his God and his conscience. I wasn't saying Greg's method was a bad one, but it sure wasn't a normal man's choice. Insuring your livelihood (literally) by the use of magic had to be against some kind of rule.

"I mean, I'm a good agent," he said, defending himself, though I hadn't said a word. "I'm careful about what I insure. I'm careful about checking things out. It's not all the magic."

"Oh, no," I said, because he would just explode with anxiety if I didn't. "People have accidents anyway, right?"

"Regardless of what spells I use," he agreed gloomily. "They drive drunk. And sometimes metal parts give way, no matter what."

The idea of conventional Greg Aubert going around Bon Temps putting spells on cars was almost enough to distract me from the ruin of my house . . . but not quite.

In the clear chilly daylight, I could see the damage in full. Though I kept telling myself it could have been much worse—and that I was very lucky that the kitchen had extended off the back of the house, since it had been built at a later date—it had also been the room that had held big-ticket items. I'd have to replace the stove, the refrigerator, the hot water heater, and the microwave, and the back porch had been home to my washer and drier.

After the loss of those major appliances, there came the dishes and the pots and the pans and the silverware, some of it very old indeed. One of my greats had come from a family with a little money, and she'd brought a set of fine china and a silver tea service that had been a pain to polish. I'd never have to polish it again, I realized, but there was no joy in the thought. My Nova was old, and I'd needed to replace it for a long time, but I hadn't planned on that being now.

Well, I had insurance, and I had money in the bank, thanks to the vampires who'd paid me for keeping Eric when he'd lost his memory.

"And you had smoke detectors?" Greg was asking.

"Yes, I did," I said, remembering the high-pitched pulsing that had started up right after Claudine had woken me.

"If the ceiling in the hall is still there, you'll be able to see one."

There were no more back steps to get us up onto the porch, and the porch floorboards looked very unsteady. In fact, the washer had half fallen through and was tilted at an odd angle. It made me sick, seeing my everyday things, things I'd touched and used hundreds of times, exposed to the world and ruined.

"We'll go through from the front door," Greg suggested, and I was glad to agree.

It was still unlocked, and I felt a flutter of alarm before I realized how ludicrous that was. I stepped in. The first thing I noticed was the smell. Everything reeked of smoke. I opened the windows, and the cool breeze that blew through began to clear the smell out until it was just tolerable.

This end of the house was better than I'd expected. The furniture would need cleaning, of course. But the floor was solid and undamaged. I didn't even go up the stairs; I seldom used the rooms up there, so whatever had happened up there could wait.

My arms were crossed under my breasts. I looked from side to side, moving slowly across the room toward the hall. I felt the floor vibrate as someone else came in. I knew without looking around that Jason was behind me. He and Greg said something to each other, but after a second Jason fell silent, as shocked as I was.

We passed into the hall. The door to my bedroom and the door to the bedroom across the hall were both open. My bedding was still thrown back. My slippers were beside the night table. All the windows were smudged with smoke and moisture, and the dreadful odor grew even stronger. There was the smoke detector on the hall ceiling. I pointed to it silently. I opened the door to the linen closet and found that everything in it felt damp. Well, these things could be washed. I went into my room and opened my closet door. My closet shared a wall with the kitchen. At first glance my clothes looked intact, until I noticed that each garment hanging on a wire hanger had a line across the shoulders where the heated hanger had singed the cloth. My shoes had baked. Maybe three pairs were usable.

I gulped.

Though I felt shakier by the second, I joined my brother and the insurance agent as they carefully continued down the hall to the kitchen.

The floor closest to the old part of the house seemed okay. The kitchen had been a large room, since it had also served as the family dining room. The table was partially burned, as were two of the chairs. The linoleum on the floor was all broken up, and some of it was charred. The hot water heater had gone through the floor, and the curtains that had covered the window over the sink were hanging in strips. I remembered Gran making those curtains; she hadn't enjoyed sewing, but the ones from JCPenney that she'd liked were just too much. So she'd gotten out her mother's old sewing machine and bought some cheap but pretty flowered material at Hancock's, and she'd measured, and cursed under her breath, and worked and worked until finally she'd gotten them done. Jason and I had admired them extravagantly to make her feel it had been worth the effort, and she'd been so pleased.

I opened one drawer, the one that had held all the keys. They were melted together. I pressed my lips together, hard. Jason stood beside me, looked down.

"Shit," he said, his voice low and vicious. That helped me push the tears back.

I held on to his arm for just a minute. He patted me awkwardly. Seeing items so familiar, items made dear by use, irrevocably altered by fire was a terrible shock, no matter how many times I reminded myself that the whole house could have been consumed by the flames; that I could have died, too. Even if the smoke detector had wakened me in time, there was every likelihood I would have run outside to be confronted by the arsonist, Jeff Marriot.

Almost everything on the east side of the kitchen was ruined. The floor was unstable. The kitchen roof was gone.

"It's lucky the rooms upstairs don't extend over the kitchen," Greg said when he came down from examining the two bedrooms and the attic. "You'll have to get a builder to let you know, but I think the second story is essentially sound."

I talked to Greg about money after that. When would it come? How much would it be? What deductible would I have to pay?

Jason wandered around the yard while Greg and I stood by his car. I could interpret my brother's posture and movements. Jason was very angry: at my near-death escape, at what had happened to the house. After Greg drove off, leaving me with an exhausting list of things to do and phone calls to make (from where?) and work to get ready for (wearing what?), Jason meandered over to me and said, "If I'd been here, I coulda killed him."

"In your new body?" I asked.

"Yeah. It would've given that sumbitch the scare of his life before he left it."

"I think Charles probably was pretty scary, but I appreciate the thought."

"They put the vamp in jail?"

"No, Bud Dearborn just told him not to leave town. After all, the Bon Temps jail doesn't have a vampire cell. And regular cells don't hold 'em, plus they have windows."

"That's where the guy was from—Fellowship of the Sun? Just a stranger who came to town to do you in?"

"That's what it looks like."

"What they got against you? Other than you dating Bill and associating with some of the other vamps?"

Actually, the Fellowship had quite a bit against me. I'd been responsible for their huge Dallas church being raided and one of their main leaders going underground. The papers had been full of what the police had found in the Fellowship building in Texas. Arriving to find the members dashing in turmoil around their building, claiming vampires had attacked them, the police entered the building to search it and found a basement torture chamber, illegal arms adapted to shoot wooden stakes into vampires, and a corpse. The police failed to see a single vampire. Steve and Sarah Newlin, the leaders of the Fellowship church in Dallas, had been missing since that night.

I'd seen Steve Newlin since then. He'd been at Club Dead in Jackson. He and one of his cronies had been preparing to stake a vampire in the club when I'd prevented them. Newlin had escaped; his buddy hadn't.

It appeared that the Newlins' followers had tracked me down. I hadn't foreseen such a thing, but then, I'd never foreseen anything that had happened to me in the past year. When Bill had been learning how to use his computer, he'd told me that with a little knowledge and money, anyone could be found through a computer.

Maybe the Fellowship had hired private detectives, like the couple who had been in my house yesterday. Maybe Jack and Lily Leeds had just been pretending to be hired by the Pelt family? Maybe the Newlins were their real employers? They hadn't struck me as politicized people, but the power of the color green is universal.

"I guess dating a vampire was enough for them to hate me," I told Jason. We were sitting on the tailgate of his truck, staring dismally at the house. "Who do you think I should call about rebuilding the kitchen?"

I didn't think I needed an architect; I just wanted to replace what was missing. The house was raised up off the ground, so slab size wasn't a factor. Since the floor was burned through in the kitchen and would have to be completely replaced, it wouldn't cost much more to make the kitchen a little bigger and enclose the back porch completely. The washer and dryer wouldn't be so awful to use in bad weather, I thought longingly. I had more than enough money to satisfy the deductible, and I was sure the insurance would pay for most of the rest.

After a while, we heard another truck coming. Maxine Fortenberry, Hoyt's mother, got out with a couple of laundry baskets. "Where's your clothes, girl?" she called. "I'm gonna take them home and wash them, so you'll have something to wear that don't smell like smoke."

After I protested and she insisted, we went into the chokingly unpleasant air of the house to get some clothes. Maxine also insisted on getting an armful of linens out of the linen closet to see if some of them could be resurrected.

Right after Maxine left, Tara drove her new car into the clearing, followed by her part-time help, a tall young woman called McKenna, who was driving Tara's old car.

After a hug and a few words of sympathy, Tara said, "You drive this old Malibu while you're getting your insurance stuff straightened out. It's just sitting in my carport doing nothing, and I was just about to put it in the paper in the For Sale column. You can be using it."

"Thank you," I said in a daze. "Tara, that's so nice of you." She didn't look good, I noticed vaguely, but I was too sunk in my own troubles to really evaluate Tara's demeanor. When she and McKenna left, I gave them a limp wave good-bye.

After that, Terry Bellefleur arrived. He offered to demolish the burned part for a very nominal sum, and for a little bit more he'd haul all the resultant trash to the parish dump. He'd start as soon as the police gave him the go-ahead, he said, and to my astonishment he gave me a little hug.

Sam came after that, driven by Arlene. He stood and looked at the back of the house for a few minutes. His lips were tightly compressed. Almost any man would have said, "Pretty lucky I sent the vampire home with you, huh?" But Sam didn't. "What can I do?" he said instead.

"Keep me working," I said, smiling. "Forgive me coming to work in something besides my actual work clothes." Arlene walked all around the house, and then hugged me wordlessly.

"That's easily done," he said. He still wasn't smiling. "I hear that the guy who started the fire was a Fellowship member, that this is some kind of payback for you dating Bill."

"He had the card in his wallet, and he had a gas can." I shrugged.

"But how'd he find you? I mean, no one around here . . ." Sam's voice trailed off as he considered the possibility more closely.

He was thinking, as I had, that though the arson could be just because I'd dated Bill, it seemed a drastic overreaction. A more typical retaliation was a Fellowship member throwing pig's blood on humans who dated, or had a work partnership with, a vampire. That had happened more than once, most notably to a designer from Dior who'd employed all vampire models for one spring show. Such incidents usually occurred in big cities, cities that hosted large Fellowship "churches" and a bigger vampire population.

What if the man had been hired to set fire to my house by someone else? What if the Fellowship card in his wallet was planted there for misdirection?

Any of these things could be true; or all of them, or none of them. I couldn't decide what I believed. So, was I the target of an assassin, like the shape-shifters? Should I, too, fear the shot from the dark, now that the fire had failed?

That was such a frightening prospect that I flinched from pursuing it. Those were waters too deep for me.

The state police arson investigator appeared while Sam and Arlene were there. I was eating a lunch plate Arlene had brought me. That Arlene was not much of a food person is the nicest way to put it, so my sandwich was made of cheap bologna and plastic cheese, and my canned drink was off-brand sugared tea. But she'd thought of me and she'd brought them to me, and her kids had drawn a picture for me. I would have been happy if she'd brought me just a slice of bread under those conditions.

Automatically, Arlene made eyes at the arson investigator. He was a lean man in his late forties named Dennis Pettibone. Dennis had a camera, a notebook, and a grim outlook. It took Arlene maybe two minutes of conversation to coax a little smile from Mr. Pettibone's lips, and his brown eyes were admiring her curves after two more minutes had passed. Before Arlene drove Sam home, she had a promise from the investigator that he'd drop by the bar that evening.

Also before she left, Arlene offered me the foldout couch in her trailer, which was sweet of her, but I knew it would crowd her and throw off her get-the-kids-to-school morning routine, so I told her I had a place to stay. I didn't think Bill would evict me. Jason had mentioned his house was open to me, and to my amazement, before he left, Sam said, "You can stay with me, Sookie. No strings. I have two empty bedrooms in the double-wide. There's actually a bed in one of them."

"That's so nice of you," I said, putting all my sincerity into my voice. "Every soul in Bon Temps would have us on the way to being married if I did that, but I sure do appreciate it."

"You don't think they won't make assumptions if you stay with Bill?"

"I can't marry Bill. Not legal," I replied, cutting off that argument. "Besides, Charles is there, too."

"Fuel to the fire," Sam pointed out. "That's even spicier."

"That's kind of flattering, crediting me with enough pizzazz to take care of two vampires at a go."

Sam grinned, which knocked about ten years off his age. He looked over my shoulder as we heard the sound of gravel crunching under yet another vehicle. "Look who's coming," he said.

A huge and ancient pickup lumbered to a stop. Out of it stepped Dawson, the huge Were who'd been acting as Calvin Norris's bodyguard.

"Sookie," he rumbled, his voice so deep I expected the ground to vibrate.

"Hey, Dawson." I wanted to ask, "What are you doing here?" but I figured that would sound plain rude.

"Calvin heard about your fire," Dawson said, not wasting time with preliminaries. "He told me to come by here and see was you hurt, and to tell you that he is thinking about you and that if he were well, he would be here pounding nails already."

I saw from the corner of my eye that Dennis Pettibone was eyeing Dawson with interest. Dawson might as well have been wearing a sign that said DANGEROUS DUDE on it.

"You tell him I'm real grateful for the thought. I wish he were well, too. How's he doing, Dawson?"

"He got a couple of things unhooked this morning, and he's been walking a little. It was a bad wound," Dawson said. "It'll take a bit." He glanced over to see how far away the arson investigator was. "Even for one of us," he added.

"Of course," I said. "I appreciate your coming by."

"Also, Calvin says his house is empty while he's in the hospital, if you need a place to stay. He'd be glad to give you the use of it."

That, too, was kind, and I said so. But I would feel very awkward, being obliged to Calvin in such a significant way.

Dennis Pettibone called me over. "See, Ms. Stackhouse," he said. "You can see where he used the gasoline on your porch. See the way the fire ran out from the splash he made on the door?"

I gulped. "Yes, I see."

"You're lucky there wasn't any wind last night. And most of all, you're lucky that you had that door shut, the one between the kitchen and the rest of the house. The fire would have gone right down that hall if you hadn't shut the door. When the firefighters smashed that window on the north side, the fire ran that way looking for oxygen, instead of trying to make it into the rest of the house."

I remembered the impulse that had pushed me back into the house against all common sense, the last-minute slam of that door.

"After a couple of days, I don't think the bulk of the house will even smell as bad," the investigator told me. "Open the windows now, pray it don't rain, and fairly soon I don't think you'll have much problem. Course, you got to call the power company and talk to them about the electricity. And the propane company needs to take a look at the tank. So the house ain't livable, from that point of view."

The gist of what he was saying was, I could just sleep there to have a roof over my head. No electricity, no heat, no hot water, no cooking. I thanked Dennis Pettibone and excused myself to have a last word with Dawson, who'd been listening in.

"I'll try to come see Calvin in a day or two, once I get this straightened out," I said, nodding toward the blackened back of my house.

"Oh, yeah," the bodyguard said, one foot already in his pickup. "Calvin said let him know who done this, if it was ordered by someone besides the sumbitch dead at the scene."

I looked at what remained of my kitchen and could almost count the feet from the flames to my bedroom. "I appreciate that most of all," I said, before my Christian self could smother the thought. Dawson's brown eyes met mine in a moment of perfect accord.

9

THANKS TO MAXINE, I HAD CLEAN-SMELLING
clothes to wear to work, but I had to go buy some footwear
at Payless. Normally, I put a little money into my shoes
since I have to stand up so much, but there was no time to
go to Clarice to the one good shoe shop there or to drive
over to Monroe to the mall. When I got to work, Sweetie
Des Arts came out of the kitchen to hug me, her thin body
wrapped in a white cook's apron. Even the boy who bussed
the tables told me he was sorry. Holly and Danielle, who
were switching off shifts, each gave me a pat on the shoulder
and told me they hoped things got better for me.

Arlene asked me if I thought that handsome Dennis Pettibone would be coming by, and I told her I was sure he
would.

"I guess he has to travel a lot," she said thoughtfully. "I
wonder where he's based."

"I got his business card. He's based in Shreveport. He told me he bought himself a small farm right outside of Shreveport, now that I think about it."

Arlene's eyes narrowed. "Sounds like you and Dennis had a nice talk."

I started to protest that the arson investigator was a little long in the tooth for me, but since Arlene had stuck to saying she was thirty-six for the past three years, I figured that would be less than tactful. "He was just passing the time of day," I told her. "He asked me how long I'd worked with you, and did you have any kids."

"Oh. He did?" Arlene beamed. "Well, well." She went to check on her tables with a cheerful strut to her walk.

I set about my work, having to take longer than usual to do everything because of the constant interruptions. I knew some other town sensation would soon eclipse my house fire. Though I couldn't hope anyone else would experience a similar disaster, I would be glad when I wasn't the object of discussion of every single bar patron.

Terry hadn't been able to handle the light daytime bar duties today, so Arlene and I pitched in to cover it. Being busy helped me feel less self-conscious.

Though I was coasting on three hours of sleep, I managed okay until Sam called me from the hallway that led to his office and the public bathrooms.

Two people had come in earlier and gone up to his corner table to talk to him; I'd noted them only in passing. The woman was in her sixties, very round and short. She used a cane. The young man with her was brown haired, with a sharp nose and heavy brows to give his face some character. He reminded me of someone, but I couldn't make the reference pop to the top of my head. Sam had ushered them back into his office.

"Sookie," Sam said unhappily, "the people in my office want to talk to you."

"Who are they?"

"She's Jeff Marriot's mother. The man is his twin."

"Oh my God," I said, realizing the man reminded me of the corpse. "Why do they want to talk to me?"

"They don't think he ever had anything to do with the Fellowship. They don't understand anything about his death."

To say I dreaded this encounter was putting it mildly. "Why talk to me?" I said in a kind of subdued wail. I was nearly at the end of my emotional endurance.

"They just . . . want answers. They're grieving."

"So am I," I said. "My home."

"Their loved one."

I stared at Sam. "Why should I talk to them?" I asked. "What is it you want from me?"

"You need to hear what they have to say," Sam said with a note of finality in his voice. He wouldn't push any more, and he wouldn't explain any more. Now the decision was up to me.

Because I trusted Sam, I nodded. "I'll talk to them when I get off work," I said. I secretly hoped they'd leave by then. But when my shift was over, the two were still sitting in Sam's office. I took off my apron, tossed it in the big trash can labeled DIRTY LINEN (reflecting for the hundredth time that the trash can would probably implode if anyone put some actual linen in it), and plodded into the office.

I looked the Marriots over more carefully now that we were face-to-face. Mrs. Marriot (I assumed) was in bad shape. Her skin was grayish, and her whole body seemed to sag. Her glasses were smeared because she'd been weeping so much, and she was clutching damp tissues in her hands. Her son was shocked expressionless. He'd lost his twin, and he was sending me so much misery I could hardly absorb it.

"Thanks for talking to us," he said. He rose from his seat automatically and extended his hand. "I'm Jay Marriot, and this is my mother, Justine."

This was a family that found a letter of the alphabet it liked and stuck to it.

I didn't know what to say. Could I tell them I was sorry their loved one was dead, when he'd tried to kill me? There was no rule of etiquette for this; even my grandmother would have been stymied.

"Miss—Ms.—Stackhouse, had you ever met my brother before?"

"No," I said. Sam took my hand. Since the Marriots were seated in the only two chairs Sam's office could boast, he and I leaned against the front of his desk. I hoped his leg wasn't hurting.

"Why would he set fire to your house? He'd never been arrested before, for anything," Justine spoke for the first time. Her voice was rough and choked with tears; it had an undertone of pleading. She was asking me to let this not be true, this allegation about her son Jeff.

"I sure don't know."

"Could you tell us how this happened? His—death, I mean?"

I felt a flare of anger at being obliged to pity them—at the necessity for being delicate, for treating them specially. After all, who had almost died here? Who had lost part of her home? Who was facing a financial crunch that only chance had reduced from a disaster? Rage surged through me, and Sam let go of my hand and put his arm around me. He could feel the tension in my body. He was hoping I would control the impulse to lash out.

I held on to my better nature by my fingernails, but I held on.

"A friend woke me up," I said. "When we got outside, we found a vampire who is staying with my neighbor—also a vampire—standing by Mr. Marriot's body. There was a gasoline can near to the . . . nearby. The doctor who came said there was gas on his hands."

"What killed him?" The mother again.

"The vampire."

"Bit him?"

"No, he . . . no. No biting."

"How, then?" Jay was showing some of his own anger.

"Broke his neck, I think."

"That was what we heard at the sheriff's office," Jay said. "But we just didn't know if they were telling the truth."

Oh, for goodness's sake.

Sweetie Des Arts stuck her head in to ask Sam if she could borrow the storeroom keys because she needed a case of pickles. She apologized for interrupting. Arlene waved a hand at me as she went down the hall to the employees' door, and I wondered if Dennis Pettibone had come in the bar. I'd been so sunk in my own problems, I hadn't noticed. When the outside door clunked shut behind her, the silence seemed to gather in the little room.

"So why was the vampire in your yard?" Jay asked impatiently. "In the middle of the night?"

I did not tell him it was none of his business. Sam's hand stroked my arm. "That's when they're up. And he was staying at the only other house out by mine." That's what we'd told the police. "I guess he heard someone in my yard while he was close and came to investigate."

"We don't know how Jeff got there," Justine said. "Where is his car?"

"I don't know."

"And there was a card in his wallet?"

"Yes, a Fellowship of the Sun membership card," I told her.

"But he had nothing particular against vampires," Jay protested. "We're twins. I would have known if he'd had some big grudge. This just doesn't make any sense."

"He did give a woman in the bar a fake name and hometown," I said, as gently as I could.

"Well, he was just passing through," Jay said. "I'm a married man, but Jeff's divorced. I don't like to say this in front of my mother, but it's not unknown for men to give a false name and history when they meet a woman in a bar."

This was true. Though Merlotte's was primarily a neighborhood bar, I'd listened to many a tale from out-of-towners who'd dropped in; and I'd known for sure they were lying.

"Where was the wallet?" Justine asked. She looked up at me like an old beaten dog, and it made my heart sick.

"In his jacket pocket," I said.

Jay stood up abruptly. He began to move, pacing in the small space he had at his disposal. "There again," he said, his voice more animated, "that's just not like Jeff. He kept his billfold in his jeans, same as me. We never put our wallets in our jacket."

"What are you saying?" Sam asked.

"I'm saying that I don't think Jeff did this," his twin said. "Even those people at the Fina station, they could be mistaken."

"Someone at the Fina says he bought a can of gas there?" Sam asked.

Justine flinched again, the soft skin of her chin shaking.

I'd been wondering if there might be something to the Marriots' suspicions, but that idea was extinguished now. The phone rang, and all of us jumped. Sam picked it up and said, "Merlotte's," in a calm voice. He listened, said,

"Um-hum," and "That right?" and finally, "I'll tell her." He hung up.

"Your brother's car's been found," he told Jay Marriot. "It's on a little road almost directly across from Sookie's driveway."

The light went out completely on the little family's ray of hope, and I could only feel sorry for them. Justine seemed ten years older than she had when she'd come into the bar, and Jay looked like he'd gone days without sleep or food. They left without another word to me, which was a mercy. From the few sentences they exchanged with each other, I gathered they were going to see Jeff's car and ask if they could remove any of his belongings from it. I thought they would meet another blank wall there.

Eric had told me that that little road, a dirt track leading back to a deer camp, was where Debbie Pelt had hidden her car when she'd come to kill me. Might as well put up a sign: PARKING FOR SOOKIE STACKHOUSE NIGHTTIME ATTACKS.

Sam came swinging back into the room. He'd been seeing the Marriots out. He stood by me propped against his desk and set his crutches aside. He put his arm around me. I turned to him and slid my arms around his waist. He held me to him, and I felt peaceful for a wonderful minute. The heat of his body warmed me, and the knowledge of his affection comforted me.

"Does your leg hurt?" I asked when he moved restlessly.

"Not my leg," he said.

I looked up, puzzled, to meet his eyes. He looked rueful. Suddenly, I became aware of exactly what was hurting Sam, and I flushed red. But I didn't let go of him. I was reluctant to end the comfort of being close to someone—no, of being close to Sam. When I didn't move away, he slowly put his lips to mine, giving me every chance to step out of reach. His mouth brushed mine once, twice. Then he settled in to kissing me, and the heat of his tongue filled my mouth, stroking.

That felt incredibly good. With the visit of the Marriot family, I'd been browsing the Mystery section. Now I'd definitely wandered over to the Romances.

His height was close enough to mine that I didn't have to strain upward to meet his mouth. His kiss became more urgent. His lips strayed down my neck, to the vulnerable and sensitive place just at the base, and his teeth nipped very gently.

I gasped. I just couldn't help it. If I'd had the gift of teleportation, I would've had us somewhere more private in an instant. Remotely, I felt there was something kind of tacky at feeling this lustful in a messy office in a bar. But the heat surged as he kissed me again. We'd always had something between us, and the smoldering ember had just burst into flame.

I struggled to hold on to some sense. Was this survivor lust? What about his leg? Did he really need the buttons on his shirt?

"Not good enough for you here," he said, doing a little gasping of his own. He pulled away and reached for his crutches, but then he hauled me back and kissed me again. "Sookie, I'm going to—"

"What are you going to do?" asked a cold voice from the doorway.

If I was shocked senseless, Sam was enraged. In a split second I was pushed to one side, and he launched himself at the intruder, broken leg and all.

My heart was thumping like a scared rabbit's, and I put one hand over it to make sure it stayed in my chest. Sam's sudden attack had knocked Bill to the floor. Sam pulled back his fist to get in a punch, but Bill used his greater weight and strength to roll Sam until he was on the bottom. Bill's fangs were out and his eyes were glowing.

"Stop!" I yelled at a reduced volume, scared the patrons would come running. In a little fast action of my own, I gripped Bill's smooth dark hair with both hands and used it to yank his head back. In the excitement of the moment, Bill reached behind him to catch my wrists in his hands, and he began twisting. I choked with pain. Both my arms were about to break when Sam took the opportunity to sock Bill in the jaw with all his power. Shifters are not as powerful as Weres and vampires, but they can pack quite a punch, and Bill was rocked sideways. He also came to his senses. Releasing my arms, he rose and turned to me in one graceful movement.

My eyes welled full of tears from the pain, and I opened them wide, determined not to let the drops roll down my cheeks. But I'm sure I looked exactly like someone who was trying hard not to cry. I was holding my arms out in front of me, wondering when they'd stop hurting.

"Since your car was burned, I came to get you because it was time for you to get off work," Bill said, his fingers gently evaluating the marks on my forearms. "I swear I just intended to do you a favor. I swear I wasn't spying on you. I swear I never intended you any harm."

That was a pretty good apology, and I was glad he'd spoken first. Not only was I in pain, I was totally embarrassed. Naturally, Bill had no way of knowing that Tara had loaned me a car. I should have left him a note or left a message on his answering machine, but I'd driven straight to work from the burned house, and it simply hadn't crossed my mind. Something else did occur to me, as it should have right away.

"Oh, Sam, did your leg get hurt worse?" I brushed past Bill to help Sam to his feet. I took as much of his weight as I could, knowing he'd rather lie on the floor forever than accept any assistance from Bill. Finally, with some difficulty, I maneuvered Sam upright, and I saw he was careful to keep his weight on his good leg. I couldn't even imagine how Sam must be feeling.

He was feeling pretty pissed off, I discovered directly. He glared past me at Bill. "You come in without calling out, without knocking? I'm sure you don't expect me to say I'm sorry for jumping you." I'd never seen Sam so angry. I could tell that he was embarrassed that he hadn't "protected" me more effectively, that he was humiliated that Bill had gained the upper hand and furthermore had hurt me. Last but not least, Sam was coping with the backwash from all those hormones that had been exploding when we'd been interrupted.

"Oh, no. I don't expect that." Bill's voice dropped in temperature when he spoke to Sam. I expected to see icicles form on the walls.

I wished I were a thousand miles away. I longed for the ability to walk out, get into my own car, and drive to my own home. Of course, I couldn't. At least I had the use of a car, and I explained that to Bill.

"Then I needn't have gone to the trouble of coming to get you, and you two could have continued uninterrupted," he said in an absolutely lethal tone. "Where are you going to spend the night, if I may ask? I was going to go to the store to buy food for you."

Since Bill hated grocery shopping, that would have been a major effort, and he wanted to be sure I knew about it. (Of course, it was also possible that he was making this up on the spot to be sure I felt as guilty as possible.)

I reviewed my options. Though I never knew what I'd walk into over at my brother's, that seemed my safest choice. "I'm going to run by my house to get some makeup out of the bathroom, and then I'm going to Jason's," I said.

"Thank you for putting me up last night, Bill. I guess you brought Charles to work? Tell him if he wants to spend the night at my house, I guess the, ah, hole is okay."

"Tell him yourself. He's right outside," Bill said in a voice I can only characterize as grumpy. Bill's imagination had evidently spun a whole different scenario for the evening. The way events were unfolding was making him mighty unhappy.

Sam was in so much pain (I could see it hovering like a red glow around him) that the most merciful thing I could do was clear out of there before he gave into it. "I'll see you tomorrow, Sam," I said, and kissed him on the cheek.

He tried to smile at me. I didn't dare offer to help him over to his trailer while the vampires were there, because I knew Sam's pride would suffer. At the moment, that was more important to him than the state of his injured leg.

Charles was behind the bar and already busy. When Bill offered accommodations again for a second day, Charles accepted rather than opting for my untested hidey hole. "We have to check your hiding place, Sookie, for cracks that may have occurred during the fire," Charles said seriously.

I could understand the necessity, and without saying a word to Bill, I got into the loaner car and drove to my house. We'd left the windows open all day, and the smell had largely dissipated. That was a welcome development. Thanks to the strategy of the firefighters and the inexpert way the fire had been set, the bulk of my house would be livable in short order. I'd called a contractor, Randall Shurtliff, that evening from the bar, and he'd agreed to stop by the next day at noon. Terry Bellefleur had promised to start removing the remains of the kitchen early the next day. I would have to be there to set aside anything I could salvage. I felt like I had two jobs now.

I was suddenly and completely exhausted, and my arms

ached. I would have huge bruises the next day. It was almost too warm to justify long sleeves, but I'd have to wear them. Armed with a flashlight from the glove compartment of Tara's car, I got my makeup and some more clothes from my bedroom, throwing them all into a sport duffle I'd won at the Relay for Life. I tossed in a couple of paperbacks I hadn't read yet—books I'd traded for at the library swap rack. That prompted another line of thought. Did I have any movies that needed to go back to the rental place? No. Library books? Yes, had to return some, and I needed to air them out first. Anything else that belonged to another person? Thank goodness I'd dropped Tara's suit at the cleaner's.

There was no point in closing and locking the windows, which I'd left open to dissipate the odor, as the house was easily accessible through the burned kitchen. But when I went out my front door, I locked it behind me. I'd gotten to Hummingbird Road before I realized how silly that had been, and as I drove to Jason's, I found myself smiling for the first time in many, many hours.

~ 10

My melancholy brother was glad to see me. The fact that his new "family" didn't trust him had been eating away at Jason all day. Even his panther girlfriend, Crystal, was nervous about seeing him while the cloud of suspicion hung around him. She'd sent him packing when he'd shown up on her front doorstep this evening. When I found out he'd actually driven out to Hotshot, I exploded. I told my brother in no uncertain terms that he apparently had a death wish and I was not responsible for whatever happened to him. He responded that I'd never been responsible for anything that he did, anyway, so why would I start now?

It went on like that for a while.

After he'd grudgingly agreed to stay away from his fellow shifters, I carried my bag down the short hall to the guest bedroom. This was where he kept his computer, his old high school trophies from the baseball team and the football team, and an ancient foldout couch on hand primarily for visitors who drank too much and couldn't drive home. I didn't even bother to unfold it but spread out an ancient quilt over the glossy Naugahyde. I pulled another one over me.

After I said my prayers, I reviewed my day. It had been so full of incident that I got tired trying to remember everything. In about three minutes, I was out like a light. I dreamed about growling animals that night: they were all around me in the fog, and I was scared. I could hear Jason screaming somewhere in the mist, though I couldn't find him to defend him.

Sometimes you don't need a psychiatrist to interpret a dream, right?

I woke up just a bit when Jason left for work in the morning, mostly because he slammed the door behind him. I dozed off again for another hour, but then I woke up decisively. Terry would be coming to my house to begin tearing down the ruined part, and I needed to see if any of my kitchen things could be saved.

Since this was liable to be a dirty job, I borrowed Jason's blue jumpsuit, the one he put on when he worked on his car. I looked in his closet and pulled out an old leather jacket Jason wore for rough work. I also appropriated a box of garbage bags. As I started Tara's car, I wondered how on earth I could repay her for its use. I reminded myself to pick up her suit. Since it was on my mind, I made a slight detour to retrieve it from the dry cleaner's.

Terry was in a stable mood today, to my relief. He was smiling as he smacked away at the charred boards of the back porch with a sledgehammer. Though the day was very cool, Terry wore only a sleeveless T-shirt tucked in his jeans. It covered most of the dreadful scars. After greeting him and registering that he didn't want to talk, I went in through the front door. I was drawn down the hall to the kitchen to look again at the damage.

The firefighters had said the floor was safe. It made me nervous to step out onto the scorched linoleum, but after a moment or two, I felt easier. I pulled on gloves and began to work, going through cabinets and cupboards and drawers. Some things had melted or twisted with the heat. A few things, like my plastic colander, were so warped it took me a second or two to identify what I was holding.

I tossed the ruined things directly out the south kitchen window, away from Terry.

I didn't trust any of the food that had been in the cabinets that were on the outer wall. The flour, the rice, the sugar—they'd all been in Tupperware containers, and though the seals had held, I just didn't want to use the contents. The same held true of the canned goods; for some reason, I felt uneasy about using food from cans that had gotten so hot.

Fortunately, my everyday stoneware and the good china that had belonged to my great-great-grandmother had survived, since they were in the cabinet farthest from the flames. Her sterling silver was in fine shape, too. My far more useful stainless tableware, much closer to the fire, was warped and twisted. Some of the pots and pans were usable.

I worked for two or three hours, consigning things to the growing pile outside the window or bagging them in Jason's garbage bags for future use in a new kitchen. Terry worked hard, too, taking a break every now and then to drink bottled water while he perched on the tailgate of his pickup. The temperature rose to the upper sixties. We might have a few more hard frosts, and there was always the chance of an ice storm, but it was possible to count on spring coming soon.

It wasn't a bad morning. I felt like I was taking a step toward regaining my home. Terry was an undemanding companion, since he didn't like to talk, and he was exorcising his demons with hard work. Terry was in his late fifties now. Some of the chest hair I could see above his T-shirt neck was gray. The hair on his head, once auburn, was fading as he aged. But he was a strong man, and he swung his sledge-hammer with vigor and loaded boards onto the flatbed of his truck with no sign of strain.

Terry left to take a load to the parish dump. While he was gone, I went into my bedroom and made my bed—a strange and foolish thing to do, I know. I would have to take the sheets off and wash them; in fact, I'd have to wash almost every piece of fabric in the house to completely rid it of the smell of burning. I'd even have to wash the walls and repaint the hall, though the paint in the rest of the house seemed clean enough.

I was taking a break out in the yard when I heard a truck approaching a moment before it appeared, coming out of the trees that surrounded the driveway. To my astonishment, I recognized it as Alcide's truck, and I felt a pang of dismay. I'd told him to stay away.

He seemed miffed about something when he leaped out of the cab. I'd been sitting in the sunshine on one of my aluminum lawn chairs, wondering what time it was and wondering when the contractor would get here. After the all-round discomfort of my night at Jason's, I was also planning on finding somewhere else to stay while the kitchen was being rebuilt. I couldn't imagine the rest of my house being habitable until the work was complete, and that might be months from now. Jason wouldn't want me around that long, I was sure. He'd have to put up with me if I wanted to stay—he was my brother, after all—but I didn't want to strain his fraternal spirit. There wasn't *anyone* I wanted to stay with for a couple of months, when I came to consider the matter.

"Why didn't you tell me?" Alcide bellowed as his feet touched the ground.

I sighed. Another angry man.

"We aren't big buddies right now," I reminded him. "But I would have gotten around to it. It's only been a couple of days."

"You should have called me first thing," he told me, striding around the house to survey the damage. He stopped right in front of me. "You could have died," he said, as if it was big news.

"Yes," I said. "I know that."

"A vampire had to save you." There was disgust in his voice. Vamps and Weres just didn't get along.

"Yes," I agreed, though actually my savior had been Claudine. But Charles had killed the arsonist. "Oh, would you rather I'd burned?"

"No, of course not!" He turned away, looked at the mostly dismantled porch. "Someone's working on tearing down the damaged part already?"

"Yes."

"I could have gotten a whole crew out here."

"Terry volunteered."

"I can get you a good rate on the reconstruction."

"I've lined up a contractor."

"I can loan you the money to do it."

"I have the money, thank you very much."

That startled him. "You do? Where'd—" He stopped before saying something inexcusable. "I didn't think your grandmother had had much to leave you," he said, which was almost as bad.

"I earned the money," I said.

"You earned the money from Eric?" he guessed accurately.

Alcide's green eyes were hot with anger. I thought he was going to shake me.

"You just calm down, Alcide Herveaux," I said sharply. "How I earned it is none of your damn business. I'm glad to have it. If you'll get down off your high horse, I'll tell you that I'm glad you're concerned about me, and I'm grateful you're offering help. But don't treat me like I'm a slow fifth grader in the special class."

Alcide stared down at me while my speech soaked in. "I'm sorry. I thought you—I thought we were close enough for you to've called me that night. I thought . . . maybe you needed help."

He was playing the "you hurt my feelings" card.

"I don't mind asking for help when I need it. I'm not that proud," I said. "And I'm glad to see you." (Not totally true.) "But don't act like I can't do things for myself, because I can, and I am."

"The vampires paid you for keeping Eric while the witches were in Shreveport?"

"Yes," I said. "My brother's idea. It embarrassed me. But now I'm grateful I've got the money. I won't have to borrow any to get the house put into shape."

Terry Bellefleur returned with his pickup just then, and I introduced the two men. Terry didn't seem at all impressed by meeting Alcide. In fact, he went right back to work after he gave Alcide's hand a perfunctory shake. Alcide eyed Terry doubtfully.

"Where are you staying?" Alcide had decided not to ask questions about Terry's scars, thank goodness.

"I'm staying with Jason," I said promptly, leaving out the fact that I hoped that would be temporary.

"How long is it gonna take to rebuild?"

"Here's the guy who can tell me," I said gratefully. Randall Shurtliff was in a pickup, too, and he had his wife and partner with him. Delia Shurtliff was younger than Randall, pretty as a picture, and tough as nails. She was Randall's second wife. When he'd gotten divorced from his "starter" wife, the one who'd had three children and cleaned his house for twelve years, Delia had already been working for Randall and had gradually begun to run his business for him far more efficiently than he'd ever done. He was able to give his first wife and sons more advantages with the money his second wife had helped him earn than he otherwise might have, had he married someone else. It was common knowledge (by which I mean I wasn't the only one who knew this) that Delia was very ready for Mary Helen to remarry and for the three Shurtliff boys to graduate from high school.

I shut out Delia's thoughts with a firm resolve to work on keeping my shields up. Randall was pleased to meet Alcide, whom he'd known by sight, and Randall was even more eager to take on rebuilding my kitchen when he knew I was a friend of Alcide's. The Herveaux family carried a lot of weight personally and financially in the building trade. To my irritation, Randall began addressing all his remarks to Alcide instead of to me. Alcide accepted this quite naturally.

I looked at Delia. Delia looked at me. We were very unlike, but we were of one mind at that moment.

"What do you think, Delia?" I asked her. "How long?"

"He'll huff and he'll puff," she said. Her hair was paler than mine, courtesy of the beauty salon, and she wore emphatic eye makeup, but she was dressed sensibly in khakis and a polo shirt with "Shurtliff Construction" in script above her left breast. "But he's got that house over on Robin Egg to finish. He can work on your kitchen before he begins a house in Clarice. So, say, three to four months from now, you'll have you a usable kitchen."

"Thanks, Delia. Do I need to sign something?"

"We'll get an estimate ready for you. I'll bring it to the bar for you to check. We'll include the new appliances, because we can get a dealer discount. But I'll tell you right now, you're looking at this ballpark."

She showed me the estimate on a kitchen renovation they had done a month before.

"I have it," I said, though I gave one long shriek deep inside. Even with the insurance money, I'd be using up a big chunk of what I had in the bank.

I should be thankful, I reminded myself sternly, that Eric had paid me all that money, that I had it to spend. I wouldn't have to borrow from the bank or sell the land or take any other drastic step. I should think of that money as just passing through my account rather than living there. I hadn't actually owned it. I'd just had custody of it for a while.

"You and Alcide good friends?" Delia asked, our business concluded.

I gave it some thought. "Some days," I answered honestly.

She laughed, a harsh cackle that was somehow sexy. Both men looked around, Randall smiling, Alcide quizzical. They were too far away to hear what we were saying.

"I'll tell you something," Delia Shurtliff said to me quietly. "Just between you and me and the fencepost. Jackson Herveaux's secretary, Connie Babcock—you met her?"

I nodded. I'd at least seen her and talked to her when I'd dropped by Alcide's office in Shreveport.

"She got arrested this morning for stealing from Herveaux and Son."

"What did she take?" I was all ears.

"This is what I don't understand. She was caught sneaking some papers out of Jackson Herveaux's office. Not business papers, but personal, the way I heard it. She said she'd been paid to do it."

"By?"

"Some guy who owns a motorcycle dealership. Now, does that make sense?"

It did if you knew that Connie Babcock had been sleeping with Jackson Herveaux, as well as working in his office. It did if you suddenly realized that Jackson had taken Christine Larrabee, a pure Were and influential, to the funeral of Colonel Flood, instead of taking the powerless human Connie Babcock.

While Delia elaborated on the story, I stood, lost in thought. Jackson Herveaux was without a doubt a clever businessman, but he was proving to be a stupid politician. Having Connie arrested was dumb. It drew attention to the Weres, had the potential to expose them. A people so secretive would not appreciate a leader who couldn't manage a problem with more finesse than that.

As a matter of fact, since Alcide and Randall were still discussing the rebuilding of my house with each other instead of with me, a lack of finesse appeared to run in the Herveaux family.

Then I frowned. It occurred to me that Patrick Furnan might be devious and clever enough to have engineered the whole thing—bribing the spurned Connie to steal Jackson's private papers, then ensuring she was caught—knowing that Jackson would react with a hot head. Patrick Furnan might be much smarter than he looked, and Jackson Herveaux much stupider, at least in the way that mattered if you wanted to be packmaster. I tried to shake off these disturbing speculations. Alcide hadn't said a word about Connie's arrest, so I had to conclude that he considered it none of my business. Okay, maybe he thought I had enough to worry about, and he was right. I turned my mind back to the moment.

"You think they'd notice if we left?" I asked Delia.

"Oh, yeah," Delia said confidently. "It might take Randall a minute, but he'd look around for me. He'd get lost if he couldn't find me."

Here was a woman who knew her own worth. I sighed and thought about getting in my borrowed car and driving away. Alcide, catching sight of my face, broke off his discussion with my contractor and looked guilty. "Sorry," he called. "Habit."

Randall came back to where I was standing quite a bit faster than he'd wandered away. "Sorry," he apologized. "We were talking shop. What did you have in mind, Sookie?"

"I want the same dimensions for the kitchen as before," I said, having dropped visions of a larger room after seeing the estimate. "But I want the new back porch to be just as wide as the kitchen, and I want to enclose it."

Randall produced a tablet, and I sketched what I wanted.

"You want the sinks where they were? You want all the appliances where they were?"

After some discussion, I drew everything I wanted, and Randall said he'd call me when it was time to pick out the cabinets and the sinks and all the other incidentals.

"One thing I wish you'd do for me today or tomorrow is fix the door from the hall into the kitchen," I said. "I want to be able to lock the house."

Randall rummaged around in the back of his pickup for a minute or two and came up with a brand-new doorknob with a lock, still in its package. "This won't keep out anyone really determined," he said, still in the apologetic vein, "but it's better'n nothing." He had it installed within fifteen minutes, and I was able to lock the sound part of the house away from the burned part. I felt much better, though I knew this lock wasn't worth much. I needed to put a dead bolt on the inside of the door; that would be even better. I wondered if I could do it myself, but I recalled that would entail cutting away some of the door frame, and I wasn't anything of a carpenter. Surely I could find someone who'd help me with that task.

Randall and Delia left with many assurances that I would be next on the list, and Terry resumed work. Alcide said, "You're never alone," in mildly exasperated tones.

"What did you want to talk about? Terry can't hear us over here." I led the way over to where my aluminum chair was sitting under a tree. Its companion was leaning up against the rough bark of the oak, and Alcide unfolded it. It creaked a little under his weight as he settled into it. I assumed he was going to tell me about the arrest of Connie Babcock.

"I upset you the last time I talked to you," he said directly.

I had to change mental gears at the unexpected opening. Okay, I liked a man who could apologize. "Yes, you did."

"You didn't want me to tell you I knew about Debbie?"

"I just hate that the whole thing happened. I hate that her family is taking it so hard. I hate that they don't know, that they're suffering. But I'm glad to be alive, and I'm not going to jail for defending myself."

"If it'll make you feel any better, Debbie wasn't that close to her family. Her parents always preferred Debbie's little sister, though she didn't inherit any shifter characteristics. Sandra is the apple of their eye, and the only reason they're pursuing this with such vigor is that Sandra expected it."

"You think they'll give up?"

"They think I did it," Alcide said. "The Pelts think that because Debbie got engaged to another man, I killed her. I got an e-mail from Sandra in response to mine about the private eyes."

I could only gape at him. I had a horrible vista of the future in which I saw myself going down to the police station and confessing to save Alcide from a jail term. Even to be suspected of a murder he hadn't committed was an awful thing, and I couldn't permit it. It just hadn't occurred to me that someone else would be blamed for what I'd done.

"But," Alcide continued, "I can prove I didn't. Four pack members have sworn I was at Pam's house after Debbie left, and one female will swear I spent the night with her."

He had been with the pack members, just somewhere else. I slumped with relief. I was not going to have a jealous spasm about the female. He wouldn't have called her that if he'd actually had sex with her.

"So the Pelts will just have to suspect someone else. That's not what I wanted to talk to you about, anyway."

Alcide took my hand. His were big, and hard, and enclosed mine like he was holding something wild that would fly away if he relaxed his grip. "I want you to think about seeing me on a steady basis," Alcide said. "As in, every day."

Once again, the world seemed to rearrange itself around me. "Huh?" I said.

"I like you very much," he said. "I think you like me, too. We want each other." He leaned over to kiss me once on the cheek and then, when I didn't move, on the mouth. I was too surprised to get into it and unsure whether I wanted to anyway. It's not often a mind reader gets taken by surprise, but Alcide had achieved it.

He took a deep breath and continued. "We enjoy each other's company. I want to see you in my bed so much it makes me ache. I wouldn't have spoken this soon, without us being together more, but you need a place to live right now. I have a condo in Shreveport. I want you to think about staying with me."

If he'd whomped me upside the head with a two-by-four, I couldn't have been more stunned. Instead of trying so hard to stay out of people's heads, I should consider getting back into them. I started several sentences in my head, discarded them all. The warmth of him, the attraction of his big body, was something I had to fight as I struggled to sort my thoughts.

"Alcide," I began at last, speaking over the background noise of Terry's sledgehammer knocking down the boards of my burned kitchen, "you're right that I like you. In fact, I more than like you." I couldn't even look at his face. I looked instead at his big hands, with their dusting of dark hair across the backs. If I looked down past his hands, I could see his muscular thighs and his . . . Well, back to the hands. "But the timing seems all wrong. I think you need more time to get over your relationship with Debbie, since you seemed so enslaved to her. You may feel that just saying the words 'I abjure you' got rid of all your feelings for Debbie, but I'm not convinced that's so."

"It's a powerful ritual of my people," Alcide said stiffly, and I risked a quick glance at his face.

"I could tell it was a powerful ritual," I assured him, "and it had a big effect on everyone there. But I can't believe that, quick as a flash, every single feeling you had for Debbie was uprooted when you said the words. That's just not how people work."

"That's how werewolves work." He looked stubborn. And determined.

I thought very hard about what I wanted to say.

"I'd love for someone to step in and solve all my problems," I told him. "But I don't want to accept your offer because I need a place to live and we're hot for each other. When my house is rebuilt, then we'll talk, if you still feel the same."

"This is when you need me the most," he protested, the words spilling out of his mouth in his haste to persuade me. "You need me *now*. I need you *now*. We're right for each other. You know it."

"No, I don't. I know that you're worried about a lot of

things right now. You lost your lover, however it happened. I don't think it's sunk into you yet that you'll never see her again."

He flinched.

"I shot her, Alcide. With a shotgun."

His whole face clenched.

"See? Alcide, I've seen you rip into a person's flesh when you were being a wolf. And it didn't make me scared of you. Because *I'm on your side.* But you loved Debbie, at least for a time. We get into a relationship now, at some point you're going to look up and say, 'Here's the one who ended her life.'"

Alcide opened his mouth to protest, but I held up a hand. I wanted to finish.

"Plus, Alcide, your dad's in this succession struggle. He wants to win the election. Maybe you being in a settled relationship would help his ambitions. I don't know. But I don't want any part of Were politics. I didn't appreciate you dragging me into it cold last week at the funeral. You should have let me decide."

"I wanted them to get used to the sight of you by my side," Alcide said, his face stiffening with offense. "I meant it as an honor to you."

"I might have appreciated that honor more if I'd known about it," I snapped. It was a relief to hear another vehicle approaching, to see Andy Bellefleur get out of his Ford and watch his cousin knocking down my kitchen. For the first time in months, I was glad to see Andy.

I introduced Andy to Alcide, of course, and watched them size each other up. I like men in general, and some men in specific, but when I saw them practically circle each other as they sniffed each other's butts—excuse me, exchanged greetings—I just had to shake my head. Alcide was the taller by a good four inches, but Andy Bellefleur had been on his college wrestling team, and he was still a block of muscle. They were about the same age. I would put even money on them in a fight, providing that Alcide kept his human form.

"Sookie, you asked me to keep you posted on the man who died here," Andy said.

Sure, but it had never occurred to me he'd actually do it. Andy did not have any very high opinion of me, though he'd always been a big fan of my rear end. It's wonderful being telepathic, huh?

"He has no prior record," Andy said, looking down at the little notebook he'd produced. "He has no known association with the Fellowship of the Sun."

"But that doesn't make sense," I said into the little silence that followed. "Why would he set the fire otherwise?"

"I was hoping you could tell me that," Andy said, his clear gray eyes meeting mine.

I'd had it with Andy, abruptly and finally. In our dealings over the years, he'd insulted me and wounded me, and now I'd encountered that last straw.

"Listen to me, Andy," I said, and I looked right back into his eyes. "I never did anything to you that I know of. I've never been arrested. I've never even jaywalked, or been late paying my taxes, or sold a drink to an underage teen. I've never even had a speeding ticket. Now someone tried to barbecue me inside my own home. Where do you get off, making me feel like I've done something wrong?" *Other than shoot Debbie Pelt,* a voice whispered in my head. It was the voice of my conscience.

"I don't think there's anything in this guy's past that would indicate he'd do this to you."

"Fine! Then find out who did! Because someone burned my house, and it sure wasn't me!" I was yelling when I got to the last part, partly to drown the voice. My only recourse was to turn and walk away, striding around the house until I was out of Andy's sight. Terry gave me a sidelong look, but he didn't stop swinging his sledgehammer.

After a minute, I heard someone picking his way through the debris behind me. "He's gone," Alcide said, his deep voice just a tiny bit amused. "I guess you're not interested in going any further with our conversation."

"You're right," I said briefly.

"Then I'll go back to Shreveport. Call me if you need me."

"Sure." I made myself be more polite. "Thanks for your offer of help."

" 'Help'? I asked you to live with me!"

"Then thank you for asking me to live with you." I couldn't help it if I didn't sound completely sincere. I said the right words. Then my grandmother's voice sounded in my head, telling me that I was acting like I was seven years old. I made myself turn around.

"I do appreciate your . . . affection," I said, looking up into Alcide's face. Even this early in the spring, he had a tan line from wearing a hard hat. His olive complexion would be shades darker in a few weeks. "I do appreciate . . ." I trailed off, not sure how to put it. I appreciated his willingness to consider me as an eligible woman to mate with, which so many men didn't, as well as his assumption that I would make a good mate and a good ally. This was as close as I could get to phrasing what I meant.

"But you're not having any." The green eyes regarded me steadily.

"I'm not saying that." I drew a breath. "I'm saying now is not the time to work on a relationship with you." *Though I wouldn't mind jumping your bones,* I added to myself wistfully.

But I wasn't going to do that on a whim, and certainly not with a man like Alcide. The new Sookie, the rebound

Sookie, wasn't going to make the same mistake twice in a row. I was double rebounding. (If you rebound from the two men you've had so far, do you end up a virgin again? To what state are you rebounding?) Alcide gave me a hard hug and dropped a kiss on my cheek. He left while I was still mulling that over. Soon after Alcide left, Terry knocked off for the day. I changed from the jumpsuit into my work clothes. The afternoon had chilled, so I pulled on the jacket I'd borrowed from Jason's closet. It smelled faintly of Jason.

I detoured on the way to work to drop off the pink and black suit at Tara's house. Her car wasn't there, so I figured she was still at the shop. I let myself in and went back to her bedroom to put the plastic bag in her closet. The house was dusky and deep shadowed. It was almost dark outside. Suddenly my nerves thrummed with alarm. I shouldn't be here. I turned away from the closet and stared around the room. When my eyes got to the doorway, it was filled with a slim figure. I gasped before I could stop myself. Showing them you're scared is like waving a red flag in front of a bull.

I couldn't see Mickey's face to read his expression, if he had any.

"Where did that new bartender at Merlotte's come from?" he asked.

If I'd expected anything, it wasn't that.

"When Sam got shot, we needed another bartender in a hurry. We borrowed him from Shreveport," I said. "From the vampire bar."

"Had he been there long?"

"No," I said, managing to feel surprised even through my creeping fear. "He hadn't been there long at all."

Mickey nodded, as if that confirmed some conclusion he'd reached. "Get out of here," he said, his deep voice quite calm. "You're a bad influence on Tara. She doesn't need anything but me, until I'm tired of her. Don't come back."

The only way out of the room was through the door he was filling. I didn't trust myself to speak. I walked toward him as confidently as I could, and I wondered if he would move when I reached him. It felt like three hours later by the time I rounded Tara's bed and eased my way around her dressing table. When I showed no sign of slowing down, the vampire stepped aside. I couldn't stop myself from looking up at his face as I passed him, and he was showing fang. I shuddered. I felt so sick for Tara that I couldn't stop myself. How had this happened to her?

When he saw my revulsion, he smiled.

I tucked the problem of Tara away in my heart to pull out later. Maybe I could think of something to do for her, but as long as she seemed willing to stay with this monstrous creature, I didn't see what I could do to help.

Sweetie Des Arts was outside smoking a cigarette when I parked my car at the back of Merlotte's. She looked pretty good, despite being wrapped in a stained white apron. The outside floodlights lit up every little crease in her skin, revealing that Sweetie was a little older than I'd thought, but she still looked very fit for someone who cooked most of the day. In fact, if it hadn't been for the white apron swathing her and the lingering perfume of cooking oil, Sweetie might have been a sexy woman. She certainly carried herself like a person who was used to being noticed.

We'd had such a succession of cooks that I hadn't made much effort to know her. I was sure she'd drift away sooner or later—probably sooner. But she raised a hand in greeting and seemed to want to talk to me, so I paused.

"I'm sorry about your house," she said. Her eyes were shining in the artificial light. It didn't smell so great here by the Dumpster, but Sweetie was as relaxed as if she were on an Acapulco beach.

"Thanks," I said. I just didn't want to talk about it. "How are you today?"

"Fine, thanks." She waved the hand with the cigarette around, indicating the parking lot. "Enjoying the view. Hey, you got something on your jacket." Holding her hand carefully to one side so she wouldn't get ash on me, she leaned forward, closer than my comfort zone permitted, and flicked something off my shoulder. She sniffed. Maybe the smokey smell of the burned wood clung to me, despite all my efforts.

"I need to go in. Time for my shift," I said.

"Yeah, I gotta get back in myself. It's a busy night." But Sweetie stayed where she was. "You know, Sam's just nuts about you."

"I've worked for him for a long time."

"No, I think it goes a little beyond that."

"Ah, I don't think so, Sweetie." I couldn't think of any polite way to conclude a conversation that had gotten way too personal.

"You were with him when he got shot, right?"

"Yeah, he was heading for his trailer and I was heading for my car." I wanted to make it clear we were going in different directions.

"You didn't notice anything?" Sweetie leaned against the wall and tilted her head back, her eyes closed as if she were sunbathing.

"No. I wish I had. I'd like the police to catch whoever's doing this."

"Did you ever think there might be a reason those people were targeted?"

"No," I lied stoutly. "Heather and Sam and Calvin have nothing in common."

Sweetie opened one brown eye and squinted up at me. "If we were in a mystery, they'd all know the same secret, or they'd have witnessed the same accident, or something. Or the police would find out they all had the same dry cleaner." Sweetie flicked the ashes off her cigarette.

I relaxed a little. "I see what you're getting at," I said. "But I think real life doesn't have as many patterns as a serial killer book. I think they were all chosen at random."

Sweetie shrugged. "You're probably right." I saw she'd been reading a Tami Hoag suspense novel, now tucked into an apron pocket. She tapped her book with one blunt fingernail. "Fiction just makes it all more interesting. Truth is so boring."

"Not in my world," I said.

11

BILL BROUGHT A DATE INTO MERLOTTE'S THAT
night. I assumed this was payback for my kissing Sam, or
maybe I was just being proud. This possible payback was in
the form of a woman from Clarice. I'd seen her in the bar before every once in a while. She was a slim brunette with
shoulder-length hair, and Danielle could hardly wait to tell
me she was Selah Pumphrey, a real estate saleswoman who'd
gotten the million-dollar sales award the year before.

I hated her instantly, utterly, and passionately.

So I smiled as brightly as a thousand-watt bulb and
brought them Bill's warm TrueBlood and her cold screwdriver quick as a wink. I didn't spit in the screwdriver, either. That was beneath me, I told myself. Also, I didn't have
enough privacy.

Not only was the bar crowded, but Charles was eyeing me
watchfully. The pirate was in fine form tonight, wearing a

white shirt with billowing sleeves and navy blue Dockers, a
bright scarf pulled through the belt loops for a dash of color.
His eye patch matched the Dockers, and it was embroidered
with a gold star. This was as exotic as Bon Temps could get.

Sam beckoned me over to his tiny table, which we'd
wedged into a corner. He had his bad leg propped up on another chair. "Are you all right, Sookie?" Sam murmured,
turning away from the crowd at the bar so no one could even
read his lips.

"Sure, Sam!" I gave him an amazed expression. "Why
not?" At that moment, I hated him for kissing me, and I
hated me for responding.

He rolled his eyes and smiled for a fleeting second. "I
think I've solved your housing problem," he said to distract
me. "I'll tell you later." I hurried off to take an order. We
were swamped that night. The warming weather and the attraction of a new bartender had combined to fill Merlotte's
with the optimistic and the curious.

I'd left *Bill,* I reminded myself proudly. Though he'd
cheated on me, he hadn't wanted us to break up. I had to
keep telling myself that, so I wouldn't hate everyone present
who was witnessing my humiliation. Of course, none of the
people knew any of the circumstances, so they were free to
imagine that Bill had dropped me for this brunette bitch.
Which was *so* not the case.

I stiffened my back, broadened my smile, and hustled
drinks. After the first ten minutes, I began to relax and see
that I was behaving like a fool. Like millions of couples, Bill
and I had broken up. Naturally, he'd begun dating someone
else. If I'd had the normal run of boyfriends, starting when I
was thirteen or fourteen, my relationship with Bill would
just be another in a long line of relationships that hadn't
panned out. I'd be able to take this in stride, or at least in
perspective.

I had no perspective. Bill was my first love, in every sense.

The second time I brought drinks to their table, Selah Pumphrey looked at me uneasily when I beamed at her. "Thanks," she said uncertainly.

"Don't mention it," I advised her through clenched teeth, and she blanched.

Bill turned away. I hoped he wasn't hiding a smile. I went back to the bar.

Charles said, "Shall I give her a good scare, if she spends the night with him?"

I'd been standing behind the bar with him, staring into the glass-fronted refrigerator we kept back there. It held soft drinks, bottled blood, and sliced lemons and limes. I'd come to get a slice of lemon and a cherry to put on a Tom Collins, and I'd just stayed. He was entirely too perceptive.

"Yes, please," I said gratefully. The vampire pirate was turning into an ally. He'd saved me from burning, he'd killed the man who'd set fire to my house, and now he was offering to scare Bill's date. You had to like that.

"Consider her terrified," he said in a courtly way, bowing with a florid sweep of his arm, his other hand on his heart.

"Oh, you," I said with a more natural smile, and got out the bowl of sliced lemons.

It took every ounce of self-control I had to stay out of Selah Pumphrey's head. I was proud of myself for making the effort.

To my horror, the next time the door opened, Eric came in. My heart rate picked up immediately, and I felt almost faint. I was going to have to stop reacting like this. I wished I could forget our "time together" (as one of my favorite romance novels might term it) as thoroughly as Eric had. Maybe I should track down a witch, or a hypnotherapist, and give myself a dose of amnesia. I bit down on the inside of my cheek, hard, and carried two pitchers of beer over to a table of young couples who were celebrating the promotion of one of the men to supervisor—of someone, somewhere.

Eric was talking to Charles when I turned around, and though vampires can be pretty stone-faced when they're dealing with each other, it seemed apparent to me that Eric wasn't happy with his loaned-out bartender. Charles was nearly a foot shorter than his boss, and his head was tilted up as they talked. But his back was stiff, his fangs protruded a bit, and his eyes were glowing. Eric was pretty scary when he was mad, too. He was now definitely looking toothy. The humans around the bar were tending to find something to do somewhere else in the room, and any minute they'd start finding something to do at some other bar.

I saw Sam grabbing at a cane—an improvement over the crutches—so he could get up and go over to the pair, and I sped over to his table in the corner. "You stay put," I told him in a very firm low voice. "Don't you think about intervening."

I heel and toed it over to the bar. "Hi, Eric! How you doing? Is there anything I can help you with?" I smiled up at him.

"Yes. I need to talk to you, too," he growled.

"Then why don't you come with me? I was just going to step out back to take a break," I offered.

I took hold of his arm and towed him through the door and down the hall to the employees' entrance. We were outside in the night-cold air before you could say Jack Robinson.

"You better not be about to tell me what to do," I said instantly. "I've had enough of that for one day, and Bill's in here with a woman, and I lost my kitchen. I'm in a bad mood." I underlined this by squeezing Eric's arm, which was like gripping a small tree trunk.

"I care nothing about your mood," he said instantly, and

he was showing fang. "I pay Charles Twining to watch you and keep you safe, and who hauls you out of the fire? A fairy. While Charles is out in the yard, killing the fire setter rather than saving his hostess's life. Stupid Englishman!"

"He's supposed to be here as a favor to Sam. He's supposed to be here helping Sam out." I peered at Eric doubtfully.

"Like I give a damn about a shifter," the vampire said impatiently.

I stared up at him.

"There's something about you," Eric said. His voice was cold, but his eyes were not. "There is something I am almost on the verge of knowing about you, and it's under my skin, this feeling that something happened while I was cursed, something I should know about. Did we have sex, Sookie? But I can't think that was it, or it alone. Something happened. Your coat was ruined with brain tissue. Did I kill someone, Sookie? Is that it? You're protecting me from what I did while I was cursed?" His eyes were glowing like lamps in the darkness.

I'd never thought he might be wondering whom he'd killed. But frankly, if it had occurred to me, I wouldn't have thought Eric would care; what difference would one human life make to a vampire as old as this one? But he seemed mighty upset. Now that I understood what he was worried about, I said, "Eric, you did not kill anyone at my house that night." I stopped short.

"You have to tell me what happened." He bent a little to look into my face. "I hate not knowing what I did. I've had a life longer than you can even imagine, and I remember every second of it, except for those days I spent with you."

"I can't make you remember," I said as calmly as I could. "I can only tell you that you stayed with me for several days, and then Pam came to get you."

Eric stared into my eyes a little longer. "I wish I could

get in your head and get the truth out of you," he said, which alarmed me more than I wanted to show. "You've had my blood. I can tell you're concealing things from me." After a moment's silence, he said, "I wish I knew who's trying to kill you. And I hear you had a visit from some private detectives. What did they want of you?"

"Who told you that?" Now I had something else to worry about. Someone was informing on me. I could feel my blood pressure rise. I wondered if Charles was reporting to Eric every night.

"Is this something to do with the woman who's missing, that bitch the Were loved so much? Are you protecting him? If I didn't kill her, did he? Did she die in front of us?"

Eric had gripped my shoulders, and the pressure was excruciating.

"Listen, you're hurting me! Let go."

Eric's grip loosened, but he didn't remove his hands.

My breath began to come faster and shallower, and the air was full of the crackling of danger. I was sick to death of being threatened.

"Tell me now," he demanded.

He would have power over me for the rest of my life if I told him he'd seen me kill someone. Eric already knew more about me than I wanted him to, because I'd had his blood, and he'd had mine. Now I rued our blood exchange more than ever. Eric was sure I was concealing something important.

"You were so sweet when you didn't know who you were," I said, and whatever he'd been expecting me to say, it wasn't that. Astonishment played tag with outrage across his handsome face. Finally, he was amused.

"Sweet?" he said, one corner of his mouth turning up in a smile.

"Very," I said, trying to smile back. "We gossiped like old buddies." My shoulders ached. Probably everyone in the bar needed a new drink. But I couldn't go back in just yet. "You were scared and alone, and you liked to talk to me. It was fun having you around."

"Fun," he said thoughtfully. "I'm not fun now?"

"No, Eric. You're too busy being . . . yourself." Head boss vampire, political animal, budding tycoon.

He shrugged. "Is myself so bad? Many women seem to think not."

"I'm sure they do." I was tired to the bone.

The back door opened. "Sookie, are you all right?" Sam had hobbled to my rescue. His face was stiff with pain.

"Shifter, she doesn't need your assistance," Eric said.

Sam didn't say anything. He just kept Eric's attention.

"I was rude," Eric said, not exactly apologetically, but civilly enough. "I'm on your premises. I'll be gone. Sookie," he said to me, "we haven't finished this conversation, but I see this isn't the time or place."

"I'll see you," I said, since I knew I had no choice.

Eric melted into the darkness, a neat trick that I'd love to master someday.

"What is he so upset about?" Sam asked. He hobbled out of the doorway and leaned against the wall.

"He doesn't remember what happened while he was cursed," I said, speaking slowly out of sheer weariness. "That makes him feel like he's lost control. Vampires are big on having control. I guess you noticed."

Sam smiled—a small smile, but genuine. "Yes, that had come to my attention," he admitted. "I'd also noticed they're pretty possessive."

"You're referring to Bill's reaction when he walked in on us?" Sam nodded. "Well, he seems to have gotten over it."

"I think he's just repaying you in kind."

I felt awkward. Last night, I'd been on the verge of going to bed with Sam. But I was far from feeling passionate at this moment, and Sam's leg had been hurt badly in his fall. He didn't look as if he could romance a rag doll, much less a robust woman like me. I knew it was wrong to think of indulging in some sex play with my boss, though Sam and I had been teetering on a fine edge for months. Coming down on the "no" side was the safest, sanest thing to do. Tonight, particularly after the emotionally jangling events of the past hour, I wanted to be safe.

"He stopped us in time," I said.

Sam raised a fine red-gold eyebrow. "Did you want to be stopped?"

"Not at that moment," I admitted. "But I guess it was for the best."

Sam just looked at me for a moment. "What I was going to tell you, though I was going to wait until after the bar closed, is that one of my rental houses is empty right now. It's the one next to—well, you remember, the one where Dawn . . ."

"Died," I finished.

"Right. I had that one redone, and it's rented out now. So you'd have a neighbor, and you're not used to that. But the empty side is furnished. You'd only have to bring a few linens, your clothes, and some pots and pans." Sam smiled. "You could get that in a car. By the way, where'd you get this?" He nodded at the Malibu.

I told him how generous Tara had been, and I also told him I was worried about her. I repeated the warning Eric had given me about Mickey.

When I saw how anxious Sam looked, I felt like a selfish creep for burdening him with all this. Sam had enough to worry about. I said, "I'm sorry. You don't need to hear more troubles. Come on, let's go back inside."

Sam stared at me. "I do need to sit down," he said after a moment.

"Thanks for the rental. Of course I'll pay you. I'm so glad to have a place to live where I can come and go without bothering anyone! How much is it? I think my insurance will pay for me renting a place to live while my house is being fixed."

Sam gave me a hard look, and then named a price that I was sure was well below his usual rate. I slid my arm around him because his limp was so bad. He accepted the help without a struggle, which made me think even better of him. He hobbled down the hall with my help and settled in the rolling chair behind his desk with a sigh. I pushed over one of the visitor chairs so he could put his leg up on it if he wanted, and he used it immediately. Under the strong fluorescent light in his office, my boss looked haggard.

"Get back to work," he said mock-threateningly. "I'll bet they're mobbing Charles."

The bar was just as chaotic as I'd feared, and I began tending to my tables immediately. Danielle shot me a dirty look, and even Charles looked less than happy. But gradually, moving as fast as I could, I served fresh drinks, took away empty glasses, dumped the occasional ashtray, wiped the sticky tables, and smiled at and spoke to as many people as I could. I could kiss my tips good-bye, but at least peace was restored.

Bit by bit, the pulse of the bar slowed and returned to normal. Bill and his date were deep in conversation, I noticed . . . though I made a great effort not to keep glancing their way. To my dismay, every single time I saw them as a couple, I felt a wave of rage that did not speak well for my character. For another thing, though my feelings were a matter of indifference to almost ninety percent of the bar's patrons, the other ten percent were watching like hawks to see if Bill's date was making me suffer. Some of them would be glad to see it, and some wouldn't—but it was no one's business, either way.

As I was cleaning off a table that had just been vacated, I felt a tap on my shoulder. I picked up a foreshadowing just as I turned, and that enabled me to keep my smile in place. Selah Pumphrey was waiting for my attention, her own smile bright and armor plated.

She was taller than I, and perhaps ten pounds lighter. Her makeup was expensive and expert, and she smelled like a million bucks. I reached out and touched her brain without even thinking twice.

Selah was thinking she had it all over me, unless I was fantastic in bed. Selah thought that lower-class women must always be better in bed, because they were less inhibited. She knew she was slimmer, was smarter, made more money, and was far more educated and better read than the waitress she was looking at. But Selah Pumphrey doubted her own sexual skill and had a terror of making herself vulnerable. I blinked. This was more than I wanted to know.

It was interesting to discover that (in Selah's mind) since I was poor and uneducated, I was more in touch with my nature as a sexual being. I'd have to tell all the other poor people in Bon Temps. Here we'd been having a wonderful time screwing one another, having much better sex than smart upper-class people, and we hadn't even appreciated it.

"Yes?" I asked.

"Where is the ladies' room?" she asked.

"Through that door there. The one with 'Restrooms' on the sign above it." I should be grateful I was clever enough to read signs.

"Oh! Sorry, I didn't notice."

I just waited.

"So, um, you got any tips for me? About dating a vampire?" She waited, looking nervous and defiant all at once.

"Sure," I said. "Don't eat any garlic." And I turned away from her to wipe down the table.

Once I was certain she was out of the room, I swung around to carry two empty beer mugs to the bar, and when I turned back, Bill was standing there. I gave a gasp of surprise. Bill has dark brown hair and of course the whitest skin you can imagine. His eyes are as dark as his hair. Right at the moment, those eyes were fixed on mine.

"Why did she talk to you?" he asked.

"Wanted to know the way to the bathroom."

He cocked an eyebrow, glancing up at the sign.

"She just wanted to take my measure," I said. "At least, that's my guess." I felt oddly comfortable with Bill at that moment, no matter what had passed between us.

"Did you scare her?"

"I didn't try to."

"Did you scare her?" he asked again in a sterner voice. But he smiled at me.

"No," I said. "Did you want me to?"

He shook his head in mock disgust. "Are you jealous?"

"Yes." Honesty was always safest. "I hate her skinny thighs and her elitist attitude. I hope she's a dreadful bitch who makes you so miserable that you howl when you remember me."

"Good," said Bill. "That's good to hear." He gave me a brush of lips on my cheek. At the touch of his cool flesh, I shivered, remembering. He did, too. I saw the heat flare in his eyes, the fangs begin to run out. Then Catfish Hunter yelled to me to stir my stumps and bring him another bourbon and Coke, and I walked away from my first lover.

It had been a long, long day, not only from a physical-energy-expended measurement, but also from an emotional-depths-plumbed point of view. When I let myself into my brother's house, there were giggles and squeakings coming from his bedroom, and I deduced Jason was consoling himself in the usual way. Jason might be upset that his new community suspected him of a foul crime, but he was not so upset that it affected his libido.

I spent as brief a time in the bathroom as I could and went into the guest room, shutting the door firmly behind me. Tonight the couch looked a lot more inviting than it had the evening before. As I curled up on my side and pulled the quilt over me, I realized that the woman spending the night with my brother was a shifter; I could feel it in the faint pulsing redness of her brain.

I hoped she was Crystal Norris. I hoped Jason had somehow persuaded the girl that he had nothing to do with the shootings. If Jason wanted to compound his troubles, the best way possible would be to cheat on Crystal, the woman he'd chosen from the werepanther community. And surely even Jason wasn't that stupid. Surely.

He wasn't. I met Crystal in the kitchen the next morning after ten o'clock. Jason was long gone, since he had to be at work by seven forty-five. I was drinking my first mug of coffee when Crystal stumbled in, wearing one of Jason's shirts, her face blurry with sleep.

Crystal was not my favorite person, and I was not hers, but she said, "Morning" civilly enough. I agreed that it was morning, and I got out a mug for her. She grimaced and got out a glass, filling it with ice and then Coca-Cola. I shuddered.

"How's your uncle?" I asked, when she seemed conscious.

"He's doing better," she said. "You ought to go see him. He liked having you visit."

"I guess you're sure Jason didn't shoot him."

"I am," she said briefly. "I didn't want to talk to him at first, but once he got me on the phone, he just talked his way out of me suspecting him."

I wanted to ask her if the other inhabitants of Hotshot were willing to give Jason the benefit of the doubt, but I hated to bring up a touchy subject.

I thought of what I had to do today: I had to go get enough clothes, some sheets and blankets, and some kitchen gear from the house, and get those things installed in Sam's duplex.

Moving into a small, furnished place was a perfect solution to my housing problem. I had forgotten Sam owned several small houses on Berry Street, three of them duplexes. He worked on them himself, though sometimes he hired JB du Rone, a high school friend of mine, to do simple repairs and maintenance chores. Simple was the best way to keep it, with JB.

After I retrieved my things, I might have time to go see Calvin. I showered and dressed, and Crystal was sitting in the living room watching TV when I left. I assumed that was okay with Jason.

Terry was hard at work when I pulled into the clearing. I walked around back to check his progress, and I was delighted to see he'd done more than I'd have thought possible. He smiled when I said so, and paused in loading broken boards into his truck. "Tearing down is always easier than building up," he said. This was no big philosophical statement, but a builder's summary. "I should be done in two more days, if nothing happens to slow me down. There's no rain in the forecast."

"Great. How much will I owe you?"

"Oh," he muttered, shrugging and looking embarrassed. "A hundred? Fifty?"

"No, not enough." I ran a quick estimate of his hours in my head, multiplied. "More like three."

"Sookie, I'm not charging you that much." Terry got his stubborn face on. "I wouldn't charge you anything, but I got to get a new dog."

Terry bought a very expensive Catahoula hunting dog about every four years. He wasn't turning in the old models for new ones. Something always seemed to happen to Terry's dogs, though he took great care of them. After he'd had the first hound about three years, a truck had hit him. Someone had fed poisoned meat to the second. The third one, the one he'd named Molly, had gotten snake-bit, and the bite had turned septic. For months now, Terry had been on the list for one in the next litter born at the kennel in Clarice that bred Catahoulas.

"You bring that puppy around for me to hug," I suggested, and he smiled. Terry was at his best in the outdoors, I realized for the first time. He always seemed more comfortable mentally and physically when he was not under a roof, and when he was outside with a dog, he seemed quite normal.

I unlocked the house and went in to gather what I might need. It was a sunny day, so the absence of electric light wasn't a problem. I filled a big plastic laundry basket with two sets of sheets and an old chenille bedspread, some more clothes, and a few pots and pans. I would have to get a new coffeepot. My old one had melted.

And then, standing there looking out the window at the coffeemaker, which I'd pitched to the top of the trash heap, I understood how close I'd come to dying. The realization hit me broadside.

One minute I was standing at my bedroom window, looking out at the misshaped bit of plastic; the next I was sitting on the floor, staring at the painted boards and trying to breathe.

Why did it hit me now, after three days? I don't know. Maybe there was something about the way the Mr. Coffee looked: cord charred, plastic warped with the heat. The plastic had literally bubbled. I looked at the skin of my hands and shuddered. I stayed on the floor, shivering and shaking, for an unmeasured bit of time. For the first minute or two after that, I had no thoughts at all. The closeness of my brush with death simply overwhelmed me.

Claudine had not only most probably saved my life; she had certainly saved me from pain so excruciating that I would have wanted to be dead. I owed her a debt I would never be able to repay.

Maybe she really was my fairy godmother.

I got up, shook myself. Grabbing up the plastic basket, I left to go move into my new home.

12 ~

I LET MYSELF IN WITH THE KEY I'D GOTTEN FROM SAM.
I was on the right side of a duplex, the mirror of the one
next door presently occupied by Halleigh Robinson, the
young schoolteacher dating Andy Bellefleur. I figured I was
likely to have police protection at least part of the time, and
Halleigh would be gone during most of the day, which was
nice considering my late hours.

The living room was small and contained a flowered
couch, a low coffee table, and an armchair. The next room
was the kitchen, which was tiny, of course. But it had a
stove, a refrigerator, and a microwave. No dishwasher, but
I'd never had one. Two plastic chairs were tucked under a
tiny table.

After I'd glanced at the kitchen I went through into the
small hall that separated the larger (but still small) bedroom on the right from the smaller (tiny) bedroom and the

bathroom on the left. At the end of the hall there was a door to the little back porch.

This was a very basic accommodation, but it was quite clean. There was central heating and cooling, and the floors were level. I ran a hand around the windows. They fit well. Nice. I reminded myself I'd have to keep the venetian blinds drawn down, since I had neighbors.

I made up the double bed in the larger bedroom. I put my clothes away in the freshly painted chest of drawers. I started a list of other things I needed: a mop, a broom, a bucket, some cleaning products . . . those had been on the back porch. I'd have to get my vacuum cleaner out of the house. It had been in the closet in the living room, so it should be fine. I'd brought one of my phones to plug in over here, so I would have to arrange with the phone company for them to route calls to this address. I'd loaded my television into my car, but I had to arrange for my cable to be hooked up here. I'd have to call from Merlotte's. Since the fire, all my time was being absorbed with the mechanics of living.

I sat on the hard couch, staring into space. I tried to think of something fun, something I could look forward to. Well, in two months, it'd be sunbathing time. That made me smile. I enjoyed lying in the sun in a little bikini, timing myself carefully so I didn't burn. I loved the smell of coconut oil. I took pleasure in shaving my legs and removing most of my other body hair so I'd look smooth as a baby's bottom. And I don't want to hear any lectures about how bad tanning is for you. That's my vice. Everybody gets one.

More immediately, it was time to go to the library and get another batch of books; I'd retrieved my last bagful while I was at the house, and I'd spread them out on my tiny porch here so they'd air out. So going to the library—that would be fun.

Before I went to work, I decided I'd cook myself something in my new kitchen. That necessitated a trip to the grocery store, which took longer than I'd planned because I kept seeing staples I was sure I'd need. Putting the groceries away in the duplex cabinets made me feel that I really lived there. I browned a couple of pork chops and put them in the oven, microwaved a potato, and heated some peas. When I had to work nights, I usually went to Merlotte's at about five, so my home meal on those days was a combination lunch and dinner.

After I'd eaten and cleaned up, I thought I just had time to drive down to visit Calvin in the Grainger hospital.

The twins had not arrived to take up their post in the lobby again, if they were still keeping vigil. Dawson was still stationed outside Calvin's room. He nodded to me, gestured to me to stop while I was several feet away, and stuck his head in Calvin's room. To my relief, Dawson swung the door wide open for me to enter and even patted my shoulder as I went in.

Calvin was sitting up in the padded chair. He clicked off the television as I came in. His color was better, his beard and hair were clean and trimmed, and he looked altogether more like himself. He was wearing pajamas of blue broadcloth. He still had a tube or two in, I saw. He actually tried to push himself up out of the chair.

"No, don't you dare get up!" I pulled over a straight chair and sat in front of him. "Tell me how you are."

"Glad to see you," he said. Even his voice was stronger. "Dawson said you wouldn't take any help. Tell me who set that fire."

"That's the strange thing, Calvin. I don't know why this man set the fire. His family came to see me . . ." I hesitated, because Calvin was recuperating from his own brush with death, and he shouldn't have to worry about other stuff.

But he said, "Tell me what you're thinking," and he sounded so interested that I ended up relating everything to the wounded shifter: my doubts about the arsonist's motives, my relief that the damage could be repaired, my concern about the trouble between Eric and Charles Twining. And I told Calvin that the police here had learned of more clusters of sniper activity.

"That would clear Jason," I pointed out, and he nodded. I didn't push it.

"At least no one else has been shot," I said, trying to think of something positive to throw in with the dismal mix.

"That we know of," Calvin said.

"What?"

"That we know of. Maybe someone else has been shot, and no one's found 'em yet."

I was astonished at the thought, and yet it made sense. "How'd you think of that?"

"I don't have nothing else to do," he said with a small smile. "I don't read, like you do. I'm not much one for television, except for sports." Sure enough, the station he'd had on when I'd entered had been ESPN.

"What do you do in your spare time?" I asked out of sheer curiosity.

Calvin was pleased I'd asked him a personal question. "I work pretty long hours at Norcross," he said. "I like to hunt, though I'd rather hunt at the full moon." In his panther body. Well, I could understand that. "I like to fish. I love mornings when I can just sit in my boat on the water and not worry about a thing."

"Uh-huh," I said encouragingly. "What else?"

"I like to cook. We have shrimp boils sometimes, or we cook up a whole mess of catfish and we eat outside—catfish and hush puppies and slaw and watermelon. In the summer, of course."

It made my mouth water just to think about it.

"In the winter, I work on the inside of my house. I go out and cut wood for the people in our community who can't cut their own. I've always got something to do, seems like."

Now I knew twice as much about Calvin Norris as I had.

"Tell me how you're recovering," I asked.

"I've still got the damn IV in," he said, gesturing with his arm. "Other than that, I'm a lot better. We heal pretty good, you know."

"How are you explaining Dawson to the people from your work who come to visit?" There were flower arrangements and bowls of fruit and even a stuffed cat crowding the level surfaces in the room.

"Just tell 'em he's my cousin here to make sure I won't get too wore out with visitors."

I was pretty sure no one would question Dawson directly.

"I have to get to work," I said, catching a glimpse of the clock on the wall. I was oddly reluctant to leave. I'd enjoyed having a regular conversation with someone. Little moments like these were rare in my life.

"Are you still worried about your brother?" he asked.

"Yes." But I'd made my mind up I wouldn't beg again. Calvin had heard me out the first time. There wasn't any need for a repeat.

"We're keeping an eye on him."

I wondered if the watcher had reported to Calvin that Crystal was spending the night with Jason. Or maybe Crystal herself was the watcher? If so, she was certainly taking her job seriously. She was watching Jason about as close as he could be watched.

"That's good," I said. "That's the best way to find out he didn't do it." I was relieved to hear Calvin's news, and the longer I pondered it, the more I realized I should have figured it out myself.

"Calvin, you take care." I rose to leave, and he held up his cheek. Rather reluctantly, I touched my lips to it.

He was thinking that my lips were soft and that I smelled good. I couldn't help but smile as I left. Knowing someone simply finds you attractive is always a boost to the spirits.

I drove back to Bon Temps and stopped by the library before I went to work. The Renard Parish library is an old ugly brown-brick building erected in the thirties. It looks every minute of its age. The librarians had made many justified complaints about the heating and cooling, and the electrical wiring left a lot to be desired. The library's parking lot was in bad shape, and the old clinic next door, which had opened its doors in 1918, now had boarded-up windows—always a depressing sight. The long-closed clinic's overgrown lot looked more like a jungle than a part of downtown.

I had allotted myself ten minutes to exchange my books. I was in and out in eight. The library parking lot was almost empty, since it was just before five o'clock. People were shopping at Wal-Mart or already home cooking supper.

The winter light was fading. I was not thinking about anything in particular, and that saved my life. In the nick of time, I identified intense excitement pulsing from another brain, and reflexively I ducked, feeling a sharp shove in my shoulder as I did so, and then a hot lance of blinding pain, and then wetness and a big noise. This all happened so fast I could not definitely sequence it when I later tried to reconstruct the moment.

A scream came from behind me, and then another. Though I didn't know how it had happened, I found myself on my knees beside my car, and blood was spattered over the front of my white T-shirt.

Oddly, my first thought was *Thank God I didn't have my new coat on.*

The person who'd screamed was Portia Bellefleur. Portia was not her usual collected self as she skidded across the parking lot to crouch beside me. Her eyes went one way, then another, as she tried to spot danger coming from any direction.

"Hold still," she said sharply, as though I'd proposed running a marathon. I was still on my knees, but keeling over appeared to be a pleasant option. Blood was trickling down my arm. "Someone shot you, Sookie. Oh my God, oh my God."

"Take the books," I said. "I don't want to get blood on the books. I'll have to pay for them."

Portia ignored me. She was talking into her cell phone. People talked on their phones at the damnedest times! In the library, for goodness's sake, or at the optometrist. Or in the bar. Jabber, jabber, jabber. As if everything was so important it couldn't wait. So I put the books on the ground beside me all by myself.

Instead of kneeling, I found myself sitting, my back against my car. And then, as if someone had taken a slice out of my life, I discovered I was lying on the pavement of the library parking lot, staring at someone's big old oil stain. People should take better care of their cars. . . .

Out.

"Wake up," a voice was saying. I wasn't in the parking lot, but in a bed. I thought my house was on fire again, and Claudine was trying to get me out. People were always trying to get me out of bed. Though this didn't sound like Claudine; this sounded more like . . .

"Jason?" I tried to open my eyes. I managed to peer through my barely parted lids to identify my brother. I was in a dimly lit blue room, and I hurt so bad I wanted to cry.

"You got shot," he said. "You got shot, and I was at Merlotte's, waiting for you to get there."

"You sound . . . happy," I said through lips that felt oddly thick and stiff. Hospital.

"I couldn't have done it! I was with people the whole time! I had Hoyt in the truck with me from work to Merlotte's, because his truck's in the shop. I am *covered*."

"Oh, good. I'm glad I got shot, then. As long as you're okay." It was such an effort to say it, I was glad when Jason picked up on the sarcasm.

"Yeah, hey, I'm sorry about that. At least it wasn't serious."

"It isn't?"

"I forgot to tell you. Your shoulder got creased, and it's going to hurt for a while. Press this button if it hurts. You can give yourself pain medication. Cool, huh? Listen, Andy's outside."

I pondered that, finally deduced Andy Bellefleur was there in his official capacity. "Okay," I said. "He can come in." I stretched out a finger and carefully pushed the button.

I blinked then, and it must have been a long blink, because when I pried my eyes open again, Jason was gone and Andy was in his place, a little notebook and a pen in his hands. There was something I had to tell him, and after a moment's reflection, I knew what it was.

"Tell Portia I said thank you," I told him.

"I will," he said seriously. "She's pretty shook up. She's never been that close to violence before. She thought you were gonna die."

I could think of nothing to say to that. I waited for him to ask me what he wanted to know. His mouth moved, and I guess I answered him.

". . . said you ducked at the last second?"

"I heard something, I guess," I whispered. That was the truth, too. I just hadn't heard something with my ears. . . . But Andy knew what I meant, and he was a believer. His eyes met mine and widened.

And out again. The ER doctor had certainly given me some excellent painkiller. I wondered which hospital I was in. The one in Clarice was a little closer to the library; the one in Grainger had a higher-rated ER. If I was in Grainger, I might as well have saved myself the time driving back to Bon Temps and going to the library. I could have been shot right in the hospital parking lot when I left from visiting Calvin, and that would have saved me the trip.

"Sookie," said a quiet, familiar voice. It was cool and dark, like water running in a stream on a moonless night.

"Bill," I said, feeling happy and safe. "Don't go."

"I'll be right here."

And he was there, reading, in a chair by my bed when I woke up at three in the morning. I could feel the minds in the rooms around me all shut down in sleep. But the brain in the head of the man next to me was a blank. At that moment, I realized that the person who'd shot me had not been a vampire, though all the shootings had taken place at dusk or full dark. I'd heard the shooter's brain in the second before the shot, and that had saved my life.

Bill looked up the instant I moved. "How are you feeling?" he asked.

I pushed the button to raise the head of the bed. "Like hell warmed over," I said frankly after evaluating my shoulder. "My pain stuff has lapsed, and my shoulder aches like it's going to fall off. My mouth feels like an army has marched through it, and I need to go to the bathroom in the worst way."

"I can help you take care of that," he said, and before I could get embarrassed, he'd moved the IV pole around the bed and helped me up. I stood cautiously, gauging how steady my legs were. He said, "I won't let you fall."

"I know," I said, and we started across the floor to the bathroom. When he got me settled on the toilet, he tactfully stepped out, but left the door cracked while he waited just outside. I managed everything awkwardly, but I became profoundly aware I was lucky I'd been shot in my left shoulder instead of my right. Of course, the shooter must have been aiming for my heart.

Bill got me back into the bed as deftly as if he'd been nursing people all his life. He'd already smoothed the bed and shaken the pillows, and I felt much more comfortable. But the shoulder continued to nag me, and I pressed the pain button. My mouth was dry, and I asked Bill if there was water in the plastic pitcher. Bill pressed the Nurse button. When her tinny voice came over the intercom, Bill said, "Some water for Miss Stackhouse," and the voice squawked back that she'd be right down. She was, too. Bill's presence might have had something to do with her speed. People might have accepted the reality of vampires, but that didn't meant they liked undead Americans. Lots of middle-class Americans just couldn't relax around vamps. Which was smart of them, I thought.

"Where are we?" I asked.

"Grainger," he said. "I get to sit with you in a different hospital this time." Last time, I'd been in Renard Parish Hospital in Clarice.

"You can go down the hall and visit Calvin."

"If I had any interest in doing so."

He sat on the bed. Something about the deadness of the hour, the strangeness of the night, made me feel like being frank. Maybe it was just the drugs.

"I never was in a hospital till I knew you," I said.

"Do you blame me?"

"Sometimes." I watched his face glow. Other people didn't always know a vamp when they saw one; that was hard for me to understand.

"When I met you, that first night I came into Merlotte's,

I didn't know what to think of you," he said. "You were so pretty, so full of vitality. And I could tell there was something different about you. You were interesting."

"My curse," I said.

"Or your blessing." He put one of his cool hands on my cheek. "No fever," he said to himself. "You'll heal." Then he sat up straighter. "You slept with Eric while he was staying with you."

"Why are you asking, if you already know?" There was such a thing as too much honesty.

"I'm not asking. I knew when I saw you together. I smelled him all over you; I could tell how you felt about him. We've had each other's blood. It's hard to resist Eric," Bill went on in a detached way. "He's as vital as you are, and you share a zest for life. But I'm sure you know that . . ." He paused, seemed to be trying to think how to frame what he wanted to say.

"I know that you'd be happy if I never slept with anyone else in my life," I said, putting his thoughts into words for him.

"And how do you feel about me?"

"The same. Oh, but wait, you already *did* sleep with someone else. Before we even broke up." Bill looked away, the line of his jaw like granite. "Okay, that's water under the bridge. No, I don't want to think about you with Selah, or with anyone. But my head knows that's unreasonable."

"Is it unreasonable to hope that we'll be together again?"

I considered the circumstances that had turned me against Bill. I thought of his infidelity with Lorena; but she had been his maker, and he had had to obey her. Everything I'd heard from other vamps had confirmed what he'd told me about that relationship. I thought of his near-rape of me in the trunk of a car; but he'd been starved and tortured, and hadn't known what he was doing. The minute he'd come to his senses, he'd stopped.

I remembered how happy I'd been when I'd had what I thought was his love. I'd never felt more secure in my life. How false a feeling that had been: He'd become so absorbed in his work for the Queen of Louisiana that I'd begun to come in a distant second. Out of all the vampires who could have walked into Merlotte's Bar, I'd gotten the workaholic.

"I don't know if we can ever have the same relationship again," I said. "It might be possible, when I'm a little less raw from the pain of it. But I'm glad you're here tonight, and I wish you would lie down with me for a little while . . . if you want to." I moved over on the narrow bed and turned on my right side, so the wounded shoulder was up. Bill lay down behind me and put his arm over me. No one could approach me without him knowing. I felt perfectly secure, absolutely safe, and cherished. "I'm so glad you're here," I mumbled as the medicine kicked in. As I was drifting off to sleep again, I remembered my New Year's Eve resolution: I wanted not to get beaten up. Note to self: I should have included "shot."

I was released the next morning. When I went to the business office, the clerk, whose name tag read MS. BEESON, said, "It's already been taken care of."

"By who?" I asked.

"The person wishes to remain anonymous," the clerk said, her round brown face set in a way that implied I shouldn't look gift horses in the mouth.

This made me uneasy, very uneasy. I actually had the money in the bank to pay the whole bill, instead of sending a check each month. And nothing comes without a price. There were some people to whom I just didn't want to be beholden. When I absorbed the total at the bottom of the bill, I was shocked to find how very beholden I'd be.

Maybe I should have stayed in the office longer and argued with Ms. Beeson more forcefully, but I just didn't feel up to it. I wanted to shower, or at least bathe—something more thorough than the high-spots scrub I'd given myself (very slowly and carefully) that morning. I wanted to eat my own food. I wanted some solitude and peace. So I got back in the wheelchair and let the aide wheel me out of the main entrance. I felt like the biggest idiot when it occurred to me that I didn't have a way home. My car was still in the library parking lot in Bon Temps—not that I was supposed to drive it for a couple of days.

Just as I was about to ask the aide to wheel me back inside so I could ride up to Calvin's room (maybe Dawson could give me a lift), a sleek red Impala came to a halt in front of me. Claudine's brother, Claude, leaned over to push open the passenger door. I sat gaping at him. He said irritably, "Well, are you going to get in?"

"Wow," muttered the aide. "Wow." I thought her blouse buttons were going to pop open, she was breathing so hard.

I'd met Claudine's brother Claude only once before. I'd forgotten what an impact he made. Claude was absolutely breathtaking, so lovely that his proximity made me tense as a high wire. Relaxing around Claude was like trying to be nonchalant with Brad Pitt.

Claude had been a stripper on ladies' night at Hooligans, a club in Monroe, but lately he'd not only moved into managing the club, he'd also branched into print and runway modeling. The opportunities for such work were few and far between in northern Louisiana, so Claude (according to Claudine) had decided to compete for Mr. Romance at a romance readers' convention. He'd even had his ears surgically altered so they weren't pointed anymore. The big payoff was the chance to appear on a romance cover. I didn't know too much about the contest, but I knew what I saw when I looked at Claude. I felt pretty confident Claude would win by acclamation.

Claudine had mentioned that Claude had just broken up with his boyfriend, too, so he was unattached: all six feet of him, accessorized with rippling black hair and rippling muscles and a six-pack that could have been featured in *Abs Weekly*. Mentally add to that a pair of brown velour-soft eyes, a chiseled jaw, and a sensuous mouth with a pouty bottom lip, and you've got Claude. Not that I was noticing.

Without the help of the aide, who was still saying, "Wow, wow, wow," very quietly, I got out of the wheelchair and eased myself into the car. "Thanks," I said to Claude, trying not to sound as astonished as I felt.

"Claudine couldn't get off work, so she called me and woke me up so I'd be here to chauffeur you," Claude said, sounding totally put out.

"I'm grateful for the ride," I said, after considering several possible responses.

I noticed that Claude didn't have to ask me for directions to Bon Temps, though I'd never seen him in the area—and I think I've made the point that he was hard to miss.

"How is your shoulder?" he said abruptly, as if he'd remembered that was the polite question to ask.

"On the mend," I said. "And I have a prescription for some painkillers to fill."

"So I guess you need to do that, too?"

"Um, well, that would be nice, since I'm not supposed to drive for another day or two."

When we reached Bon Temps, I directed Claude to the pharmacy, where he found a parking slot right in front. I managed to get out of the car and take in the prescription, since Claude didn't offer. The pharmacist, of course, had heard what had happened already and wanted to know what this world was coming to. I couldn't tell him.

I passed the time while he was filling my prescription by speculating on the possibility that Claude was bisexual— even a little bit? Every woman who came into the pharmacy had a glazed look on her face. Of course, they hadn't had the privilege of having an actual conversation with Claude, so they hadn't had the benefit of his sparkling personality.

"Took you long enough," Claude said as I got back in the car.

"Yes, Mr. Social Skills," I snapped. "I'll try to hurry from now on. Why should getting shot slow me down? I apologize."

Out of the corner of my eye, I noticed Claude's cheeks reddening.

"I'm sorry," he said stiffly. "I was abrupt. People tell me I'm rude."

"No! Really?"

"Yes," he admitted, and then realized I'd been a tad sarcastic. He gave me a look I would have called a glower from a less beautiful creature. "Listen, I have a favor to ask you."

"You're certainly off to a good start. You've softened me up now."

"Would you stop that? I know I'm not . . . not . . ."

"Polite? Minimally courteous? Gallant? Going about this the right way?"

"Sookie!" he bellowed. "Be quiet!"

I wanted one of my pain pills. "Yes, Claude?" I said in a quiet, reasonable voice.

"The people running the pageant want a portfolio. I'll go to the studio in Ruston for some glamour shots, but I think it might be a good idea to do some posed pictures, too. Like the covers of the books Claudine is always reading. Claudine says I should have a blonde pose with me, since I'm dark. I thought of you."

I guess if Claude had told me he wanted me to have his baby I could have been more surprised, but only just. Though Claude was the surliest man I'd ever encountered, Claudine had a habit of saving my life. For her sake, I wanted to oblige.

"Would I need, like, a costume?"

"Yes. But the photographer also does amateur dramatics and he rents out Halloween costumes, so he thought he might have some things that would do. What size do you wear?"

"An eight." Sometimes more like a ten. But then again, once in a blue moon, a six, okay?

"So when can you do this?"

"My shoulder has to heal," I said gently. "The bandage wouldn't look good in the pictures."

"Oh, right. So you'll call me?"

"Yes."

"You won't forget?"

"No. I'm so looking forward to it." Actually, at the moment what I wanted was my own space, free and clear of any other person, and a Diet Coke, and one of the pills I was clutching in my hand: Maybe I'd have a little nap before I took the shower that also featured on my list.

"I've met the cook at Merlotte's before," Claude said, the floodgates evidently now wide open.

"Uh-huh. Sweetie."

"That's what she's calling herself? She used to work at the Foxy Femmes."

"She was a stripper?"

"Yeah, until the accident."

"Sweetie was in an accident?" I was getting more worn out by the second.

"Yeah, so she got scarred and didn't want to strip anymore. It would've required too much makeup, she said. Besides, by then she was getting a little on the, ah, old side to be stripping."

"Poor thing," I said. I tried to picture Sweetie parading down a runway in high heels and feathers. Disturbing.

"I'd never let her hear you say that," he advised.

We parked in front of the duplex. Someone had brought my car back from the library parking lot. The door to the other side of the duplex opened, and Halleigh Robinson stepped out, my keys in her hand. I was wearing the black pants I'd had on since I had been on my way to work, but my Merlotte's T-shirt had been ruined so the hospital had given me a white sweatshirt that someone had left there once upon a time. It was huge on me, but that wasn't why Halleigh was standing stock-still, catching flies with her mouth. Claude had actually gotten out to help me into the house, and the sight of him had paralyzed the young schoolteacher.

Claude eased his arm tenderly around my shoulders, bent his head to look adoringly into my face, and winked.

This was the first hint I'd had that Claude had a sense of humor. It pleased me to find he wasn't universally disagreeable.

"Thanks for bringing me my keys," I called, and Halleigh suddenly remembered she could walk.

"Um," she said. "Um, sure." She put the keys somewhere in the vicinity of my hand, and I snagged them.

"Halleigh, this is my friend Claude," I said with what I hoped was a meaningful smile.

Claude moved his arm down to circle my waist and gave her a distracted smile of his own, hardly moving his eyes from mine. Oh, brother. "Hello, Halleigh," he said in his richest baritone.

"You're lucky to have someone to bring you home from

the hospital," Halleigh said. "That's very nice of you, uh, Claude."

"I would do anything for Sookie," Claude said softly.

"Really?" Halleigh shook herself. "Well, how nice. Andy drove your car back over here, Sookie, and he asked if I'd give you your keys. It's lucky you caught me. I just ran home to eat lunch. I, um, I have to go back to . . ." She gave Claude a final comprehensive stare before getting into her own little Mazda to drive back to the elementary school.

I unlocked my door clumsily and stepped into my little living room. "This is where I'm staying while my house is being rebuilt," I told Claude. I felt vaguely embarrassed at the small sterile room. "I just moved in the day I got shot. Yesterday," I said with some wonder.

Claude, his faux admiration having been dropped when Halleigh pulled away, eyed me with some disparagement. "You have mighty bad luck," he observed.

"In some ways," I said. But I thought of all the help I'd already gotten, and of my friends. I remembered the simple pleasure of sleeping close to Bill the night before. "My luck could definitely be worse," I added, more or less to myself.

Claude was massively uninterested in my philosophy.

After I thanked him again and asked him to give Claudine a hug from me, I repeated my promise to call him when my wound had healed enough for the posing session.

My shoulder was beginning to ache now. When I locked the door behind him, I swallowed a pill. I'd called the phone company from the library the afternoon before, and to my surprise and pleasure I got a dial tone when I picked up my phone. I called Jason's cell to tell him I was out of the hospital, but he didn't answer so I left a message on his voice mail. Then I called the bar to tell Sam I'd be back at work the next day. I'd missed two days' worth of pay and tips, and I couldn't afford any more.

I stretched out on the bed and took a long nap.

When I woke up, the sky was darkening in a way that meant rain. In the front yard of the house across the street, a small maple was whipping around in an alarming way. I thought of the tin roof my Gran had loved and of the clatter the rain made when it hit the hard surface. Rain here in town was sure to be quieter.

I was looking out my bedroom window at the identical duplex next door, wondering who my neighbor was, when I heard a sharp knock. Arlene was breathless from running through the first drops of rain. She had a bag from Wendy's in her hand, and the smell of the food made my stomach wake up with a growl.

"I didn't have time to cook you anything," she said apologetically as I stood aside to let her in. "But I remembered you liked to get the double hamburger with bacon when you were feeling low, and I figured you'd be feeling pretty low."

"You figured right," I said, though I was discovering I was much better than I'd been that morning. I went to the kitchen to get a plate, and Arlene followed, her eyes going to every corner.

"Hey, this is nice!" she said. Though it looked barren to me, my temporary home must have looked wonderfully un-cluttered to her.

"What was it like?" Arlene asked. I tried not to hear that she was thinking that I got into more trouble than anyone she knew. "You must have been so scared!"

"Yes." I was serious, and my voice showed it. "I was very scared."

"The whole town is talking about it," Arlene said artlessly. That was just what I wanted to hear: that I was the subject of many conversations. "Hey, you remember that Dennis Petti-bone?"

"The arson expert?" I said. "Sure."

"We've got a date tomorrow night."

"Way to go, Arlene. What are you all gonna do?"

"We're taking the kids to the roller rink in Grainger. He's got a girl, Katy. She's thirteen."

"Well, that sounds like fun."

"He's on stakeout tonight," Arlene said importantly.

I blinked. "What's he staking out?"

"They needed all the officers they could call in. They're staking out different parking lots around town to see if they can catch this sniper in the act."

I could see a flaw in their plan. "What if the sniper sees them first?"

"These are professionally trained men, Sookie. I think they know how to handle this." Arlene looked, and sounded, quite huffy. All of a sudden, she was Ms. Law Enforcement.

"Chill," I said. "I'm just concerned." Besides, unless the lawmen were Weres, they weren't in danger. Of course, the big flaw in that theory was that I had been shot. And I was no Were, no shifter. I still hadn't figured out how to work that into my scenario.

"Where's the mirror?" Arlene asked, and I looked around.

"I guess the only big one's in the bathroom," I said, and it felt strange to have to think about the location of an item in my own place. While Arlene fussed with her hair, I put my food on a plate, hoping I'd get to eat while it was still warm. I caught myself standing like a fool with the empty food bag in my hand, wondering where the garbage can was. Of course there wasn't a garbage can until I went out to buy one. I'd never lived anywhere but my Gran's house for the past nineteen years. I'd never had to start housekeeping from the ground up.

"Sam's still not driving, so he can't come to see you, but

he's thinking about you," Arlene called. "You gonna be able to work tomorrow night?"

"I'm planning on it."

"Good. I'm scheduled to be off, Charlsie's granddaughter's in the hospital with pneumonia, so she's gone, and Holly doesn't always show up when she's scheduled. Danielle's going to be out of town. That new girl, Jada—she's better than Danielle, anyway."

"You think?"

"Yeah." Arlene snorted. "I don't know if you've noticed, but Danielle just doesn't seem to care anymore. People can be wanting drinks and calling to her, and it doesn't make a smidge of difference to her. She'll just stand there talking to her boyfriend while people holler at her."

It was true that Danielle had been less than scrupulous about her work habits since she'd started steady-dating a guy from Arcadia. "You think she's gonna quit?" I asked, and that opened up another conversational pit we mined for about five minutes, though Arlene had said she was in a hurry. She'd ordered me to eat while the food was good, so I chewed and swallowed while she talked. We didn't say anything startlingly new or original, but we had a good time. I could tell that Arlene (for once) was just enjoying sitting with me, being idle.

One of the many downsides to telepathy is the fact that you can tell the difference between when someone's really listening to you, and when you're talking to just a face instead of a mind.

Andy Bellefleur arrived as Arlene was getting into her car. I was glad I'd stuffed the bag from Wendy's in a cabinet just to get it out of the way.

"You're right next to Halleigh," Andy said—an obvious opening gambit.

"Thanks for leaving my keys with her and getting my car over here," I said. Andy had his moments.

"She says the guy that brought you home from the hospital was really, ah, interesting." Andy was obviously fishing. I smiled at Andy. Whatever Halleigh had said had made him curious and maybe a little jealous.

"You could say that," I agreed.

He waited to see if I'd expound. When I didn't, he became all business.

"The reason I'm here, I wanted to find out if you remembered any more about yesterday."

"Andy, I didn't know anything then, much less now."

"But you ducked."

"Oh, Andy," I said, exasperated, since he knew good and well about my condition, "you don't have to ask why I ducked."

He turned red, slowly and unbecomingly. Andy was a fireplug of a man and an intelligent police detective, but he had such ambiguity toward things he knew to be true, even if those things weren't completely conventional items of common knowledge.

"We're here all by ourselves," I pointed out. "And the walls are thick enough that I don't hear Halleigh moving around."

"Is there more?" he asked suddenly, his eyes alight with curiosity. "Sookie, is there more?"

I knew exactly what he meant. He would never spell it out, but he wanted to know if there was even more in this world than humans, and vampires, and telepaths. "So much more," I said, keeping my voice quiet and even. "Another world."

Andy's eyes met mine. His suspicions had been confirmed, and he was intrigued. He was right on the edge of asking me about the people who'd been shot—right on the verge of making the leap—but at the last instant, he drew back. "You didn't see anything or hear anything that would help us? Was there anything different about the night Sam was shot?"

"No," I said. "Nothing. Why?"

He didn't answer, but I could read his mind like a book. The bullet from Sam's leg didn't match the other recovered bullets.

After he left, I tried to dissect that quick impression I'd gotten, the one that had prompted me to duck. If the parking lot hadn't been empty, I might not have caught it at all, since the brain that had made it had been at some distance. And what I'd felt had been a tangle of determination, anger, and above all, disgust. The person who'd been shooting had been sure I was loathsome and inhuman. Stupidly enough, my first reaction was hurt—after all, no one likes to be despised. Then I considered the strange fact that Sam's bullet didn't match any of the previous Were shootings. I couldn't understand that at all. I could think of many explanations, but all of them seemed far-fetched.

The rain began to pour down outside, hitting the north-facing windows with a hiss. I didn't have a reason to call anyone, but I felt like making one up. It wasn't a good night to be out of touch. As the pounding of the rain increased, I became more and more anxious. The sky was a leaden gray; soon it would be full dark.

I wondered why I was so twitchy. I was used to being by myself, and it seldom bothered me. Now I was physically closer to people than I'd ever been in my house on Hummingbird Road, but I felt more alone.

Though I wasn't supposed to drive, I needed things for the duplex. I would have made the errand a necessity and gone to Wal-Mart despite the rain—or because of the rain—if the nurse hadn't made such a big deal out of resting my shoulder. I went restlessly from room to room until the crunch of gravel told me that I was having yet more company. This was town living, for sure.

When I opened the door, Tara was standing there in a leopard-print raincoat with a hood. Of course I asked her in, and she tried her best to shake out the coat on the little front porch. I carried it into the kitchen to drip on the linoleum.

She hugged me very gently and said, "Tell me how you are."

After I went over the story once again, she said, "I've been worried about you. I couldn't get away from the shop until now, but I just had to come see you. I saw the suit in my closet. Did you come to my house?"

"Yes," I said. "The day before yesterday. Didn't Mickey tell you?"

"He was in the house when you were there? I warned you," she said, almost panic-stricken. "He didn't hurt you, did he? He didn't have anything to do with you getting shot?"

"Not that I know of. But I did go into your house kind of late, and I know you told me not to. It was just dumb. He did, ah, try to scare me. I wouldn't let him know you've been to see me, if I were you. How were you able to come here tonight?"

A shutter dropped over Tara's face. Her big dark eyes hardened, and she pulled away from me. "He's out somewhere," she said.

"Tara, can you tell me how you came to be involved with him? What happened to Franklin?" I tried to ask these questions as gently as I could, because I knew I was treading on delicate ground.

Tara's eyes filled with tears. She was struggling to answer me, but she was ashamed. "Sookie," she began at last, almost whispering, "I thought Franklin really cared about me, you know? I mean, I thought he respected me. As a person."

I nodded, intent on her face. I was scared of disrupting the flow of her story now that she'd finally begun to talk to me.

"But he . . . he just passed me along when he was through with me."

"Oh, no, Tara! He . . . surely he explained to you why you two were breaking up. Or did you have a big fight?" I didn't want to believe Tara had been passed from vamp to vamp like some fang-banger at a bloodsucker's party.

"He said, 'Tara, you're a pretty girl and you've been good company, but I owe a debt to Mickey's master, and Mickey wants you now.'"

I knew my mouth was hanging open, and I didn't care. I could scarcely believe what Tara was telling me. I could hear the humiliation rolling off of her in waves of self-loathing. "You couldn't do anything about it?" I asked. I was trying to keep the incredulity out of my voice.

"Believe me, I tried," Tara said bitterly. She wasn't blaming me for my question, which was a relief. "I told him I wouldn't. I told him I wasn't a whore, that I'd been dating him because I liked him." Her shoulders collapsed. "But you know, Sookie, I wasn't telling the whole truth, and he knew it. I took all the presents he gave me. They were expensive things. But they were freely given, and he didn't tell me there were strings attached! I never asked for anything!"

"So he was saying that because you'd accepted his gifts, you were bound to do as he said?"

"He said—" Tara began weeping, and her sobs made everything come out in little jerks. "He said that I was acting like a mistress, and he'd paid for everything I had, and that I might as well be of more use to him. I said I wouldn't, that I'd give him back everything, and he said he didn't want it. He told me this vamp named Mickey had seen me out with him, that Franklin owed Mickey a big favor."

"But this is America," I protested. "How can they do that?"

"Vampires are awful," Tara said dismally. "I don't know how you can stand hanging out with them. I thought I was so cool, having a vamp boyfriend. Okay, he was more like a sugar daddy, I guess." Tara sighed at the admission. "It was just so nice being, you know, treated so well. I'm not used to that. I really thought he liked me, too. I wasn't just being greedy."

"Did he take blood from you?" I asked.

"Don't they always?" she asked, surprised. "During sex?"

"As far as I know," I said. "Yeah. But you know, after he had your blood, he could tell how you felt about him."

"He could?"

"After they've had your blood, they're tuned in to your feelings." I was quite sure that Tara hadn't been as fond of Franklin Mott as she'd been saying, that she was much more interested in his lavish gifts and courteous treatment than in him. Of course, he'd known that. He might not have much cared if Tara liked him for himself or not, but that had surely made him more inclined to trade her off. "So how'd it happen?"

"Well, it wasn't so abrupt as I've made it sound," she said. She stared down at her hands. "First Franklin said he couldn't go somewhere with me, so would it be okay if this other guy took me instead? I thought he was thinking of me, of how disappointed I'd be if I didn't get to go—it was a concert—so I really didn't brood over it. Mickey was on his best behavior, and it wasn't a bad evening. He left me at the door, like a gentleman."

I tried not to raise my eyebrows in disbelief. The snakelike Mickey, whose every pore breathed "bad to the bone," had persuaded Tara he was a gentleman? "Okay, so then what?"

"Then Franklin had to go out of town, so Mickey came by to see if I had everything I needed, and he brought me a present, which I thought was from Franklin."

Tara was lying to me, and halfway lying to herself. She had surely known the present, a bracelet, was from Mickey. She had persuaded herself it was kind of a vassal's tribute to his lord's lady, but she had known it wasn't from Franklin.

"So I took it, and we went out, and then when we came back that night, he started making advances. And I broke that off." She gave me a calm and regal face.

She may have repulsed his advances that night, but she hadn't done it instantly and decisively.

Even Tara forgot I could read her mind.

"So that time he left," she said. She took a deep breath. "The next time, he didn't."

He'd given plenty of advance warning of his intentions.

I looked at her. She flinched. "I know," she wailed. "I know, I did wrong!"

"So, is he living at your place?"

"He's got a day place somewhere close," she said, limp with misery. "He shows up at dark, and we're together the whole night. He takes me to meetings, he takes me out, and he . . ."

"Okay, okay." I patted her hand. That didn't seem like enough, and I hugged her closer. Tara was taller than I, so it wasn't a very maternal hug, but I just wanted my friend to know I was on her side.

"He's real rough," Tara said very quietly. "He's going to kill me some day."

"Not if we kill him first."

"Oh, we can't."

"You think he's too strong?"

"I think I can't kill someone, even him."

"Oh." I had thought Tara had more grit to her, after what her parents had put her through. "Then we have to think of a way to pry him off you."

"What about your friend?"

"Which one?"

"Eric. Everyone says that Eric has a thing for you."

"Everyone?"

"The vampires around here. Did Bill pass you to Eric?"

He'd told me once I should go to Eric if anything happened to him, but I hadn't taken that as meaning Eric should assume the same role that Bill had in my life. As it turned out, I had had a fling with Eric, but under entirely different circumstances.

"No, he didn't," I said with absolute clarity. "Let me think." I mulled it over, feeling the terrible pressure of Tara's eyes. "Who's Mickey's boss?" I asked. "Or his sire?"

"I think it's a woman," Tara said. "At least, Mickey's taken me to a place in Baton Rouge a couple of times, a casino, where he's met with a female vamp. Her name is Salome."

"Like in the Bible?"

"Yeah. Imagine naming your kid that."

"So, is this Salome a sheriff?"

"What?"

"Is she a regional boss?"

"I don't know. Mickey and Franklin never talked about that stuff."

I tried not to look as exasperated as I felt. "What's the name of the casino?"

"Seven Veils."

Hmmm. "Okay, did he treat her with deference?" That was a good Word of the Day entry from my calendar, which I hadn't seen since the fire.

"Well, he kind of bowed to her."

"Just his head, or from the waist?"

"From the waist. Well, more than the head. I mean, he bent over."

"Okay. What did he call her?"

"Mistress."

"Okay." I hesitated, and then asked again, "You're sure we can't kill him?"

"Maybe you can," she said morosely. "I stood over him with an ice pick for fifteen minutes one night when he went to sleep after, you know, sex. But I was too scared. If he finds out I've been here to see you, he'll get mad. He doesn't like you at all. He thinks you're a bad influence."

"He got that right," I said with a confidence I was far from feeling. "Let me see what I can think of."

Tara left after another hug. She even managed a little smile, but I didn't know how justified her flash of optimism might be.

There was only one thing I could do.

The next night I'd be working. It was full dark by now, and he'd be up.

I had to call Eric.

13

"Fangtasia," said a bored feminine voice. "Where all your bloody dreams come true."

"Pam, it's Sookie."

"Oh, hello," she said more cheerfully. "I hear you're in even more trouble. Got your house burned. You won't live much longer if you keep that up."

"No, maybe not," I agreed. "Listen, is Eric there?"

"Yes, he's in his office."

"Can you transfer me to him?"

"I don't know how," she said disdainfully.

"Could you take the phone to him, please, ma'am?"

"Of course. Something always happens around here after you call. It's quite the break in routine." Pam was carrying the phone through the bar; I could tell by the change in the ambient noise. There was music in the background. KDED again: "The Night Has a Thousand Eyes" this time. "What's happening in Bon Temps, Sookie?" Pam asked, saying in a clear aside to some bar patron, "Step aside, you son of a misbegotten whore!

"They like that kind of talk," she said to me conversationally. "Now, what's up?"

"I got shot."

"Oh, too bad," she said. "Eric, do you know what Sookie is telling me? Someone shot her."

"Don't get so emotional, Pam," I said. "Someone might think you care."

She laughed. "Here is the man," she said.

Sounding just as matter-of-fact as Pam had, Eric said, "It can't be critical or you wouldn't be talking to me."

This was true, though I would have enjoyed a more horrified reaction. But this was no time to think of little issues. I took a deep breath. I knew, sure as shooting, what was coming, but I had to help Tara. "Eric," I said with a feeling of doom, "I need a favor."

"Really?" he said. Then, after a notable pause, "Really?"

He began to laugh.

"Gotcha," he said.

He arrived at the duplex an hour later and paused on the doorsill after I'd responded to his knock. "New building," he reminded me.

"You are welcome to come in," I said insincerely, and he stepped in, his white face practically blazing with—triumph? Excitement? Eric's hair was wet with rain and straggled over his shoulders in rattails. He was wearing a golden brown silk T-shirt and brown pleated trousers with a magnificent belt that was just barbaric: lots of leather, and gold, and dangling tassels. You can take the man out of the Viking era, but you can't take the Viking out of the man.

"Can I get you a drink?" I said. "I'm sorry, I don't have any

TrueBlood, and I'm not supposed to drive, so I couldn't go get any." I knew that was a big breach of hospitality, but there was nothing I could do about it. I hadn't been about to ask anyone to bring me blood for Eric.

"Not important," he said smoothly, looking around the small room.

"Please sit down."

Eric said onto the couch, his right ankle on the knee of his left leg. His big hands were restless. "What's the favor you need, Sookie?" He was openly gleeful.

I sighed. At least I was pretty sure he'd help, since he could practically taste the leverage he'd have over me.

I perched on the edge of the lumpy armchair. I explained about Tara, about Franklin, about Mickey. Eric got serious in a hurry. "She could leave during the day and she doesn't," he pointed out.

"Why should she leave her business and her home? He's the one should leave," I argued. (Though I have to confess, I'd wondered to myself why Tara didn't just take a vacation. Surely Mickey wouldn't stick around too long if his free ride was gone?) "Tara would be looking over her shoulder for the rest of her life if she tried to shake him loose by running," I said firmly.

"I've learned more about Franklin since I met him in Mississippi," Eric said. I wondered if Eric had learned this from Bill's database. "Franklin has an outdated mind-set."

This was rich, coming from a Viking warrior whose happiest days had been spent pillaging and raping and laying waste.

"Vampires used to pass willing humans around," Eric explained. "When our existence was secret, it was convenient to have a human lover, to maintain that person . . . that is, not to take too much blood . . . and then, when there was no one left who wanted her—or him," Eric added hastily, so my feminist side would not be offended, "that person would be, ah, completely used."

I was disgusted and showed it. "You mean drained," I said.

"Sookie, you have to understand that for hundreds, thousands, of years we have considered ourselves better than humans, separate from humans." He thought for a second. "Very much in the same relationship to humans as humans have to, say, cows. Edible like cows, but cute, too."

I was knocked speechless. I had sensed this, of course, but to have it spelled out was just . . . nauseating. Food that walked and talked, that was us. McPeople.

"I'll just go to Bill. He knows Tara, and she rents her business premises from him, so I bet he'll feel obliged to help her," I said furiously.

"Yes. He'd be obliged to try to kill Salome's underling. Bill doesn't rank any higher than Mickey, so he can't order him to leave. Who do you think would survive the fight?"

The idea paralyzed me for a minute. I shuddered. What if Mickey won?

"No, I'm afraid I'm your best hope here, Sookie." Eric gave me a brilliant smile. "I'll talk to Salome and ask her to call her dog off. Franklin is not her child, but Mickey is. Since he's been poaching in my area, she'll be obliged to re-call him."

He raised a blond eyebrow. "And since you're asking me to do this for you, of course, you owe me."

"Gosh, I wonder what you want in return?" I asked, maybe a little on the dry and sarcastic side.

He grinned at me broadly, giving me a flash of fang. "Tell me what happened while I was staying with you. Tell me completely, leaving out nothing. After that, I'll do what you want." He put both feet on the floor and leaned forward, focused on me.

"All right." Talk about being caught between a rock and a hard place. I looked down at my hands clasped in my lap.

"Did we have sex?" he asked directly.

For about two minutes, this might actually be fun. "Eric," I said, "we had sex in every position I could imagine, and some I couldn't. We had sex in every room in my house, and we had sex outdoors. You told me it was the best you'd ever had." (At the time he couldn't recall all the sex he'd ever had. But he'd paid me a compliment.) "Too bad you can't remember it," I concluded with a modest smile.

Eric looked like I'd hit him in the forehead with a mallet. For all of thirty seconds his reaction was completely gratifying. Then I began to be uneasy.

"Is there anything else I should know?" he said in a voice so level and even that it was simply scary.

"Um, yes."

"Then perhaps you'll enlighten me."

"You offered to give up your position as sheriff and come to live with me. And get a job."

Okay, maybe this *wasn't* going so well. Eric couldn't get any whiter or stiller. "Ah," he said. "Anything else?"

"Yes." I ducked my head because I'd gotten to the absolutely un-fun part. "When we came home that last night, the night we'd had the battle with the witches in Shreveport, we came in the back door, right, like I always do. And Debbie Pelt—you remember her. Alcide's—oh, whatever she was to him . . . Debbie was sitting at my kitchen table. And she had a gun and was gonna shoot me." I risked a glance and found Eric's brows had drawn in together in an ominous frown. "But you threw yourself in front of me." I leaned forward very quickly and patted him on the knee. Then I retreated into my own space. "And you took the bullet, which was really, really sweet of you. But she was going to shoot again, and I pulled out my brother's shotgun, and I killed her." I hadn't cried at all that night, but I felt a tear run down my cheek now. "I killed her," I said, and gasped for breath.

Eric's mouth opened as though he was going to ask a question, but I held up a hand in a *wait* gesture. I had to finish. "We gathered up the body and bagged it, and you took it and buried her somewhere while I cleaned the kitchen. And you found her car and you hid it. I don't know where. It took me hours to get the blood out of the kitchen. It was on everything." I grabbed desperately at my self-possession. I rubbed my eyes with the back of my wrist. My shoulder ached, and I shifted in the chair, trying to ease it.

"And now someone else has shot at you and I wasn't there to take the bullet," Eric said. "You must be living wrong. Do you think the Pelt family is trying to get revenge?"

"No," I said. I was pleased that Eric was taking all this so calmly. I don't know what I'd expected, but it wasn't this. He seemed, if anything, subdued. "They hired private detectives, and as far as I know, the private detectives didn't find any reason to suspect me any more than anyone else. The only reason I was a suspect anyway was because when Alcide and I found that body in Shreveport at Verena Rose's, we told the police we were engaged. We had to explain why we went together to a bridal shop. Since he had such an on-and-off relationship with Debbie, him saying we were getting married naturally raised a red flag when the detectives checked it out. He had a good alibi for the time she died, as it turned out. But if they ever seriously suspect me, I'll be in trouble. I can't give you as an alibi, because of course you weren't even here, as far as anyone knows. You can't give me an alibi because you don't remember that night; and of course, I'm just plain old guilty. I killed her. I had to do it." I'm sure Cain had said that when he'd killed Abel.

"You're talking too much," Eric said.

I pressed my lips together. One minute he wanted me to tell him everything; the next minute he wanted me to stop talking.

For maybe five minutes, Eric just looked at me. I wasn't always sure he was seeing me. He was lost in some deep thoughts.

"I told you I would leave everything for you?" he said at the end of all this rumination.

I snorted. Trust Eric to select that as the pertinent idea.

"And how did you respond?"

Okay, that astonished me. "You couldn't just stay with me, not remembering. That wouldn't be right."

He narrowed his eyes. I got tired of being regarded through slits of blue. "So," I said, curiously deflated. Maybe I'd expected a more emotional scene than this. Maybe I'd expected Eric to grab me and kiss me silly and tell me he still felt the same. Maybe I was too fond of daydreams. "I did your favor. Now you do mine."

Not taking his eyes off me, Eric whipped a cell phone from his pocket and dialed a number from memory. "Rose-Anne," he said. "Are you well? Yes, please, if she's free. Tell her I have information that will interest her." I couldn't hear the response on the other end, but Eric nodded, as he would if the speaker had been present. "Of course I'll hold. Briefly." In a minute, he said, "And hello to you, too, most beautiful princess. Yes, it keeps me busy. How's business at the casino? Right, right. There's one born every minute. I called to tell you something about your minion, that one named Mickey. He has some business connection with Franklin Mott?"

Then Eric's eyebrows rose, and he smiled slightly. "Is that right? I don't blame you. Mott is trying to stick to the old ways, and this is America." He listened again. "Yes, I'm giving you this information for free. If you choose not to

grant me a small favor in return, of course that's of no consequence. You know in what esteem I hold you." Eric smiled
charmingly at the telephone. "I did think you should know
about Mott's passing on a human woman to Mickey.
Mickey's keeping her under his thumb by threatening her
life and property. She's quite unwilling."

After another silence, during which his smile widened,
Eric said, "The small favor is removing Mickey. Yes, that's
all. Just make sure he knows he should never again approach
this woman, Tara Thornton. He should have nothing more to
do with her, or her belongings and friends. The connection
should be completely severed. Or I'll have to see about sev-
ering some part of Mickey. He's done this in my area, without the courtesy of coming to visit me. I really expected
better manners of any child of yours. Have I covered all the
bases?"

That Americanism sounded strange, coming from Eric
Northman. I wondered if he'd ever played baseball.

"No, you don't need to thank me, Salome. I'm glad to be
of service. And if you could let me know when the thing is
accomplished? Thanks. Well, back to the grindstone." Eric
flipped the phone shut and began tossing it in the air and
catching it, over and over.

"You knew Mickey and Franklin were doing something
wrong to start with," I said, shocked but oddly unsurprised.
"You know their boss would be glad to find out they were
breaking the rules, since her vamp was violating your territory. So this won't affect you at all."

"I only realized that when you told me what you wanted,"
Eric pointed out, the very essence of reason. He grinned at
me. "How could I know that your heart's desire would be for
me to help someone else?"

"What did you think I wanted?"

"I thought maybe you wanted me to pay for rebuilding

your house, or you would ask me to help find out who's shooting the Weres. Someone who could have mistaken you for a Were," Eric told me, as if I should have known that. "Who had you been with before you were shot?"

"I'd been to visit Calvin Norris," I said, and Eric looked displeased.

"So you had his smell on you."

"Well, I gave him a hug good-bye, so yeah."

Eric eyed me skeptically. "Had Alcide Herveaux been there?

"He came by the house site," I said.

"Did he hug you, too?"

"I don't remember," I said. "It's no big deal."

"It is for someone looking for shifters and Weres to shoot. And you are hugging too many people."

"Maybe it was Claude's smell," I said thoughtfully. "Gosh, I didn't think of that. No, wait, Claude hugged me after the shooting. So I guess the fairy smell didn't matter."

"A fairy," Eric said, the pupils of his eyes actually dilating. "Come here, Sookie."

Ah-oh. I might have overplayed my hand out of sheer irritation.

"No," I said. "I told you what you wanted, you did what I asked, and now you can go back to Shreveport and let me get some sleep. Remember?" I pointed to my bandaged shoulder.

"Then I'll come to you," Eric said, and knelt in front of me. He pressed against my legs and leaned over so his head was against my neck. He inhaled, held it, exhaled. I had to choke back a nervous laugh at the similarity the process held to smoking dope. "You reek," Eric said, and I stiffened. "You smell of shifter and Were and fairy. A cocktail of other races."

I stayed completely immobile. His lips were about two millimeters from my ear. "Should I just bite you, and end it all?" he whispered. "I would never have to think about you again. Thinking about you is an annoying habit, and one I want to be rid of. Or should I start arousing you, and discover if sex with you was really the best I've ever had?"

I didn't think I was going to get a vote on this. I cleared my throat. "Eric," I said, a little hoarsely, "we need to talk about something."

"No. No. No," he said. With each "no" his lips brushed my skin.

I was looking past his shoulder at the window. "Eric," I breathed, "someone's watching us."

"Where?" His posture didn't change, but Eric had shifted from a mood that was definitely dangerous to me to one that was dangerous for someone else.

Since the eyes-at-the-window scenario was an eerie echo of the situation the night my house had burned, and that night the skulker had proved to be Bill, I hoped the watcher might be Bill again. Maybe he was jealous, or curious, or just checking up on me. If the trespasser was a human, I could have read his brain and found out who he was, or at least what he intended; but this was a vampire, as the blank hole where the brain pattern should be had informed me.

"It's a vampire," I told Eric in the tiniest whisper I could manage, and he put his arms around me and pulled me into him.

"You're so much trouble," Eric said, and yet he didn't sound exasperated. He sounded excited. Eric loved the action moments.

By then, I was sure that the lurker wasn't Bill, who would have made himself known. And Charles was presumably busy at Merlotte's, mixing daiquiris. That left one vampire in the area unaccounted for. "Mickey," I breathed, my fingers gripping Eric's shirt.

"Salome moved more quickly than I thought," Eric said

in a regular voice. "He's too angry to obey her, I suppose. He's never been in here, correct?"

"Correct." Thank God.

"Then he can't come inside."

"But he can break the window," I said as glass shattered to our left. Mickey had thrown a large rock as big as my fist, and to my dismay the rock hit Eric squarely in the head. He went down like a—well, like a rock. He lay without moving. Dark blood welled from a deep cut in his temple. I leaped to my feet, completely stunned at seeing the powerful Eric apparently out cold.

"Invite me in," said Mickey, just outside the window. His face, white and angry, shone in the pelting rain. His black hair was plastered to his head.

"Of course not," I said, kneeling beside Eric, who blinked, to my relief. Not that he could be dead, of course, but still, when you see someone take a blow like that, vampire or not, it's just plain terrifying. Eric had fallen in front of the armchair, which had its back to the window, so Mickey couldn't see him.

But now I could see what Mickey was holding by one hand: Tara. She was almost as pale as he was, and she'd been beaten to a pulp. Blood was running out of the corner of her mouth. The lean vampire had a merciless grip on her arm. "I'll kill her if you don't let me in," he said, and to prove his point, he put both hands around her neck and began to squeeze. A clap of thunder and a bolt of lightning lit up Tara's desperate face as she clawed weakly at his arms. He smiled, fangs completely exposed.

If I let him in, he'd kill all of us. If I left him out there, I would have to watch him kill Tara. I felt Eric's hands take hold of my arm. "Do it," I said, not moving my gaze from Mickey. Eric bit, and it hurt like hell. He wasn't finessing this at all. He was desperate to heal in a hurry.

I'd just have to swallow the pain. I tried hard to keep my face still, but then I realized I had a great reason to look upset. "Let her go!" I yelled at Mickey, trying to buy a few seconds. I wondered if any of the neighbors were up, if they could hear the ruckus, and I prayed they wouldn't come searching to find out what was going on. I was even afraid for the police, if they came. We didn't have any vampire cops to handle vampire lawbreakers, like the cities did.

"I'll let her go when you let me in," Mickey yelled. He looked like a demon out there in the rain. "How's your tame vamp doing?"

"He's still out," I lied. "You hurt him bad." It didn't take any effort at all to make my voice crack as if I were on the verge of tears. "I can see his skull," I wailed, looking down at Eric to see that he was still feeding as greedily as a hungry baby. His head was mending as I watched. I'd seen vamps heal before, but it was still amazing. "He can't even open his eyes," I added in a heartbroken way, and just then Eric's blue eyes blazed up at me. I didn't know if he was in fighting trim yet, but I could not watch Tara being choked. "Not yet," Eric said urgently, but I had already told Mickey to come in.

"Oops," I said, and then Mickey slithered through the window in an oddly boneless movement. He knocked the broken glass out of the way carelessly, like it didn't hurt him to get cut. He dragged Tara through after him, though at least he'd switched his grip from her neck to her arm. Then he dropped her on the floor, and the rain coming in the window pelted down on her, though she couldn't be any wetter than she already was. I wasn't even sure she was conscious. Her eyes were closed in her bloody face, and her bruises were turning dark. I stood, swaying with the blood loss, but keeping my wrist concealed by resting it on the back of the armchair. I'd felt Eric lick it, but it would take a few minutes to heal.

"What do you want?" I asked Mickey. As if I didn't know.

"Your head, bitch," he said, his narrow features twisted with hatred, his fangs completely out. They were white and glistening and sharp in the bright overhead light. "Get down on your knees to your betters!" Before I could react in any way—in fact before I could blink—the vampire backhanded me, and I stumbled across the small room, landing half on the couch before I slid to the floor. The air went out of me in a big whoosh, and I simply couldn't move, couldn't even gasp for air, for an agonizingly long minute. In the meantime, Mickey was on top of me, his intentions completely clear when he reached down to unzip his pants. "This is all you're good for!" he said, contempt making him even uglier. He tried to push his way into my head, too, forcing the fear of him into my brain to cow me.

And my lungs inflated. The relief of breathing was exquisite, even under the circumstances. With air came rage, as if I'd inhaled it along with oxygen. This was the trump card male bullies played, always. I was sick of it—sick of being scared of the bogeyman's dick.

"No!" I screamed up at him. *"No!"* And finally I could think again; finally the fear let loose of me. "Your invitation is *rescinded*!" I yelled, and it was his turn to panic. He reared up off of me, looking ridiculous with his pants open, and he went backward out of the window, stepping on poor Tara as he went. He tried to bend, to grip her so he could yank her with him, but I lunged across the little room to grab her ankles, and her arms were too slick with rain to give him purchase, and the magic that had hold of him was too strong. In a second, he was outside looking in, screaming with rage. Then he looked east, as if he heard someone calling, and he vanished into the darkness.

Eric pushed himself to his feat, looking almost as startled

as Mickey. "That was clearer thinking than most humans can manage," he said mildly into the sudden silence. "How are you, Sookie?" He reached down a hand and pulled me to my feet. "I myself am feeling much better. I've had your blood without having to talk you into it, and I didn't have to fight Mickey. You did all the work."

"You got hit in the head with a rock," I pointed out, content just to stand for a minute, though I knew I had to call an ambulance for Tara. I was feeling a little on the weak side myself.

"A small price to pay," Eric told me. He brought out his cell phone, flipped it open, and pressed the REDIAL button. "Salome," Eric said, "glad you answered the phone. He's trying to run. . . ."

I heard the gleeful laughter coming from the other end of the phone. It was chilling. I couldn't feel the least bit sorry for Mickey, but I was glad I wouldn't have to witness his punishment.

"Salome'll catch him?" I asked.

Eric nodded happily as he returned his phone to his pocket. "And she can do things to him more painful than anything I could imagine," he said. "Though I can imagine plenty right now."

"She's that, ah, creative?"

"He's hers. She's his sire. She can do with him what she wishes. He can't disobey her and go unpunished. He has to go to her when she calls him, and she's calling."

"Not on the phone, I take it," I ventured.

His eyes glinted down at me. "No, she won't need a phone. He's trying to run away, but he'll go to her eventually. The longer he holds out, the more severe his torture will be. Of course," he added, in case I missed the point, "that's as it should be."

"Pam is yours, right?" I asked, falling to my knees and putting my fingers to Tara's cold neck. I didn't want to look at her.

"Yes," Eric said. "She's free to leave when she wants, but she comes back when I let her know I need her help."

I didn't know how I felt about that, but it didn't really make a hell of a lot of difference. Tara gasped and moaned. "Wake up, girl," I said. "Tara! I'm gonna call an ambulance for you.

"No," she said sharply. "No." There was a lot of that word going around tonight.

"But you're bad hurt."

"I can't go to the hospital. Everyone will know."

"Everyone will know someone beat the shit out of you when you can't go to work for a couple of weeks, you idiot."

"You can have some of my blood," Eric offered. He was looking down at Tara without any obvious emotion.

"No," she said. "I'd rather die."

"You might," I said, looking her over. "Oh, but you've had blood from Franklin or Mickey." I was assuming some tit-for-tat in their lovemaking.

"Of course not," she said, shocked. The horror in her voice took me aback. I'd had vampire blood when I'd needed it. The first time, I'd have died without it.

"Then you have to go to the hospital." I was really concerned that Tara might have internal injuries. "I'm scared for you to move," I protested, when she tried to push herself to a seated position. Mr. Super Strength didn't help, which irritated me, since he could have shifted her easily.

But at last Tara managed to sit with her back against the wall, the empty window allowing the chilly wind to gust in and blow the curtains to and fro. The rain had abated until only a drop or two was coming in. The linoleum in front of the window was wet with water and blood, and the glass lay in glittering sharp fragments, some stuck to Tara's damp clothes and skin.

"Tara, listen to me," Eric said. She looked up at him. Since he was close to the fluorescent light, she had to squint. I thought she looked pitiful, but Eric didn't seem to see the same person I was seeing. "Your greed and selfishness put my—my friend Sookie in danger. You say you're her friend, too, but you don't act like it."

Hadn't Tara loaned me a suit when I needed one? Hadn't she loaned me her car when mine burned? Hadn't she helped me on other occasions when I needed it? "Eric, this isn't any of your business," I said.

"You called me and asked me for my help. That makes it my business. I called Salome and told her what her child was doing, and she's taken him away and to punish him for it. Isn't that what you wanted?"

"Yes," I said, and I'm ashamed to say I sounded sullen.

"Then I'm going to make my point with Tara." He looked back down at her. "Do you understand me?"

Tara nodded painfully. The bruises on her face and throat seemed to be darkening more every minute.

"I'm getting some ice for your throat," I told her, and ran into the kitchen to dump ice from the plastic trays into a Ziploc bag. I didn't want to listen to Eric scold her; she seemed so pitiful.

When I came back less than a minute later, Eric had finished whatever he was going to say to Tara. She was touching her neck gingerly, and she took the bag from me and held it to her throat. While I was leaning over her, anxious and scared, Eric was back on his cell phone.

I twitched with worry. "You need a doctor," I urged her.

"No," she said.

I looked up at Eric, who was just finishing his phone call. He was the injury expert.

"She'll heal without going to the hospital," he said briefly. His indifference made a chill run down my spine. Just when I thought I was used to them, vampires would show me their true face, and I would have to remind myself all over again that they were a different race. Or maybe it was centuries of conditioning that made the difference; decades of disposing of people as they chose, taking what they wanted, enduring the dichotomy of being the most powerful beings on earth in the darkness, and yet completely helpless and vulnerable during the hours of light.

"But will she have some permanent damage? Something doctors could fix if she got to them quick?"

"I'm fairly certain that her throat is only badly bruised. She has some broken ribs from the beating, possibly some loose teeth. Mickey could have broken her jaw and her neck very easily, you know. He probably wanted her to be able to talk to you when he brought her here, so he held back a little. He counted on you panicking and letting him in. He didn't think you could gather your thoughts so quickly. If I'd been him, my first move would have been to damage your mouth or neck so you couldn't rescind my entrance."

That possibility hadn't occurred to me, and I blanched.

"When he backhanded you, I think that was what he was aiming for," Eric continued dispassionately.

I'd heard enough. I thrust a broom and dustpan into his hands. He looked at them as if they were ancient artifacts and he could not fathom their use.

"Sweep up," I said, using a wet washcloth to clean the blood and dirt off my friend. I didn't know how much of this conversation Tara was absorbing, but her eyes were open and her mouth was shut, so maybe she was listening. Maybe she was just working through the pain.

Eric moved the broom experimentally and made an attempt to sweep the glass into the pan while it lay in the middle of the floor. Of course, the pan slid away. Eric scowled.

I'd finally found something Eric did poorly.

"Can you stand?" I asked Tara. She focused on my face and nodded very slightly. I squatted and took her hands. Slowly and painfully, she drew her knees up, and then she pushed as I pulled. Though the window had broken mostly in big pieces, a few bits of glass fell from her as she rose, and I flicked an eye at Eric to make sure he understood he should clean them up. He had a truculent set to his mouth.

I tried to put my arm around Tara to help her into my bedroom, but my wounded shoulder gave a throb of pain so unexpected that I flinched. Eric tossed down the dustpan. He picked up Tara in one smooth gesture and put her on the couch instead of my bed. I opened my mouth to protest and he looked at me. I shut my mouth. I went into the kitchen and fetched one of my pain pills, and I got Tara to swallow one, which took some coaxing. The medicine seemed to knock her out, or maybe she just didn't want to acknowledge Eric anymore. Anyway, she kept her eyes closed and her body slack, and gradually her breathing grew even and deep.

Eric handed me the broom with a triumphant smile. Since he'd lifted Tara, clearly I was stuck with his task. I was awkward because of my bad shoulder, but I finished sweeping up the glass and disposing of it in a garbage bag. Eric turned toward the door. I hadn't heard anyone arrive, but Eric opened the door to Bill before Bill even knocked. Eric's earlier phone conversation must have been with Bill. In a way, that made sense; Bill lived in Eric's fiefdom, or whatever they called it. Eric needed help, so Bill was obliged to supply it. My ex was burdened with a large piece of ply-wood, a hammer, and a box of nails.

"Come in," I said when Bill halted in the doorway, and without speaking a word to each other, the two vampires nailed the wood across the window. To say I felt awkward would be an understatement, though thanks to the events of the evening I wasn't as sensitive as I would've been at another time. I was mostly preoccupied with the pain in my shoulder, and Tara's recovery, and the current whereabouts of Mickey. In the extra space I had left over after worrying about those items, I crammed in some anxiety about replacing Sam's window, and whether the neighbors had heard enough of this fracas to call the police. On the whole, I thought they hadn't; someone would be here by now.

After Bill and Eric finished their temporary repair, they both watched me mopping up the water and blood on the linoleum. The silence began to weigh heavily on all three of us: at least, on my third of the three of us. Bill's tenderness in caring for me the night before had touched me. But Eric's just acquired knowledge of our intimacy raised my self-consciousness to a whole new level. I was in the same room with two guys who both knew I'd slept with the other.

I wanted to dig a hole and lie down in it and pull the opening inside with me, like a character in a cartoon. I couldn't look either of them in the face.

If I rescinded both their invitations, they'd have to walk outside without a word; but in view of the fact that they'd both just helped me, such a procedure would be rude. I'd solved my problems with them before in exactly that way. Though I was tempted to repeat it to ease my personal embarrassment, I simply couldn't. So what did we do next?

Should I pick a fight? Yelling at one another might clear the air. Or maybe a frank acknowledgment of the situation . . . no.

I had a sudden mental picture of us all three climbing in the double bed in the little bedroom. Instead of *duking* out our conflicts, or *talking* out our problems, we could . . . no. I could feel my face flame red, as I was torn between semi-hysterical amusement and a big dash of shame at even thinking the thought. Jason and his buddy Hoyt had often discussed (in my hearing) that every male's fantasy was to be in bed with two women. And men who came into the bar echoed that idea, as I knew from checking Jason's theory by reading a random sample of male minds. Surely I was allowed to entertain the same kind of fantasy? I gave a hysterical kind of giggle, which definitely startled both vampires.

"This is amusing?" Bill asked. He gestured from the plywood, to the recumbent Tara, to the bandage on my shoulder. He omitted pointing from Eric to himself. I laughed out loud.

Eric cocked a blond eyebrow. "*We* are amusing?"

I nodded wordlessly. I thought, *Instead of a cook-off, we could have a cock-off. Instead of a fishing derby, we could have a . . .*

At least in part because I was tired, and strained, and blood depleted, I went way into the silly zone. I laughed even harder when I looked at Eric's and Bill's faces. They wore almost identical expressions of exasperation.

Eric said, "Sookie, we haven't finished our discussion."

"Oh yes, we have," I said, though I was still smiling. "I asked you for a favor: releasing Tara from her bondage to Mickey. You asked me for payment for that favor: telling you what happened when you lost your memory. You performed your side of the bargain, and so did I. Bought and paid for. The end."

Bill looked from Eric to me. Now he knew that Eric knew what I knew. . . . I giggled again. Then the giddiness just poofed out of me. I was a deflated balloon, for sure. "Good night, both of you," I said. "Thanks, Eric, for taking that rock in the head, and for sticking to your phone throughout the evening. Thanks, Bill, for turning out so late with window-repair supplies. I appreciate it, even if you got volunteered by Eric." Under ordinary circumstances—if there were such things as ordinary circumstances with vampires around—I would've given them each a hug, but that just seemed too weird. "Shoo," I said. "I have to go to bed. I'm all worn out."

"Shouldn't one of us stay here with you tonight?" Bill asked.

If I'd had to say yes to that, had to pick one of them to stay with me that night, it would have been Bill—if I could have counted on him to be as undemanding and gentle as he'd been the night before. When you're down and hurting, the most wonderful thing in the world is to feel cherished. But that was too big a bunch of if's for tonight.

"I think I'll be fine," I said. "Eric assures me that Salome will scoop up Mickey in no time, and I need sleep more than anything. I appreciate both of you coming out tonight."

For a long moment I thought they might just say "No" and try to outwait each other. But Eric kissed me on the forehead and left, and Bill, not to be outdone, brushed my lips with his and took his leave. When the two vampires had departed, I was delighted to be by myself.

Of course, I wasn't exactly alone. Tara was passed out on the couch. I made sure she was comfortable—took off her shoes, got the blanket off my bed to cover her—and then I fell into my own bed.

14 ~

I SLEPT FOR HOURS.

When I woke up, Tara was gone.

I felt a stab of panic, until I realized she'd folded the blanket, washed her face in the bathroom (wet washcloth), and put her shoes on. She had left me a little note, too, on an old envelope that already held the beginnings of my shopping list. It said, "I'll call you later. T"—a terse note, and not exactly redolent of sisterly love.

I felt a little sad. I figured I wouldn't be Tara's favorite person for a while. She'd had to look more closely at herself than she wanted to look.

There are times to think, and times to lie fallow. Today was a fallow day. My shoulder felt much better, and I decided I would drive to the Wal-Mart Supercenter in Clarice and get all my shopping over with in one trip. Also, there I wouldn't see as many people I knew, and I wouldn't have to discuss getting shot.

It was very peaceful, being anonymous in the big store. I moved slowly and read labels, and I even selected a shower curtain for the duplex bathroom. I took my time completing my list. When I transferred the bags from the buggy into the car, I tried to do all the lifting with my right arm. I was practically reeking with virtue when I got back to the house on Berry Street.

The Bon Temps Florist van was in the driveway. Every woman has a little lift in her heart when the florist's van pulls up, and I was no exception.

"I have a multiple delivery here," said Bud Dearborn's wife, Greta. Greta was flat-faced like the sheriff and squatty like the sheriff, but her nature was happy and unsuspicious. "You're one lucky girl, Sookie."

"Yes, ma'am, I am," I agreed, with only a tincture of irony. After Greta had helped me carry in my bags, she began carrying in flowers.

Tara had sent me a little vase of daisies and carnations. I am very fond of daisies, and the yellow and white looked pretty in my little kitchen. The card just read "From Tara."

Calvin had sent a very small gardenia bush wrapped up in tissue and a big bow. It was ready to pop out of the plastic tub and be planted as soon as the danger of a frost was over. I was impressed with the thoughtfulness of the gift, since the gardenia bush would perfume my yard for years. Because he'd had to call in the order, the card bore the conventional sentiment "Thinking of you—Calvin."

Pam had sent a mixed bouquet, and the card read, "Don't get shot anymore. From the gang at Fangtasia." That made me laugh a little. I automatically thought of writing thank-you notes, but of course I didn't have my stationery with me. I'd stop by the pharmacy and get some. The downtown pharmacy had a corner that was a card shop, and also it accepted packages for UPS pickup. You had to be diverse in Bon Temps.

I put away my purchases, awkwardly hung the shower curtain, and got cleaned up for work.

Sweetie Des Arts was the first person I saw when I came through the employees' entrance. She had an armful of kitchen towels, and she'd tied on her apron. "You're a hard woman to kill," she remarked. "How you feeling?"

"I'm okay," I said. I felt like Sweetie had been waiting for me, and I appreciated the gesture.

"I hear you ducked just in time," she said. "How come? Did you hear something?"

"Not exactly," I said. Sam limped out of his office then, using his cane. He was scowling. I sure didn't want to explain my little quirk to Sweetie on Sam's time. I said, "I just had a feeling," and shrugged, which was unexpetedly painful.

Sweetie shook her head at my close call and turned to go through the bar and back to the kitchen.

Sam jerked his head toward his office, and with a sinking heart I followed him in. He shut the door behind us. "What were you doing when you got shot?" he asked. His eyes were bright with anger.

I wasn't going to get blamed for what had happened to me. I stood right up to Sam, got in his face. "I was just checking out library books," I said through my teeth.

"So why would he think you're a shifter?"

"I have no idea."

"Who had you been around?"

"I'd been to see Calvin, and I'd . . ." My voice trailed off as I caught at the tail end of a thought.

"So, who can tell you smell like a shifter?" I asked slowly.

"No one but another shifter, right? Or someone with shifter blood. Or a vampire. Some supernatural thing."

"But we haven't had any strange shifters around here lately."

"Have you gone to where the shooter must have been, to smell?"

"No, the only time I was on the spot at a shooting, I was too busy screaming on the ground with blood running out of my leg."

"But maybe now you could pick up something."

Sam looked down at his leg doubtfully. "It's rained, but I guess it's worth a try," he conceded. "I should have thought of it myself. Okay, tonight, after work."

"It's a date," I said flippantly as Sam sank down in his squeaky chair. I put my purse in the drawer Sam kept empty and went out to check my tables.

Charles was hard at work, and he gave me a nod and a smile before he concentrated on the level of beer in the pitcher he was holding to the tap. One of our consistent drunks, Jane Bodehouse, was seated at the bar with Charles fixed in her sights. It didn't seem to make the vampire uncomfortable. I saw that the rhythm of the bar was back to normal; the new bartender had been absorbed into the background.

After I'd worked about an hour, Jason came in. He had Crystal cuddled up in the curve of his arm. He was as happy as I'd ever seen him. He was excited by his new life and very pleased with Crystal's company. I wondered how long that would last. But Crystal herself seemed of much the same mind.

She told me that Calvin would be getting out of the hospital the next day and going home to Hotshot. I made sure to mention the flowers he'd sent and told her I'd be fixing Calvin some dish to mark his homecoming.

Crystal was pretty sure she was pregnant. Even through

the tangle of shifter brain, I could read that thought as clear as a bell. It wasn't the first time I'd learned that some girl "dating" Jason was sure he was going to be a dad, and I hoped that this time was as false as the last time. It wasn't that I had anything against Crystal . . . Well, that was a lie I was telling myself. I did have something against Crystal. Crystal was part of Hotshot, and she'd never leave it. I didn't want any niece or nephew of mine to be brought up in that strange little community, within the pulsing magic influence of the crossroads that formed its center.

Crystal was keeping her late period a secret from Jason right now, determined to stay quiet until she was sure what it meant. I approved. She nursed one beer while Jason downed two, and then they were off to the movies in Clarice. Jason gave me a hug on the way out while I was distributing drinks to a cluster of law enforcement people. Alcee Beck, Bud Dearborn, Andy Bellefleur, Kevin Pryor, and Kenya Jones, plus Arlene's new crush, arson investigator Dennis Pettibone, were all huddled around two tables pushed together in a corner. There were two strangers with them, but I picked up easily enough that the two men were cops, too, part of some task force.

Arlene might have liked to wait on them, but they were clearly in my territory, and they clearly were talking about something heap big. When I was taking drink orders, they all hushed up, and when I was walking away, they'd start their conversation back up. Of course, what they said with their mouths didn't make any difference to me, since I knew what each and every one of them was thinking.

And they all knew this good and well; and they all forgot it. Alcee Beck, in particular, was scared to death of me, but even he was quite oblivious to my ability, though I'd demonstrated it for him before. The same could be said of Andy Bellefleur.

"What's the law enforcement convention in the corner cooking up?" asked Charles. Jane had tottered off to the ladies', and he was temporarily by himself at the bar.

"Let me see," I said, closing my eyes so I could concentrate better. "Well, they're thinking of moving the stakeout for the shooter to another parking lot tonight, and they're convinced that the arson is connected to the shootings and that Jeff Marriot's death is tied in with everything, somehow. They're even wondering if the disappearance of Debbie Pelt is included in this clutch of crimes, since she was last seen getting gas on the interstate at the filling station closest to Bon Temps. And my brother, Jason, disappeared for a while a couple of weeks ago; maybe that's part of the picture, too." I shook my head and opened my eyes to find that Charles was disconcertingly close. His one good eye, his right, stared hard into my left.

"You have very unusual gifts, young woman," he said after a moment. "My last employer collected the unusual."

"Who'd you work for before you came into Eric's territory?" I asked. He turned away to get the Jack Daniel's.

"The King of Mississippi," he said.

I felt as if someone had pulled the rug out from under my feet. "Why'd you leave Mississippi and come here?" I asked, ignoring the hoots from the table five feet away.

The King of Mississippi, Russell Edgington, knew me as Alcide's girlfriend, but he didn't know me as a telepath occasionally employed by vampires. It was quite possible Edgington might have a grudge against me. Bill had been held in the former stables behind Edgington's mansion and tortured by Lorena, the creature who'd turned Bill into a vampire over a hundred and forty years before. Bill had escaped. Lorena had died. Russell Edgington didn't necessarily know I was the agent of these events. But then again, he might.

"I got tired of Russell's ways," Sir Charles said. "I'm not

of his sexual persuasion, and being surrounded by perversity became tiresome."

Edgington enjoyed the company of men, it was true. He had a house full of them, as well as a steady human companion, Talbot.

It was possible Charles had been there while I was visiting, though I hadn't noticed him. I'd been severely injured the night I was brought to the mansion. I hadn't seen all its inhabitants, and I didn't necessarily remember the ones I'd seen.

I became aware that the pirate and I were maintaining our eye contact. If they've survived for any length of time, vampires read human emotions very well, and I wondered what Charles Twining was gleaning from my face and demeanor. This was one of the few times I wished I could read a vampire's mind. I wondered, very much, if Eric was aware of Charles's background. Surely Eric wouldn't have taken him on without a background check? Eric was a cautious vampire. He'd seen history I couldn't imagine, and he'd lived through it because he was careful.

Finally I turned to answer the summons of the impatient roofers who'd been trying to get me to refill their beer pitchers for several minutes.

I avoided speaking to our new bartender for the rest of the evening. I wondered why he'd told me as much as he had. Either Charles wanted me to know he was watching me, or he really had no idea I'd been in Mississippi recently.

I had a lot to think about.

The working part of the night finally came to an end. We had to call Jane's son to come get his soused relative, but that was nothing new. The pirate bartender had been working at a good clip, never making mistakes, being sure to give every patron a good word as he filled the orders. His tip jar looked healthy.

Bill arrived to pick up his boarder as we were closing up for the night. I wanted to have a quiet word with him, but Charles was by Bill's side in a flash, so I didn't have an opportunity. Bill gave me an odd look, but they were gone without my making an opportunity to talk to him. I wasn't sure what I would say, anyway. I was reassured when I realized that of course Bill had seen the worst employees of Russell Edgington, because those employees had tortured him. If Charles Twining was unknown to Bill, he might be okay.

Sam was ready to go on our sniffing mission. It was cold and brilliant outside, the stars glittering in the night sky. Sam was bundled up, and I pulled on my pretty red coat. I had a matching set of gloves and a hat, and I would need them now. Though spring was coming closer every day, winter hadn't finished with us yet.

No one was at the bar but us. The entire parking lot was empty, except for Jane's car. The glare of the security lights made the shadows deeper. I heard a dog bark way off in the distance. Sam was moving carefully on his crutches, trying to negotiate the uneven parking lot.

Sam said, "I'm going to change." He didn't mean his clothes.

"What'll happen to your leg if you do?"

"Let's find out."

Sam was full-blood shifter on both sides. He could change when it wasn't the full moon, though the experiences were very different, he'd said. Sam could change into more than one animal, though dogs were his preference, and a collie was his choice among dogs.

Sam retired behind the hedge in front of his trailer to doff his clothes. Even in the night, I saw the air disturbance that signaled magic was working all around him. He fell to his knees and gasped, and then I couldn't see him anymore through the dense bushes. After a minute, a bloodhound trotted out, a red one, his ears swinging from side to side. I wasn't used to seeing Sam this way, and it took me a second to be sure it was him. When the dog looked up at me, I knew my boss was inside.

"Come on, Dean," I said. I'd named Sam that in his animal guise before I'd realized the man and the dog were the same being. The bloodhound trotted ahead of me across the parking lot and into the woods where the shooter had waited for Sam to come out of the club. I watched the way the dog was moving. It was favoring its right rear leg, but not drastically.

In the cold night woods, the sky was partially blocked. I had a flashlight, and I turned it on, but somehow that just made the trees creepier. The bloodhound—Sam—had already reached the place the police had decided marked the shooter's vantage point. The dog, jowls jouncing, bent its head to the ground and moved around, sorting through all the scent information he was receiving. I stayed out of the way, feeling useless. Then Dean looked up at me and said, "Rowf." He began making his way back to the parking lot. I guessed he'd gathered all he could.

As we'd arranged, I loaded Dean in the Malibu to take him to another shooting site, the place behind some old buildings opposite the Sonic where the shooter had hidden on the night poor Heather Kinman had been killed. I turned into the service alley behind the old stores and parked behind Patsy's Cleaners, which had moved to a new and more convenient location fifteen years ago. Between the cleaners and the dilapidated and long-empty Louisiana Feed and Seed, a narrow gap afforded a great view of the Sonic. The drive-in restaurant was closed for the night but still bright with light. Since the Sonic was on the town's main drag, there were lights up and down the street, and I could actually see pretty well in the areas where the structures allowed light to go; unfortunately, that made the shadows impenetrable.

Again, the bloodhound worked the area, paying particular interest to the weedy strip of ground between the two old stores, a strip so narrow it was no more than a gap wide enough for one person. He seemed pretty excited at some particular scent he found. I was excited, too, hoping that he'd found something we could translate into evidence for the police.

Suddenly Dean let out a "Whoof!" and raised his head to look past me. He was certainly focusing on something, or someone. Almost unwillingly, I turned to see. Andy Bellefleur stood at the point where the service alley crossed the gap between the buildings. Only his face and upper torso were in the light.

"Jesus Christ, Shepherd of Judea! Andy, you scared the hell out of me!" If I hadn't been watching the dog so intently, I would've sensed him coming. The stakeout, dammit. I should have remembered.

"What are you doing here, Sookie? Where'd you get the dog?"

I couldn't think of a single answer that would sound plausible. "It seemed worth a try to see if a trained dog could pick up a single scent from the places where the shooter stood," I said. Dean leaned against my legs, panting and slobbering.

"So when did you get on the parish payroll?" Andy asked conversationally. "I didn't realize you'd been hired as an investigator."

Okay, this wasn't going well.

"Andy, if you'll move out of the way, me and the dog'll just get back into my car, and we'll drive away, and you won't have to be mad at me anymore." He was plenty mad, and he was determined to have it out with me, whatever that entailed. Andy wanted to get the world realigned, with facts he knew forming the tracks it should run on. I didn't fit in that world. I wouldn't run on those tracks. I could read his mind, and I didn't like what I was hearing.

I realized, too late, that Andy'd had one drink too many during the conference at the bar. He'd had enough to remove his usual constraints.

"You shouldn't be in our town, Sookie," he said.

"I have as much right to be here as you, Andy Bellefleur."

"You're a genetic fluke or something. Your grandmother was a real nice woman, and people tell me your dad and mom were good people. What happened to you and Jason?"

"I don't think there's much wrong with me and Jason, Andy," I said calmly, but his words stung like fire ants. "I think we're regular people, no better and no worse than you and Portia."

Andy actually snorted.

Suddenly the bloodhound's side, pressed against my legs, began to vibrate. Dean was growling almost inaudibly. But he wasn't looking at Andy. The hound's heavy head was turned in another direction, toward the dark shadows of the other end of the alley. Another live mind: a human. Not a regular human, though.

"Andy," I said. My whisper pierced his self-absorption. "You armed?"

I didn't know whether I felt that much better when he drew his pistol.

"Drop it, Bellefleur," said a no-nonsense voice, one that sounded familiar.

"Bullshit," Andy sneered. "Why should I?"

"Because I got a bigger gun," said the voice, cool and sarcastic. Sweetie Des Arts stepped from the shadows, carrying a rifle. It was pointed at Andy, and I had no doubt she was ready to fire. I felt like my insides had turned to Jell-O.

"Why don't you just leave, Andy Bellefleur?" Sweetie asked. She was wearing a mechanic's coverall and a jacket, and her hands were gloved. She didn't look anything like a short-order cook. "I've got no quarrel with you. You're just a person."

Andy was shaking his head, trying to clear it. I noticed he hadn't dropped his gun yet. "You're the cook at the bar, right? Why are you doing this?"

"You should know, Bellefleur. I heard your little conversation with the shifter here. Maybe this dog is a human, someone you know." She didn't wait for Andy to answer. "And Heather Kinman was just as bad. She turned into a fox. And the guy that works at Norcross, Calvin Norris? He's a damn panther."

"And you shot them all? You shot me, too?" I wanted to be sure Andy was registering this. "There's just one thing wrong with your little vendetta, Sweetie. I'm not a shifter."

"You smell like one," Sweetie said, clearly sure she was right.

"Some of my friends are shifters, and that day I'd hugged a few of 'em. But me myself—not a shifter of any kind."

"Guilty by association," Sweetie said. "I'll bet you got a dab of shifter from somewhere."

"What about you?" I asked. I didn't want to get shot again. The evidence suggested that Sweetie was not a sharpshooter: Sam, Calvin, and I had lived. I knew aiming at night had to be difficult, but still, you would've thought she could have done better. "Why are you on this vendetta?"

"I'm just a fraction of a shifter," she said, snarling just as much as Dean. "I got bit when I had a car wreck. This half-man half-wolf . . . thing . . . ran out of the woods near where I lay bleeding, and the damn thing bit me . . . and then another car came around the curve and it ran away. But the first full moon after that, my hands changed! My parents threw up."

"What about your boyfriend? You had one?" I kept speaking, trying to distract her. Andy was moving as far away from me as he could get, so she couldn't shoot both of us quickly. She planned on shooting me first, I knew. I wanted the bloodhound to move away from me, but he stayed loyally pressed against my legs. She wasn't sure the dog was a shifter. And, oddly, she hadn't mentioned shooting Sam.

"I was a stripper then, living with a great guy," she said, rage bubbling through her voice. "He saw my hands and the extra hair and he loathed me. He left when the moon was full. He'd take business trips. He'd go golfing with his buddies. He'd be stuck at a late meeting."

"So how long have you been shooting shifters?"

"Three years," she said proudly. "I've killed twenty-two and wounded forty-one."

"That's awful," I said.

"I'm proud of it," she said. "Cleaning the vermin off the face of the earth."

"You always find work in bars?"

"Gives me a chance to see who's one of the brethren," she said, smiling. "I check out the churches and restaurants, too. The day care centers."

"Oh, no." I thought I was going to throw up.

My senses were hyperalert, as you can imagine, so I knew there was someone coming up the alley behind Sweetie. I could feel the anger roiling in a two-natured head. I didn't look, trying to keep Sweetie's attention for as long as I could. But there was a little noise, maybe the sound of a piece of paper trash rustling against the ground, and that was enough for Sweetie. She whirled around with the rifle up to her shoulder, and she fired. There was a shriek from the darkness at the south end of the alley, and then a high whining.

Andy took his moment and shot Sweetie Des Arts while her back was turned. I pressed myself against the uneven bricks of the old Feed and Seed, and as the rifle dropped from her hand, I saw the blood come out of her mouth, black in the starlight. Then she folded to the earth.

While Andy was standing over her, his gun dangling from his hand, I made my way past them to find out who had come to our aid. I switched on my flashlight to discover a werewolf, terribly wounded. Sweetie's bullet had hit him in the middle of the chest, as best I could tell through the thick fur, and I yelled at Andy, "Use your cell phone! Call for help!" I was pressing down on the bubbling wound as hard as I could, hoping I was doing the right thing. The wound kept moving in a very disconcerting way, since the Were was in the process of changing back into a human. I glanced back to see that Andy was still lost in his own little vale of horror at what he'd done. "Bite him," I told Dean, and Dean padded over to the policeman and nipped his hand.

Andy cried out, of course, and raised his gun as if he were going to shoot the bloodhound. "No!" I yelled, jumping up from the dying Were. "Use your phone, you idiot. Call an ambulance."

Then the gun swung around to point at me.

For a long, tense moment I thought for sure the end of my life had come. We'd all like to kill what we don't understand, what scares us, and I powerfully scared Andy Bellefleur.

But then the gun faltered and dropped back to Andy's side. His broad face stared at me with dawning comprehension. He fumbled in his pocket, withdrew a cell phone. To my profound relief, he holstered the gun after he punched in a number.

I turned back to the Were, now wholly human and naked, while Andy said, "There's been a multiple shooting in the alley behind the old Feed and Seed and Patsy's Cleaners, across Magnolia Street from Sonic. Right. Two ambulances, two gunshot wounds. No, I'm fine."

The wounded Were was Dawson. His eyes flickered open, and he tried to gasp. I couldn't even imagine the pain he must be suffering. "Calvin," he tried to say.

"Don't worry now. Help's on the way," I told the big man. My flashlight was lying on the ground beside me, and by its oddly skewed light I could see his huge muscles and bare hairy chest. He looked cold, of course, and I wondered where his clothes were. I would have been glad to have his shirt to wad up over the wound, which was steadily leaking blood. My hands were covered in it.

"Told me to finish out my last day by watching over you," Dawson said. He was shuddering all over. He tried to smile. "I said, 'Piece of cake.'" And then he didn't say anything else, but lost consciousness.

Andy's heavy black shoes came to stand in my field of vision. I thought Dawson was going to die. I didn't even know his first name. I had no idea how we were going to explain a naked guy to the police. Wait . . . was that up to me? Surely Andy was the one who'd have the hard explaining to do?

As if he'd been reading my mind—for a change—Andy said, "You know this guy, right?"

"Slightly."

"Well, you're going to have to say you know him better than that, to explain his lack of clothes."

I gulped. "Okay," I said, after a brief, grim pause.

"You two were back here looking for his dog. You," Andy said to Dean. "I don't know who you are, but you stay a dog, you hear me?" Andy stepped away nervously. "And I came back here because I'd followed the woman—she was acting suspiciously."

I nodded, listening to the air rattle in Dawson's throat. If I could only give him blood to heal him, like a vampire. If I only knew a medical procedure . . . But I could already hear the police cars and the ambulances coming closer. Nothing in Bon Temps was very far from anything else, and on this side of town, the south side, the Grainger hospital would be closest.

"I heard her confess," I said. "I heard her say she shot the others."

"Tell me something, Sookie," Andy said in a rush. "Before they get here. There's nothing weird about Halleigh, right?"

I stared up at him, amazed he could think of such a thing at this moment. "Nothing aside from the stupid way she spells her name." Then I reminded myself who'd shot the bitch lying on the ground five feet away. "No, not a thing," I said. "Halleigh is just plain old normal."

"Thank God," he said. "Thank God."

And then Alcee Beck dashed down the alley and stopped in his tracks, trying to make sense of the scene before him. Right behind him was Kevin Pryor, and Kevin's partner Kenya crept along hugging the wall with her gun out. The ambulance teams were hanging back until they were sure the scene was secure. I was up against the wall getting searched before I knew what was happening. Kenya kept saying, "Sorry, Sookie" and "I have to do this," until I told her, "Just get it done. Where's my dog?"

"He run off," she said. "I guess the lights spooked him. He's a bloodhound, huh? He'll come home." When she'd done her usual thorough job, Kenya said, "Sookie? How come this guy is naked?"

This was just the beginning. My story was extremely

thin. I read disbelief written large on almost every face. It wasn't the temperature for outdoor loving, and I was completely dressed. But Andy backed me up every step of the way, and there was no one to say it hadn't happened the way I told it.

About two hours later, they let me get back in my car to return to the duplex. The first thing I did when I got inside was phone the hospital to find out how Dawson was. Somehow, Calvin got ahold of the phone. "He's alive," he said tersely.

"God bless you for sending him after me," I said. My voice was as limp as a curtain on a still summer day. "I'd be dead if it wasn't for him."

"I hear the cop shot her."

"Yes, he did."

"I hear a lot of other stuff."

"It was complicated."

"I'll see you this week."

"Yes, of course."

"Go get some sleep."

"Thanks again, Calvin."

My debt to the werepanther was piling up at a rate that scared me. I knew I'd have to work it off later. I was tired and aching. I was filthy inside from Sweetie's sad story, and filthy outside from being on my knees in the alley, helping the bloody Were. I dropped my clothes on the floor of the bedroom, went into the bathroom, and stood under the shower, trying hard to keep my bandage dry with a shower cap, the way one of the nurses had shown me.

When the doorbell rang the next morning, I cursed town living. But as it turned out, this was no neighbor who wanted to borrow a cup of flour. Alcide Herveaux was standing outside, holding an envelope.

I glared at him through eyes that felt crusty with sleep. Without saying a word, I plodded back to my bedroom and crawled into the bed. This wasn't enough to deter Alcide, who strode in after me.

"You're now doubly a friend of the pack," he said, as if he was sure that was the concern uppermost in my mind. I turned my back to him and snuggled under the covers. "Dawson says you saved his life."

"I'm glad Dawson's well enough to speak," I muttered, closing my eyes tightly and wishing Alcide would go away. "Since he got shot on my account, your pack doesn't owe me a damn thing."

From the movement of the air, I could tell that Alcide was kneeling at the side of the bed. "That's not for you to decide, but us," he said chidingly. "You're summoned to the contest for the packleader."

"What? What do I have to do?"

"You just watch the proceedings and congratulate the winner, no matter who it is."

Of course, to Alcide, this struggle for succession was the most important thing going. It was hard for him to get that I didn't have the same priorities. I was getting swamped by a wave of supernatural obligations.

The werewolf pack of Shreveport said they owed me. I owed Calvin. Andy Bellefleur owed me and Dawson and Sam for solving his case. I owed Andy for saving my life. Though I'd cleared Andy's mind about Halleigh's complete normality, so maybe that canceled my debt to him for shooting Sweetie.

Sweetie had owed payback to her assailant.

Eric and I were even, I figured.

I owed Bill slightly.

Sam and I were more or less caught up.

Alcide personally owed me, as far as I was concerned. I had showed up for this pack shit and tried to follow the rules to help him out.

In the world I lived in, the world of human people, there were ties and debts and consequences and good deeds. That was what bound people to society; maybe that was what constituted society. And I tried to live in my little niche in it the best way I could.

Joining in the secret clans of the two-natured and the undead made my life in human society much more difficult and complicated.

And interesting.

And sometimes . . . fun.

Alcide had been talking at least some of the time I'd been thinking, and I'd missed a lot of it. He was picking up on that. He said, "I'm sorry if I'm boring you, Sookie," in a stiff voice.

I rolled over to face him. His green eyes were full of hurt. "Not bored. I just have a lot to think about. Leave the invitation, okay? I'll get back with you on that." I wondered what you wore to a fighting-for-packmaster event. I wondered if the senior Mr. Herveaux and the somewhat pudgy motorcycle dealership owner would actually roll on the ground and grapple.

Alcide's green eyes were full of puzzlement. "You're acting so strange, Sookie. I felt so comfortable with you before. Now I feel like I don't know you."

Valid had been one of my Words of the Day last week. "That's a valid observation," I said, trying to sound matter-of-fact. "I felt just as comfortable with you when I first met you. Then I started to find out stuff. Like about Debbie, and shifter politics, and the servitude of some shifters to the vamps."

"No society is perfect," Alcide said defensively. "As for Debbie, I don't ever want to hear her name again."

"So be it," I said. God knew I couldn't get any sicker of hearing her name.

Leaving the cream envelope on the bedside table, Alcide took my hand, bent over it, and laid a kiss on the back of it. It was a ceremonial gesture, and I wished I knew its significance. But the moment I would have asked, Alcide was gone.

"Lock the door behind you," I called. "Just turn the little button on the doorknob." I guess he did, because I went right back to sleep, and no one woke me up until it was almost time for me to go to work. Except there was a note on my front door that said, "Got Linda T. to stand in for you. Take the night off. Sam." I went back inside and took off my waitress clothes and pulled on some jeans. I'd been ready to go to work, and now I felt oddly at a loss.

I was almost cheered to realize I had another obligation, and I went into the kitchen to start fulfilling it.

After an hour and a half of struggling to cook in an unfamiliar kitchen with about half the usual paraphernalia, I was on my way to Calvin's house in Hotshot with a dish of chicken breasts baked with rice in a sour-cream sauce, and some biscuits. I didn't call ahead. I planned to drop off the food and go. But when I reached the little community, I saw there were several cars parked on the road in front of Calvin's trim little house. "Dang," I said. I didn't want to get involved any further with Hotshot than I already was. My brother's new nature and Calvin's courting had already dragged me in too far.

Heart sinking, I parked and ran my arm through the handle of the basket full of biscuits. I took the hot dish of chicken and rice in oven-mitted hands, gritted my teeth against the ache in my shoulder, and marched my butt up to Calvin's front door. Stackhouses did the right thing.

Crystal answered the door. The surprise and pleasure on her face shamed me. "I'm so glad you're here," she said, doing her best to be offhand. "Please come in." She stood back, and now I could see that the small living room was full of people, including my brother. Most of them were werepanthers, of course. The werewolves of Shreveport had sent a representative; to my astonishment, it was Patrick Furnan, contender for the throne and Harley-Davidson salesman.

Crystal introduced me to the woman who appeared to be acting as hostess, Maryelizabeth Norris. Maryelizabeth moved as if she hadn't any bones. I was willing to bet Maryelizabeth didn't often leave Hotshot. The shifter introduced me around the room very carefully, making sure I understood the relationship Calvin bore to each individual. They all began to blur after a bit. But I could see that (with a few exceptions) the natives of Hotshot ran to two types: the small, dark-haired, quick ones like Crystal, and the fairer, stockier ones with beautiful green or golden-brown eyes, like Calvin. The surnames were mostly Norris or Hart.

Patrick Furnan was the last person Crystal reached. "Why, of course I know you," he said heartily, beaming at me as if we'd danced at a wedding together. "This here's Alcide's girlfriend," he said, making sure he was heard by everyone in the room. "Alcide's the son of the other candidate for packmaster."

There was long silence, which I would definitely characterize as "charged."

"You're mistaken," I said in a normal conversational tone. "Alcide and I are friends." I smiled at him in such a way as to let him know he better not be alone with me in an alley anytime soon.

"My mistake," he said, smooth as silk.

Calvin was receiving a hero's welcome home. There were balloons and banners and flowers and plants, and his house was meticulously clean. The kitchen had been full of food. Now Maryelizabeth stepped forward, turned her back to cut

Patrick Furnan dead, and said, "Come this way, honey. Calvin's ready to see you." If she'd had a trumpet handy, she'd have blown a flourish on it. Maryelizabeth was not a subtle woman, though she had a deceptive air of mystery due to her wide-spaced golden eyes.

I guess I could have been more uncomfortable, if there'd been a bed of red-hot coals to walk on.

Maryelizabeth ushered me into Calvin's bedroom. His furniture was very nice, with spare, clean lines. It looked Scandinavian, though I know little about furniture—or style, for that matter. He had a high bed, a queen-size, and he was propped up in it against sheets with an African motif of hunting leopards. (Someone had a sense of humor, anyway.) Against the deep colors in the sheets and the deep orange of the bedspread, Calvin looked pale. He was wearing brown pajamas, and he looked exactly like a man who'd just been released from the hospital. But he was glad to see me. I found myself thinking there was something a bit sad about Calvin Norris, something that touched me despite myself.

"Come sit," he said, indicating the bed. He moved over a little so I'd have room to perch. I guess he'd made some signal, because the man and the woman who'd been in the room—Dixie and Dixon—silently eased out through the door, shutting it behind them.

I perched, a little uneasily, on the bed beside him. He had one of those tables you most often see in hospitals, the kind that can be rolled across the bed. There was a glass of ice tea and a plate on it, steam rising from the food. I gestured that he should begin. He bowed his head and said a silent prayer while I sat quietly. I wondered to whom the prayer was addressed.

"Tell me about it," Calvin said as he unfolded his napkin, and that made me a lot more comfortable. He ate while I told him what had happened in the alley. I noticed that the food on the tray was the chicken-and-rice casserole I'd brought, with a dab of mixed vegetable casserole and two of my biscuits. He wanted me to see that he was eating the food I'd prepared for him. I was touched, which sounded a warning bell at the back of my brain.

"So, without Dawson, there's no telling what would've happened," I concluded. "I thank you for sending him. How is he?"

Calvin said, "Hanging on. They airlifted him from Grainger to Baton Rouge. He would be dead, if he wasn't a Were. He's lasted this long; I think he'll make it."

I felt terrible.

"Don't go blaming yourself for this," Calvin said, his voice suddenly sounding deeper. "This is Dawson's choice."

"Huh?" would've sounded ignorant, so I said, "How so?"

"His choice of professions. His choice of actions. Maybe he should have leaped for her a few seconds earlier. Why'd he wait? I don't know. How'd she know to aim low, given the poor light? I don't know. Choices lead to consequences." Calvin was struggling to express something. He was not naturally an articulate man, and he was trying to convey a thought both important and abstract. "There's no blame," he said finally.

"It would be nice to believe that, and I hope some day I do," I said. "Maybe I'm on my way to believing it." It was true that I was sick of self-blame and second-guessing.

"I suspect the Weres are going to invite you to their little packleader shindig," Calvin said. He took my hand. His was warm and dry.

I nodded.

"I bet you'll go," he said.

"I think I have to," I said uneasily, wondering what his goal was.

"I'm not going to tell you what to do," Calvin said. "I have no authority over you." He didn't sound too happy about that. "But if you go, please watch your back. Not for my sake; that don't mean nothing to you, yet. But for yourself."

"I can promise that," I said after a careful pause. Calvin was not a guy to whom you blurted the first idea in your head. He was a serious man.

Calvin gave me one of his rare smiles. "You're a damn fine cook," he said. I smiled back.

"Thank you, sir," I said, and got up. His hand tightened on mine and pulled. You don't fight a man who's just gotten out of the hospital, so I bent toward him and laid my cheek to his lips.

"No," he said, and when I turned a little to find out what was wrong, he kissed me on the lips.

Frankly, I expected to feel nothing. But his lips were as warm and dry as his hands, and he smelled like my cooking, familiar and homey. It was surprising, and surprisingly comfortable, to be so close to Calvin Norris. I backed off a little, and I am sure my face showed the mild shock I felt. The werepanther smiled and released my hand.

"The good thing about being in the hospital was you coming to see me," he said. "Don't be a stranger now that I'm home."

"Of course not," I said, ready to be out of the room so I could regain my composure.

The outer room had emptied of most of its crowd while I talked to Calvin. Crystal and Jason had vanished, and Maryelizabeth was gathering up plates with the help of an adolescent werepanther. "Terry," Maryelizabeth said with a sideways inclination of her head. "My daughter. We live next door."

I nodded to the girl, who gave me a darting look before turning back to her task. She was not a fan of mine. She was from the fairer bloodstock, like Maryelizabeth and Calvin, and she was a thinker. "Are you going to marry my dad?" she asked me.

"I'm not planning on marrying anyone," I said cautiously. "Who's your dad?"

Maryelizabeth gave Terry a sidelong look that promised Terry she'd be sorry later. "Terry is Calvin's," she said.

I was still puzzled for a second or two, but suddenly, the stance of both the younger and the older woman, their tasks, their air of comfort in this house, clicked into place.

I didn't say a word. My face must have shown something, for Maryelizabeth looked alarmed, and then angry.

"Don't presume to judge how we live our life," she said. "We are not like you."

"That's true," I said, swallowing my revulsion. I forced a smile to my lips. "Thank you for introducing me around. I appreciate it. Is there anything I can help you with?"

"We can take care of it," said Terry, giving me another look that was a strange combination of respect and hostility.

"We should never have sent you to school," Maryelizabeth said to the girl. Her wide-spaced golden eyes were both loving and regretful.

"Good-bye," I said, and after I recovered my coat, I left the house, trying not to hurry. To my dismay, Patrick Furnan was waiting for me beside my car. He was holding a motorcycle helmet under his arm, and I spotted the Harley a little farther down the road.

"You interested in hearing what I've got to say?" the bearded Were asked.

"No, actually not," I told him.

"He's not going to keep on helping you out for nothing," Furnan said, and my whole head snapped around so I could look at this man.

"What are you talking about?"

"A thank-you and a kiss ain't going to hold him. He's going to demand payment sooner or later. Won't be able to help it."

"I don't recall asking you for advice," I said. He stepped closer. "And you keep your distance." I let my gaze roam to the houses surrounding us. The watchful gaze of the community was full upon us; I could feel its weight.

"Sooner or later," Furnan repeated. He grinned at me suddenly. "I hope it's sooner. You can't two-time a Were, you know. Or a panther. You'll get ripped to shreds between 'em."

"I'm not two-timing *anyone*," I said, frustrated almost beyond bearing at his insistence that he knew my love life better than I did. "I'm not dating either of them."

"Then you have no protection," he said triumphantly.

I just couldn't win.

"Go to hell," I said, completely exasperated. I got in my car and drove away, letting my eyes glide over the Were as if he weren't there. (This "abjure" concept could come in handy.) The last thing I saw in my rearview mirror was Patrick Furnan sliding his helmet on, still watching my retreating car.

If I hadn't really cared who won the King of the Mountain contest between Jackson Herveaux and Patrick Furnan, I did now.

15 ~

I WAS WASHING THE DISHES I'D USED AS I COOKED FOR
Calvin. My little duplex was peaceful. If Halleigh was home,
she was being quiet as a mouse. I didn't mind washing dishes,
to tell you the truth. It was a good time to let my mind drift
around, and often I made good decisions while I was doing
something completely mundane. Not too surprisingly, I was
thinking of the night before. I was trying to remember exactly what Sweetie had said. Something about it had struck
me wrong, but at the moment I hadn't exactly been in a position to raise my hand to ask a question. It had something to
do with Sam.

I finally recalled that though she'd told Andy Bellefleur
that the dog in the alley was a shapeshifter, she hadn't known
it was Sam. There wasn't anything strange about that, since
Sam had been in a bloodhound shape, not his usual collie
form.

After I'd realized what had been bothering me, I thought my mind would be at peace. That didn't happen. There was something else—something else Sweetie had said. I thought and thought, but it just wouldn't pop to the top of my brain.

To my surprise, I found myself calling Andy Bellefleur at home. His sister Portia was just as surprised as I was when she answered, and she said rather coldly that she'd find Andy.

"Yes, Sookie?" Andy sounded neutral.

"Let me ask a question, Andy."

"I'll listen."

"When Sam was shot," I said, and paused, trying to figure out what to say.

"Okay," Andy said. "What about it?"

"Is it true that the bullet didn't match the others?"

"We didn't retrieve a bullet in every case." Not a direct answer, but probably as good as I was going to get.

"Hmmm. Okay," I said, then thanked him and hung up, uncertain if I'd learned what I wanted or not. I had to push it out of my mind and do something else. If there was a question there, it would eventually work its way to the top of the heap of the issues that burdened my thoughts.

What remained of the evening was quiet, which was getting to be a rare pleasure. With so little house to clean, and so little yard to care for, there would be lots of free hours to come. I read for an hour, worked a crossword puzzle, and went to bed at about eleven.

Amazingly, no one woke me all night. No one died, there weren't any fires, and no one had to alert me to any emergency.

The next morning I rose feeling better than I had in a week. A glance at the clock told me I'd slept all the way through to ten o'clock. Well, that wasn't so surprising. My shoulder felt nearly healed; my conscience had settled itself. I didn't think I had many secrets to keep, and that was a tremendous relief. I was used to keeping other people's secrets, but not my own.

The phone rang as I swallowed the last of my morning coffee. I put my paperback facedown on the kitchen table to mark my place and got up to answer it. "Hello," I said cheerfully.

"It's today," Alcide said, voice vibrating with excitement. "You need to come."

Thirty minutes my peace had lasted. Thirty minutes.

"I'm guessing you mean the contest for the position of packmaster."

"Of course."

"And I need to be there why?"

"You need to be there because the entire pack and all friends of the pack have to be there," Alcide said, his voice brooking no dissent. "Christine especially thought you should be a witness."

I might have argued if he hadn't added the bit about Christine. The wife of the former packmaster had struck me as a very intelligent woman with a cool head.

"All right," I said, trying not to sound grumpy. "Where and when?"

"At noon, be at the empty building at 2005 Clairemont. It used to be David & Van Such, the printing company."

I got a few directions and hung up. While I showered, I reasoned that this was a sporting event, so I dressed in my old denim skirt with a long-sleeved red tee. I pulled on some red tights (the skirt was quite short) and some black Mary Janes. They were a little scuffed, so I hoped that Christine would not look down at my shoes. I tucked my silver cross into my shirt; the religious significance wouldn't bother the Weres at all, but the silver might.

The defunct printing company of David & Van Such had been in a very modern building, in an equally modern industrial park, largely deserted this Saturday. All the businesses had been constructed to match: low gray stone and dark glass edifices, with crepe myrtle bushes all around, grass medians, and nice curbing. David & Van Such featured an ornamental bridge over an ornamental pond, and a red front door. In the spring, and after some restorative maintenance, it would be as pretty as a modern business building could get. Today, in the fading phase of winter, the dead weeds that had grown high during the previous summer waved in a chilly breeze. The skeletal crepe myrtles needed pruning back, and the water in the pond looked stagnant, with trash floating dismally here and there. The David & Van Such parking lot contained about thirty cars, including—ominously—an ambulance.

Though I wore a jacket, the day suddenly seemed colder as I went from the parking lot and across the bridge to the front door. I was sorry I'd left my heavier coat at home, but it hadn't seemed worth bringing for a brief run between enclosed spaces. The glass front of David & Van Such, broken only by the red door, reflected the clear pale blue sky and the dead grass.

It didn't seem right to knock at a business door, so I slipped inside. Two people were ahead of me, having crossed the now-empty reception area. They passed through plain gray double doors. I followed them, wondering what I was getting into.

We entered what had been the manufacturing area, I suppose; the huge presses were long gone. Or maybe this cavern of a room had been full of desks manned by clerks taking orders or doing accounting work. Skylights in the roof let in some illumination. There was a cluster of people close to the middle of the space.

Well, I hadn't gotten the clothes thing right. The women were mostly wearing nicer pants outfits, and I glimpsed a dress here and there. I shrugged. Who could have known?

There were a few people in the crowd I hadn't seen at the funeral. I nodded at a red-haired Were named Amanda (I knew her from the Witch War), and she nodded back. I was surprised to spot Claudine and Claude. The twins looked marvelous, as always. Claudine was wearing a deep green sweater and black pants, and Claude was wearing a black sweater and deep green pants. The effect was striking. Since the two fairies were the only obvious non-Weres in attendance, I went to stand with them.

Claudine bent and kissed me on the cheek, and so did Claude. Their kisses felt exactly the same.

"What's going to happen?" I whispered the question because the group was abnormally quiet. I could see things hanging from the ceiling, but in the poor light I couldn't imagine what they were.

"There will be several tests," Claudine murmured. "You're not much of a screamer, right?"

I never had been, but I wondered if I'd break new ground today.

A door opened on the far side of the room, and Jackson Herveaux and Patrick Furnan came in. They were naked. Having seen very few men naked, I didn't have much basis for comparison, but I have to say that these two Weres weren't my ideal. Jackson, though certainly fit, was an older man with skinny legs, and Patrick (though he, too, looked strong and muscular) was barrel-like in form.

After I'd adjusted to the nakedness of the men, I noticed that each was accompanied by another Were. Alcide followed his father, and a young blond man trailed Patrick. Alcide and the blond Were remained fully clothed. "It would've been nice if *they'd* been naked, huh?" Claudine whispered, nodding at the younger men. "They're the seconds."

Like in a duel. I looked to see if they carried pistols or swords, but their hands were empty.

I noticed Christine only when she went to the front of the crowd. She reached above her head and clapped her hands one time. There hadn't been much chatter before this, but now the huge space fell completely silent. The delicate woman with her silver hair commanded all attention.

She consulted a booklet before she began. "We meet to discern the next leader of the Shreveport pack, also called the Long Tooth pack. To be the leader of the pack, these Weres must compete in three tests." Christine paused to look down at the book.

Three was a good mystical number. I would have expected three.

I hoped none of these tests involved blood. Fat chance.

"The first test is the test of agility." Christine gestured behind her at a roped-off area. It looked like a giant playground in the dim light. "Then the test of endurance." She pointed at a carpeted area to her left. "Then the test of might in battle." She waved a hand at a structure behind her.

So much for no blood.

"Then the winner must mate with another Were, to ensure the survival of the pack."

I sure hoped part four would be symbolic. After all, Patrick Furnan had a wife, who was standing apart with a group that was definitely pro-Patrick.

That seemed like four tests to me, not three, unless the mating part was kind of like the winner's trophy.

Claude and Claudine took my hands and gave them a simultaneous squeeze. "This is gonna be bad," I whispered, and they nodded in unison.

I saw two uniformed paramedics standing toward the back of the crowd. They were both shifters of some kind, their brain patterns told me. With them was a person—well, maybe a creature—I hadn't seen for months: Dr. Ludwig. She caught my eye and bowed to me. Since she was around three feet tall, she didn't have far to lean. I bowed back. Dr. Ludwig had a large nose, olive skin, and thick wavy brown hair. I was glad she was there. I had no idea what Dr. Ludwig actually was, other than nonhuman, but she was a good doctor. My back would have been permanently scarred—assuming I'd lived—if Dr. Ludwig hadn't treated me after a maenad attack. I'd escaped with a couple of bad days and a fine white tracery across my shoulder blades, thanks to the tiny doctor.

The contestants entered the "ring"—actually a large square marked off by those velvet ropes and metal-topped posts that they use in hotels. I'd thought the enclosed area looked like a playground, but now, as the lights came up, I realized I was seeing something more like a jumping arena for horses crossed with a gymnastics arena—or a course for a dog agility competition for giant dogs.

Christine said, "You will change." Christine moved away to melt back into the crowd. Both candidates dropped to the ground, and the air around them began to shimmer and distort. Changing quickly at one's desire was a great source of pride among shifters. The two Weres achieved their change at nearly the same instant. Jackson Herveaux became a huge black wolf, like his son. Patrick Furnan was pale gray, broad in the chest, a bit shorter in length.

As the small crowd drew closer, hugging the velvet ropes, one of the biggest men I'd ever seen emerged from the darkest shadows to step into the arena. I recognized him as the man whom I'd last seen at Colonel Flood's funeral. At least six and half feet tall, today he was bare-chested and barefoot. He was impressively muscular, and his chest was as hairless as his head. He looked like a genie; he would have appeared quite natural with a sash and pantaloons. Instead, he was wearing aged blue jeans. His eyes were pits of pitch. Of course, he was a shape-shifter of some kind, but I could not imagine what he turned into.

"Whoa," breathed Claude.

"Hooboy," whispered Claudia.

"Wowzers," I muttered.

Standing between the contenders, the tall man led them to the start of the course.

"Once the test begins, no pack member can interrupt," he said, looking from one Were to the other.

"First contestant is Patrick, wolf of this pack," the tall man said. His bass voice was as dramatic as the distant rumble of drums.

I understood, then; he was the referee. "Patrick goes first, by coin flip," the tall man said.

Before I could think it was pretty funny that all this ceremony included a coin toss, the pale wolf was off, moving so fast that I could hardly keep track of him. He flew up a ramp, leaped three barrels, hit the ground on the far side at a dash, went up another ramp and through a ring hanging from the ceiling (which rocked violently after he was through it), and dropped down on the ground, crawling on all fours through a clear tunnel that was very narrow and twisted at intervals. It was like the one sold in pet stores for ferrets or gerbils, just bigger. Once out of the tunnel, the wolf, mouth open in a pant, came to a level area covered with Astroturf. Here, he paused and considered before putting out a foot. Every step was like that, as the wolf worked its way across the twenty yards or so of this particular area. Suddenly a section of Astroturf leaped up as a trap snapped shut, narrowly missing the wolf's hind leg. The wolf yipped in consternation, frozen in place. It must have been agonizing, trying to restrain himself from dashing for the safety of the platform that was now only a few feet away.

I was shivering, though this contest had little to do with me. The tension was clearly showing among the Weres. They didn't seem to be moving quite as humans did anymore. Even the overly made-up Mrs. Furnan had wide round eyes now, eyes that didn't look like a woman's even under all that makeup.

As the gray wolf took his final test, a leap from a dead stop that had to cover the length of perhaps two cars, a howl of triumph erupted from Patrick's mate's throat. The gray wolf stood safely on the platform. The referee checked a stopwatch in his hand.

"Second candidate," said the big man, "Jackson Herveaux, wolf of this pack." A brain close to me supplied me with the big man's name.

"Quinn," I whispered to Claudine. Her eyes opened wide. The name was significant to her in a way I could not guess.

Jackson Herveaux began the same test of skills that Patrick had already completed. He was more graceful going through the suspended hoop; it scarcely moved as he sailed through. He took a little longer, I thought, getting through the tunnel. He seemed to realize it, too, because he stepped into the trap field more hastily than I thought wise. He stopped dead, maybe coming to the same conclusion. He bent to use his nose more carefully. The information he got from this made him quiver all over. With exquisite care, the werewolf raised one black forepaw and moved it a fraction of an inch. We were holding our breath as he worked forward in a completely different style from his predecessor. Patrick Furnan had moved in big steps, with longish pauses in between for careful sniffing, a sort of hurry-up-and-wait style. Jackson Herveaux moved very steadily in small increments, his nose always busy, his movements cannily plotted.

To my relief, Alcide's father made it across unharmed, without springing any of the traps.

The black wolf gathered himself for the final long leap and launched himself into the air with all his power. His landing was less than graceful, as his hind paws had to scrabble to cling to the edge of the landing site. But he made it, and a few congratulatory yips echoed through the empty space.

"Both candidates pass the agility test," Quinn said. His eyes roamed the crowd. When they passed over our odd trio—two tall black-haired twin fairies and a much shorter blond human—his gaze may have lingered a moment, but it was hard to say.

Christine was trying to get my attention. When she saw I was looking at her, she gave a tiny, sharp nod of her head to a spot by the test-of-endurance pen. Puzzled but obedient, I eased through the crowd. I didn't know the twins had followed me until they resumed standing to either side of me. There was something about this that Christine wanted me to see, to . . . Of course. She wanted me to use my talent here. She suspected . . . skulduggery. As Alcide and his blond counterpart took their places in the pen, I noticed they were both gloved. Their attention was totally absorbed by this contest; leaving nothing for me to sieve from that focus. That left the two wolves. I'd never tried to look inside the mind of a shifted person.

With considerable anxiety, I concentrated on opening myself to their thoughts. As you might expect, the blend of human and dog thought patterns was quite challenging. At first scan I could only pick up the same kind of focus, but then I detected a difference.

As Alcide lifted an eighteen-inch-long silver rod, my stomach felt cold and shivery. Watching the blond Were next to him repeat the gesture, I felt my lips draw back in distaste. The gloves were not totally necessary, because in human form, a Were's skin would not be damaged by the silver. In wolf form, silver was terribly painful.

Furnan's blond second ran his covered hands over the silver, as if testing the bar for hidden faults.

I had no idea why silver weakened vampires and burned them, and why it could be fatal to Weres, while it had no effect on fairies—who, however, could not bear prolonged exposure to iron. But I knew these things were true, and I knew the upcoming test would be awful to watch.

However, I was there to witness it. Something was going to happen that needed my attention. I turned my mind back to the little difference I'd read in Patrick's thoughts. In his Were form, these were so primitive they hardly qualified as "thoughts."

Quinn stood between the two seconds, his smooth scalp picking up a gleam of light. He had a timing watch in his hands.

"The candidates will take the silver now," he said, and with his gloved hands Alcide put the bar in his father's mouth. The black wolf clamped down and sat, just as the light gray wolf did with his silver bar. The two seconds drew back. A high whine of pain came from Jackson Herveaux, while Patrick Furnan showed no signs of stress other than heavy panting. As the delicate skin of his gums and lips began to smoke and smell a little, Jackson's whining became louder. Patrick's skin showed the same painful symptoms, but Patrick was silent.

"They're so brave," whispered Claude, watching with fascinated horror at the torment the two wolves were enduring. It was becoming apparent that the older wolf would not win this contest. The visible signs of pain were increasing every second, and though Alcide stood there focusing solely on his father to add his support, at any moment it would be over. Except . . .

"He's cheating," I said clearly, pointing at the gray wolf.

"No member of the pack may speak." Quinn's deep voice was not angry, merely matter-of-fact.

"I'm not a pack member."

"You challenge the contest?" Quinn was looking at me now. All the pack members who'd been standing close around me dropped back until I stood alone with the two fairies, who were looking down at me with some surprise and dismay.

"You bet your ass I do. Smell the gloves Patrick's second was wearing."

The blond second looked completely blindsided. And guilty.

"Drop the bars," Quinn commanded, and the two wolves complied, Jackson Herveaux with a whimper. Alcide dropped to his knees by his father, putting his arms around the older wolf.

Quinn, moving as smoothly as if his joints were oiled, knelt to retrieve the gloves that Patrick's second had tossed to the floor. Libby Furnan's hand darted over the velvet rope to snatch them up, but a deep snarl from Quinn told her to stop. It made my own spine tingle, and I was much farther away than Libby.

Quinn picked up the gloves and smelled them.

He looked down at Patrick Furnan with a contempt so heavy that I was surprised the wolf didn't crumple under its weight.

He turned to face the rest of the crowd. "The woman is right." Quinn's deep voice gave the words the gravity of stone. "There's a drug on the gloves. It made Furnan's skin numb when the silver was placed in his mouth, so he could last longer. I declare him loser of this part of the contest.

The pack will have to decide whether he should forfeit any right to continue, and whether his second should still be a pack member." The fair-haired Were was cringing as if he expected someone to hit him. I didn't know why his punishment should be worse than Patrick's; maybe the lower your rank, the worse your punishment? Not exactly fair; but then, I wasn't a Were.

"The pack will vote," Christine called. She met my eyes and I knew this was why she wanted me here. "If the rest of you would step into the outer room?"

Quinn, Claude, Claudine, and three shape-shifters moved with me to the doors leading into the other room. There was more natural light there, which was a pleasure. Less of a pleasure was the curiosity that pooled around me. My shields were still down, and I felt the suspicion and conjecture flowing from the brains of my companions, except, of course, from the two fairies. To Claude and Claudine, my peculiarity was a rare gift, and I was a lucky woman.

"Come here," Quinn rumbled, and I thought about telling him to take his commands and shove them where the sun don't shine. But that would be childish, and I had nothing to fear. (At least that's what I told myself about seven times in rapid succession.) I made my spine stiffen, and I strode up to him and looked up into his face.

"You don't have to stick your jaw out like that," he said calmly. "I'm not going to hit you."

"I never thought you were," I said with a snap in my voice that I was proud of. I found that his round eyes were the very dark, rich, purple-brown of pansies. Wow, they were pretty! I smiled out of sheer pleasure . . . and a dollop of relief.

Unexpectedly, he smiled back. He had full lips, very even white teeth, and a sturdy column of a neck.

"How often do you have to shave?" I asked, fascinated with his smoothness.

He laughed from the belly.

"Are you scared of anything?" he asked.

"So many things," I said regretfully.

He considered that for a moment. "Do you have an extrasensitive sense of smell?"

"Nope."

"Do you know the blond one?"

"Never saw him before."

"Then how did you know?"

"Sookie is a telepath," Claude said. When he got the full weight of the big man's stare, he looked like he was sorry he'd interrupted. "My sister is her, ah, guardian," Claude concluded in a rush.

"Then you're doing a terrible job," Quinn told Claudine.

"Don't you get onto Claudine," I said indignantly. "Claudine's saved my life a bunch."

Quinn looked exasperated. "Fairies," he muttered. "The Weres aren't going to be happy about your piece of information," he told me. "At least half of them are going to wish you were dead. If your safety is Claudine's top priority, she should have held your mouth shut."

Claudine looked crushed.

"Hey," I said, "cut it out. I know you've got friends in there you're worried about, but don't take that out on Claudine. Or me," I added hastily, as his eyes fixed on mine.

"I have no friends in there. And I shave every morning," he said.

"Okay, then." I nodded, nonplussed.

"Or if I'm going out in the evening."

"Gotcha."

"To do something special."

What would Quinn consider special?

The doors opened, interrupting one of the strangest conversations I'd ever had.

"You can come back in," said a young Were in three-inch-high fuck-me shoes. She was wearing a burgundy sheath, and when we followed her back into the big room, she gave her walk some extra sway. I wondered whom she was trying to entrance, Quinn or Claude. Or maybe Claudine?

"This is our judgment," said Christine to Quinn. "We'll resume the contest where it ended. According to the vote, since Patrick cheated on the second test, he is declared the loser of that test. Of the agility test, too. However, he's allowed to stay in the running. But, to win, he has to win the last test decisively." I wasn't sure what "decisively" meant in this context. From Christine's face, I was certain it didn't bode well. For the first time, I realized that justice might not prevail.

Alcide looked very grim, when I found his face in the crowd. This judgment seemed clearly biased in favor of his father's opponent. I hadn't realized that there were more Weres in the Furnan camp than the Herveaux camp, and I wondered when that shift had occurred. The balance had seemed more even at the funeral.

Since I had already interfered, I felt free to interfere some more. I began wandering among the pack members, listening to their brains. Though the twisted and turned brains of all Weres and shifters are difficult to decipher, I began to pick up a clue here and there. The Furnans, I learned, had followed their plan of leaking stories about Jackson Herveaux's gambling habits, talking up how unreliable that made Jackson as a leader.

I knew from Alcide that the stories about his father's gambling were true. Though I didn't admire the Furnans for playing this card, I didn't consider it stacking the deck, either.

The two competitors were still in wolf form. If I had understood correctly, they had been scheduled to fight anyway. I was standing by Amanda. "What's changed about the last test?" I asked. The redhead whispered that now the fight was no longer a regular match, with the contestant left standing after five minutes declared the winner. Now, to win the fight "decisively," the loser had to be dead or disabled.

This was more than I'd bargained for, but I knew without asking that I couldn't leave.

The group gathered around a wire dome that reminded me irresistibly of *Mad Max Beyond Thunderdome*. You remember—"Two enter, one man leaves." I guess this was the wolf equivalent. Quinn opened the door, and the two large wolves slunk in, casting their gazes from side to side as they counted their supporters. Or at least, that's what I guessed they were doing.

Quinn turned and beckoned to me.

Ah-oh. I frowned. The dark, purple-brown eyes were intent. The man meant business. I approached him reluctantly.

"Go read their minds again," he told me. He laid a huge hand on my shoulder. He turned me to face him, which brought me face-to-face—well, so to speak—with his dark brown nipples. Disconcerted, I looked up. "Listen, blondie, all you have to do is go in there and do your thing," he said reassuringly.

He couldn't have had this idea while the wolves were outside the cage? What if he shut the door on me? I looked over my shoulder at Claudine, who was frantically shaking her head.

"Why do I need to? What purpose will it serve?" I asked, not being a total idiot.

"Is he gonna cheat again?" Quinn asked so softly that I knew no one else could hear him. "Does Furnan have some means of cheating that I can't see?"

"Do you guarantee my safety?"

He met my eyes. "Yes," he said without hesitation. He opened the door to the cage. Though he had to stoop, he came in behind me.

The two wolves approached me cautiously. Their smell was strong; like dog, but muskier and wilder. Nervously, I laid my hand on Patrick Furnan's head. I looked in his head as hard as I could, and I could discern nothing but rage at me for costing him his win in the endurance contest. There was a glowing coal of purpose about the coming battle, which he intended to win by sheer ruthlessness.

I sighed, shook my head, moved my hand away. To be fair, I put my hand on Jackson's shoulders, which were so high I was startled all over. The wolf was literally vibrating, a faint shiver that made his fur quiver under my touch. His whole resolve was bent toward rending his rival limb from limb. But Jackson was afraid of the younger wolf.

"All clear," I said, and Quinn turned away to open the door. He crouched to step through, and I was about to follow him when the burgundy-sheathed girl shrieked. Moving faster than I thought such a large man could move, Quinn spun on his foot, grabbed my arm with one hand, and yanked with all his might. With his other hand he slammed shut the door, and I heard something crash against it.

The noises behind me told me the battle had already started, but I was pinned against a huge expanse of smooth tan skin.

With my ear to Quinn's chest, I could hear the rumble inside as well as outside as he asked, "Did he get you?"

I had my own shaking and quivering going on. My leg was wet, and I saw that my tights were ripped, and blood was running from an abrasion on the side of my right calf. Had my leg scraped the door when Quinn had shut it so quickly, or had I been bitten? Oh my God, if I'd been bitten . . .

Everyone else was pressed against the wire cage, watching the snarling, whirling wolves. Their spittle and blood flew in fine sprays, dotting the spectators. I glanced back to see Jackson's grip on Patrick's hind leg broken when Patrick bent himself backward to bite Jackson's muzzle. I caught a glimpse of Alcide's face, intent and anguished.

I didn't want to watch this. I would rather look at this stranger's hide than watch the two men killing each other.

"I'm bleeding," I told Quinn. "It's not bad."

A high yip from the cage suggested that one of the wolves had scored a hit. I cringed.

The big man half carried me over to the wall. That was a good distance from the fight. He helped me turn and sink down into a sitting position.

Quinn lowered himself to the floor, too. He was so graceful for someone so large that I was absorbed in just watching him move. He knelt by me to pull off my shoes, and then my tights, which were ripped to shreds and dabbled with blood. I was silent and shaking as he sank down to lie on his stomach. He gripped my knee and my ankle in his huge hands as if my leg were a large drumstick. Without saying a word, Quinn began to lick the blood from my calf. I was afraid this was preparatory to taking a bite, but Dr. Ludwig trotted over, looked down, and nodded. "You'll be fine," she said dismissively. After patting me on the head as if I were an injured dog, the tiny doctor trotted back to her attendants.

Meanwhile, though I would not have thought it was possible for me to be anything but on the knife-edge of suspense, the leg-licking thing was providing an entirely unexpected diversion. I shifted restlessly, stifling a gasp. Maybe I should remove my leg from Quinn's possession? Watching the gleaming bald head bob up and down as he licked was making me think of something worlds away from the life-and-death battle taking place across the room. Quinn was working more and more slowly, his tongue warm and a little rough as he cleaned my leg. Though his brain was the most opaque shifter brain I'd ever encountered, I got the idea he was having the same reaction that I was.

When he finished, he laid his head on my thigh. He was breathing heavily, and I was trying not to. His hands released their grip but stroked my leg deliberately. He looked up at me. His eyes had changed. They were golden, solid gold. The color filled his eyes. Whoa.

I guess he could tell from my face that I was, to put it mildly, conflicted about our little interlude.

"Not our time and place, babe," he said. "God, that was . . . great." He stretched, and it wasn't an outward extension of arms and chest, the way humans stretch. He rippled from the base of his spine to his shoulders. It was one of the oddest things I'd ever seen, and I'd seen a lot of odd things. "Do you know who I am?" he asked.

I nodded. "Quinn?" I said, feeling my cheeks color.

"I've heard your name is Sookie," he said, rising to his knees.

"Sookie Stackhouse," I said.

He put his hand under my chin so I'd look up at him. I stared into his eyes as hard as I could. He didn't blink.

"I wonder what you're seeing," he said finally, and removed his hand.

I glanced down at my leg. The mark on it, now clear of blood, was almost certainly a scrape from the metal of the door. "Not a bite," I said, my voice faltering on the last word. The tension left me in a rush.

"Nope. No she-wolf in your future," he agreed, and flowed to his feet. He held out his hand. I took it, and he had me on my feet in a second. A piercing yelp from the cage yanked me back into the here and now.

"Tell me something. Why the hell can't they just vote?"
I asked him.

Quinn's round eyes, back to their purple-brown color
and properly surrounded with white, crinkled at the corners
with amusement.

"Not the way of the shifter, babe. You're going to see me
later," Quinn promised. Without another word he strode
back to the cage, and my little field trip was over. I had to
turn my attention back to the truly important thing happening in this building.

Claudine and Claude were looking anxiously over their
shoulders when I found them. They made a little space for
me to ease in between them, and wrapped their arms around
me when I was in place. They seemed very upset, and Claudine had two tears trailing down her cheeks. When I saw
the situation in the cage, I understood why.

The lighter wolf was winning. The black wolf's coat was
matted with blood. He was still on his feet, still snarling,
but one of his hind legs was giving way under his weight
from time to time. He managed to pull himself back up
twice, but the third time the leg collapsed, the younger wolf
was on him, the two spinning over and over in a terrifying
blur of teeth, torn flesh, and fur.

Forgetting the silence rules, all the Weres were screaming
their support of one contestant or the other, or just howling.
The violence and the noise blended together to make a
chaotic collage. I finally spotted Alcide pounding his hands
against the metal in futile agitation. I had never felt so sorry
for anyone in my life. I wondered if he'd try to break into the
combat cage. But another look told me that even if Alcide's
respect for pack rules broke down and he attempted to go to
his father's aid, Quinn was blocking the door. That was why
the pack had brought in an outsider, of course.

Abruptly, the fight was over. The lighter wolf had the

darker one by the throat. He was gripping, but not biting. Maybe Jackson would have gone on struggling if he hadn't been so severely wounded, but his strength was exhausted. He lay whining, quite unable to defend himself, disabled. The room fell completely silent.

"Patrick Furnan is declared the winner," said Quinn, his voice neutral.

And then Patrick Furnan bit down on Jackson Herveaux's throat and killed him.

_~ 16_

QUINN TOOK OVER THE CLEANUP WITH THE SURE AU-
thority of one who's supervised such things before. Though
I was dull and stupid with shock, I noticed he gave clear,
concise directions as to the dispersal of the testing materials.
Pack members dismantled the cage into sections and took
apart the agility arena with efficient dispatch. A cleanup
crew took care of mopping up the blood and other fluids.

Soon the building was empty of all but the people.
Patrick Furnan had reverted to his human form, and Dr.
Ludwig was attending his many wounds. I was glad he had
every one of them. I was only sorry they weren't worse. But
the pack had accepted Furnan's choice. If they would not
protest such unnecessary brutality, I couldn't.

Alcide was being comforted by Maria-Star Cooper, a
young Were I knew slightly.

Maria-Star held him and stroked his back, providing

support by her sheer closeness. He didn't have to tell me that on this occasion, he preferred another Were's companionship to mine. I'd gone to hug him, but when I'd neared him and met his eyes, I'd known. That hurt, and it hurt bad; but today wasn't about me and my feelings.

Claudine was crying in her brother's arms. "She's so tenderhearted," I whispered to Claude, feeling a bit abashed that I wasn't crying myself. My concern was for Alcide; I'd hardly known Jackson Herveaux.

"She went through the second elf war in Iowa fighting with the best of them," Claude said, shaking his head. "I've seen a decapitated goblin stick its tongue out at her in its death throes, and she laughed. But as she gets closer to the light, she becomes more sensitive."

That effectively shut me up. I was not about to ask for any explanation of yet another arcane supernatural rule. I'd had a bellyful this day.

Now that all the mess was cleared away (that mess included Jackson's body, which Dr. Ludwig had taken somewhere to be altered, to make the story of how he'd met his death more plausible), all the pack members present gathered in front of Patrick Furnan, who hadn't resumed clothes. According to his body, victory had made him feel manly. Ick.

He was standing on a blanket; it was a red plaid stadium blanket, like you'd take to a football game. I felt my lips twitch, but I became completely sober when the new packmaster's wife led a young woman to him, a brown-haired girl who seemed to be in her late teens. The girl was as bare as the packmaster, though she looked considerably better in that state.

What the hell?

Suddenly I remembered the last part of the ceremony, and I realized Patrick Furman was going to fuck this girl in front of us. No. No way was I going to watch this. I tried to turn to walk out. But Claude hissed, "You can't leave." He covered my mouth and picked me up bodily to move me to the back of the crowd. Claudine moved with us and stood in front of me, but with her back to me, so I wouldn't have to see. I made a furious sound into Claude's hand.

"Shut up," the fairy said grimly, his voice as concentrated with sincerity as he could manage. "You'll land us all in trouble. If it makes you feel any better, this is traditional. The girl volunteered. After this, Patrick'll be a faithful husband once more. But he's already bred his whelp by his wife, and he has to make the ceremonial gesture of breeding another one. May take, may not, but it has to be done."

I kept my eyes shut and was grateful when Claudine turned to me and placed her tear-wet hands over my ears. A shout went up from the crowd when the thing was completed. The two fairies relaxed and gave me some room. I didn't see what happened to the girl. Furnan remained naked, but as long as he was in a calm state, I could handle that.

To seal his status, the new packmaster began to receive the pledges of his wolves. They went in turn, oldest to youngest, I figured, after a moment's observation. Each Were licked the back of Patrick Furnan's hand and exposed his or her neck for a ritual moment. When it was Alcide's turn, I suddenly realized there was potential for even more disaster.

I found I was holding my breath.

From the profound silence, I knew I wasn't the only one.

After a long hesitation, Furnan bent over and placed his teeth on Alcide's neck; I opened my mouth to protest, but Claudine clapped her hand over it. Furnan's teeth came away from Alcide's flesh, leaving it unscathed.

Packmaster Furnan had sent a clear signal.

By the time the last Were had performed the ritual, I was

exhausted from all the emotion. Surely this was an end to it? Yes, the pack was dispersing, some members giving the Furnans congratulatory hugs, and some striding out silently.

I dodged them myself and made a beeline for the door. The next time someone told me I had to watch a supernatural rite, I was going to tell him I had to wash my hair.

Once out in the open air, I walked slowly, my feet dragging. I had to think about things I'd put to one side, like what I'd seen in Alcide's head after the whole debacle was over. Alcide thought I'd failed him. He'd told me I had to come, and I had; I should have known he had some purpose in insisting I be present.

Now I knew that he'd suspected Furnan had some underhanded trick in mind. Alcide had primed Christine, his father's ally, ahead of time. She made sure I used my telepathy on Patrick Furnan. And, sure enough, I had found that Jackson's opponent was cheating. That disclosure should have ensured Jackson's win.

Instead, the will of the pack had gone against Jackson, and the contest had continued with the stakes even higher. I'd nothing to do with that decision. But right now Alcide, in his grief and rage, was blaming me.

I was trying to be angry, but I was too sad.

Claude and Claudine said good-bye, and they hopped into Claudine's Cadillac and peeled out of the parking lot as if they couldn't wait to get back to Monroe. I was of the same mind, but I was a lot less resilient than the fairies. I had to sit behind the wheel of the borrowed Malibu for five or ten minutes, steadying myself for the drive home.

I found myself thinking of Quinn. It was a welcome relief from thinking of torn flesh and blood and death. When I'd looked into his head, I'd seen a man who knew his way. And I still didn't have a clue as to what he was.

The drive home was grim.

I might as well have phoned in to Merlotte's that evening. Oh, sure, I went through all the motions of taking orders and carrying them to the right tables, refilling pitchers of beer, popping my tips in the tip jar, wiping up spills and making sure the temporary cook (a vampire named Anthony Bolivar; he'd subbed for us before) remembered the busboy was off limits. But I didn't have any sparkle, any joy, in my work.

I did notice that Sam seemed be getting around better. He was obviously restive, sitting in his corner watching Charles work. Possibly Sam was also a little piqued, since Charles just seemed to get more and more popular with the clientele. The vamp was charming, that was for sure. He was wearing a red sequined eye patch tonight and his usual poet shirt under a black sequined vest—flashy in the extreme, but entertaining, too.

"You seem depressed, beautiful lady," he said when I came to pick up a Tom Collins and a rum and Coke.

"Just been a long day," I said, making an effort to smile. I had so many other things to digest emotionally that I didn't even mind when Bill brought Selah Pumphrey in again. Even when they sat in my section, I didn't care. But when Bill took my hand as I was turning away to get their order, I snatched it away as if he'd tried to set me on fire.

"I only want to know what's wrong," he said, and for a second I remembered how good it had felt that night at the hospital when he'd lain down with me. My mouth actually began to open, but then I caught a glimpse of Selah's indignant face, and I shut my emotional water off at the meter.

"I'll be right back with that blood," I said cheerfully, smiling wide enough to show every tooth in my head.

To heck with him, I thought righteously. *Him and the horse he rode in on.*

After that it was strictly business. I smiled and worked,

and worked and smiled. I stayed away from Sam, because I didn't want to have a long conversation with yet another shifter that evening. I was afraid—since I didn't have any reason to be mad at Sam—that if he asked me what was wrong, I'd tell him; and I just didn't want to talk about it. You ever just feel like stomping around and being miserable for a while? That was the kind of mood I was in.

But I had to go over to Sam, after all, when Catfish asked if he could pay with a check for this evening's festivities. That was Sam's rule: he had to approve checks. And I had to stand close to Sam, because the bar was very noisy.

I thought nothing of it, aside from not wanting to get into my own mood with him, but when I bent over him to explain Catfish's cash-flow problem, Sam's eyes widened. "My God, Sookie," he said, "Who have you been around?"

I backed off, speechless. He was both shocked and appalled by a smell I hadn't even known I carried. I was tired of supes pulling this on me.

"Where'd you meet up with a tiger?" he asked.

"A tiger," I repeated numbly.

So now I knew what my new acquaintance Quinn turned into when the moon was full.

"Tell me," Sam demanded.

"No," I snapped, "I won't. What about Catfish?"

"He can write a check this once. If there's a problem, he'll never write another one here again."

I didn't relay this last sentence. I took Catfish's check and his alcohol-fueled gratitude, and deposited both where they belonged.

To make my bad mood worse, I snagged my silver chain on a corner of the bar when I bent over to pick up a napkin some slob had tossed to the floor. The chain broke, and I caught it up and dropped it in my pocket. Dammit. This had been a rotten day, followed by a rotten night.

I made sure to wave at Selah as she and Bill left. He'd left me a good tip, and I stuffed it in my other pocket with so much force I almost ripped the fabric. A couple of times during the evening, I had heard the bar phone ring, and when I was taking some dirty glasses to the kitchen hatch, Charles said, "Someone keeps calling and hanging up. Very irritating."

"They'll get tired and quit," I said soothingly.

About an hour later, as I put a Coke in front of Sam, the busboy came to tell me there was someone at the employees' entrance, asking for me.

"What were you doing outside?" Sam asked sharply.

The boy looked embarrassed. "I smoke, Mr. Merlotte," he said. "I was outside taking me a break, 'cause the vamp said he'd drain me if I lit up inside, when this man walked up outta nowhere."

"What's he look like?" I asked.

"Oh, he's old, got black hair," the boy said, shrugging. Not long on the gift of description.

"Okay," I said. I was glad to take a break. I suspected who the visitor might be, and if he'd come into the bar, he'd have caused a riot. Sam found an excuse to follow me out by saying that he needed a pit stop, and he picked up his cane and used it to hobble down the hall after me. He had his own tiny bathroom off his office, and he limped into it as I continued past the men's and women's to the back door. I opened it cautiously and peered outside. But then I began smiling. The man waiting for me had one of the most famous faces in the world—except, apparently, to adolescent busboys.

"Bubba," I said, pleased to see the vampire. You couldn't call him by his former name, or he got real confused and agitated. Bubba was formerly known as . . . Well, let me just put it this way. You wondered about all those sightings after his death? This was the explanation.

The conversion hadn't been a complete success because his system had been so fuddled with drugs; but aside from his predilection for cat blood, Bubba managed pretty well. The vampire community took good care of him. Eric kept Bubba on staff as an errand boy. Bubba's glossy black hair was always combed and styled, his long sideburns sharply trimmed. Tonight he was wearing a black leather jacket, new blue jeans, and a black-and-silver plaid shirt.

"Looking good, Bubba," I said admiringly.

"You too, Miss Sookie." He beamed at me.

"Did you want to tell me something?"

"Yessum. Mr. Eric sent me over here to tell you that he's not what he seems."

I blinked.

"Who, Bubba?" I asked, trying to keep my voice gentle.

"He's a hit man."

I stared at Bubba's face not because I thought staring would get me anywhere, but because I was trying to figure out the message. This was a mistake; Bubba's eyes began darting from side to side, and his face lost its smile. I should have turned to stare at the wall—it would've given me as much information, and Bubba wouldn't have become as anxious.

"Thanks, Bubba," I said, patting him on his beefy shoulder. "You did good."

"Can I go now? Back to Shreveport?"

"Sure," I said. I would just call Eric. Why hadn't he used the phone for a message as urgent and important as this one seemed to be?

"I found me a back way into the animal shelter," Bubba confided proudly.

I gulped. "Oh, well, great," I said, trying not to feel queasy.

"See ya later, alligator," he called from the edge of the parking lot. Just when you thought Bubba was the worst vampire in the world, he did something amazing like moving at a speed you simply could not track.

"After a while, crocodile," I said dutifully.

"Was that who I think it was?" The voice was right behind me.

I jumped. I spun around to find that Charles had deserted his post at the bar.

"You scared me," I said, as though he hadn't been able to tell.

"Sorry."

"Yes, that was him."

"Thought so. I've never heard him sing in person. It must be amazing." Charles stared out at the parking lot as though he were thinking hard about something else. I had the definite impression he wasn't listening to his own words.

I opened my mouth to ask a question, but before my words reached my lips I really thought about what the English pirate had just said, and the words froze in my throat. After a long hesitation, I knew I had to speak, or he would know something was wrong.

"Well, I guess I'd better get back to work," I said, smiling the bright smile that pops onto my face when I'm nervous. And, boy, was I nervous now. The one blinding revelation I'd had made everything begin to click into place in my head. Every little hair on my arms and neck stood straight up. My fight-or-flight reflex was fixed firmly on "flight." Charles was between the outside door and me. I began to back down the hall toward the bar.

The door from the bar into the hall was usually left open, because people had to pass into the hall all the time to use the bathrooms. But now it was closed. It had been open when I'd come down the hall to talk to Bubba.

This was bad.

"Sookie," Charles said, behind me. "I truly regret this."

"It was you who shot Sam, wasn't it?" I reached behind me, fumbled for the handle that would open that door. He wouldn't kill me in front of all those people, would he? Then I remembered the night Eric and Bill had polished off a roomful of men in my house. I remembered it had taken them only three or four minutes. I remembered what the men had looked like afterward.

"Yes. It was a stroke of luck when you caught the cook, and she confessed. But she didn't confess to shooting Sam, did she?"

"No, she didn't," I said numbly. "All the others, but not Sam, and the bullet didn't match."

My fingers found the knob. If I turned it, I might live. But I might not. How much did Charles value his own life?

"You wanted the job here," I said.

"I thought there was a good chance I'd come in handy when Sam was out of the picture."

"How'd you know I'd go to Eric for help?"

"I didn't. But I knew someone would tell him the bar was in trouble. Since that would mean helping you, he would do it. I was the logical one to send."

"Why are you doing all this?"

"Eric owes a debt."

He was moving closer, though not very quickly. Maybe he was reluctant to do the deed. Maybe he was hoping for a more advantageous moment, when he could carry me off in silence.

"It looks like Eric's found out I'm not from the Jackson nest, as I'd said."

"Yeah. You picked the wrong one."

"Why? It seemed ideal to me. Many men there; you wouldn't have seen them all. No one can remember all the men who've passed through that mansion."

"But they've heard Bubba sing," I said softly. "He sang for them one night. You'd never have forgotten that. I don't know how Eric found out, but I knew as soon as you said you'd never—"

He sprang.

I was on my back on the floor in a split second, but my hand was already in my pocket, and he opened his mouth to bite. He was supporting himself on his arms, courteously trying not to actually lie on top of me. His fangs were fully out, and they glistened in the light.

"I have to do this," he said. "I'm sworn. I'm sorry."

"I'm not," I said, and thrust the silver chain into his mouth, using the heel of my hand to snap his jaw shut.

He screamed and hit at me, and I felt a rib go, and smoke was coming out of his mouth. I scrambled away and did a little yelling of my own. The door flew open, and a flood of bar patrons thundered into the little hallway. Sam shot out of the door of his office like he'd been fired from a cannon, moving very well for a man with a broken leg, and to my amazement he had a stake in his hand. By that time, the screaming vampire was weighted down by so many beefy men in jeans you couldn't even see him. Charles was trying to bite whoever he could, but his burned mouth was so painful his efforts were weak.

Catfish Hunter seemed to be on the bottom of the pile, in direct contact. "You pass me that stake here, boy!" he called back to Sam. Sam passed it to Hoyt Fortenberry, who passed it to Dago Guglielmi, who transferred it to Catfish's hairy hand.

"We gonna wait for the vampire police, or we gonna take care of this ourselves?" Catfish asked. "Sookie?"

After a horrified second of temptation, I opened my mouth to say, "Call the police." The Shreveport police had a squad of vampire policemen, as well as the necessary special transportation vehicle and special jail cells.

"End it," said Charles, somewhere below the heaving pile of men. "I failed in my mission, and I can't abide jails."

"Okeydokey," Catfish said, and staked him.

After it was over and the body had disintegrated, the men went back into the bar and settled down at the tables where they'd been before they heard the fight going on in the hall. It was beyond strange. There wasn't much laughing, and there wasn't much smiling, and no one who'd stayed in the bar asked anyone who'd left what had happened.

Of course, it was tempting to think this was an echo of the terrible old days, when black men had been lynched if there was even a rumor they'd winked at a white woman.

But, you know, the simile just didn't hold. Charles was a different race, true. But he'd been guilty as hell of trying to kill me. I would have been a dead woman in thirty more seconds, despite my diversionary tactic, if the men of Bon Temps hadn't intervened.

We were lucky in a lot of ways. There was not one law enforcement person in the bar that night. Not five minutes after everyone resumed his table, Dennis Pettibone, the arson investigator, came in to have a visit with Arlene. (The busboy was still mopping the hall, in fact.) Sam had bound my ribs with some Ace bandages in his office, and I walked out, slowly and carefully, to ask Dennis what he wanted to drink.

We were lucky that there weren't any outsiders. No college guys from Ruston, no truckers from Shreveport, no relatives who'd dropped in for a beer with a cousin or an uncle.

We were lucky there weren't many women. I don't know why, but I imagined a woman would be more likely to get squeamish about Charles's execution. In fact, I felt pretty squeamish about it, when I wasn't counting my lucky stars I was still alive.

And Eric was lucky when he dashed into the bar about thirty minutes later, because Sam didn't have any more stakes handy. As jittery as everyone was, some foolhardy soul would have volunteered to take out Eric: but he wouldn't have come out of it relatively unscathed, as those who'd tackled Charles had.

And Eric was also lucky that the first words out of his mouth were "Sookie, are you all right?" In his anxiety, he grabbed me, one hand on either side of my waist, and I cried out.

"You're hurt," he said, and then realized five or six men had jumped to their feet.

"I'm just sore," I said, making a huge effort to look okay. "Everything's fine. This here's my friend Eric," I said a little loudly. "He's been trying to get in touch with me, and now I know why it was so urgent." I met the eyes of each man, and one by one, they dropped back into their seats.

"Let's us go sit and talk," I said very quietly.

"Where is he? I will stake the bastard myself, no matter what Hot Rain sends against me." Eric was furious.

"It's been taken care of," I hissed. "Will you *chill*?"

With Sam's permission, we went to his office, the only place in the building that offered both chairs and privacy. Sam was back behind the bar, perched on a high stool with his leg on a lower stool, managing the bartending himself.

"Bill searched his database," Eric said proudly. "The bastard told me he came from Mississippi, so I wrote him down as one of Russell's discarded pretty boys. I had even called Russell, to ask him if Twining had worked well for him. Russell said he had so many new vampires in the mansion, he had only the vaguest recollection of Twining. But Russell, as I observed at Josephine's Bar, is not the kind of manager I am."

I managed a smile. That was definitely true.

"So when I found myself wondering, I asked Bill to go to

work, and Bill traced Twining from his birth as a vampire to his pledge to Hot Rain."

"This Hot Rain was the one who made him a vampire?"

"No, no," Eric said impatiently. "Hot Rain made the pirate's sire a vampire. And when Charles's sire was killed during the French and Indian War, Charles pledged himself to Hot Rain. When Hot Rain was dissatisfied with Long Shadow's death, he sent Charles to exact payment for the debt he felt was owed."

"Why would killing me cancel the debt?"

"Because he decided after listening to gossip and much reconnoitering that you were important to me, and that your death would wound me the way Long Shadow's had him."

"Ah." I could not think of one thing to say. Not one thing.

At last I asked, "So Hot Rain and Long Shadow were doing the deed, once upon a time?"

Eric said, "Yes, but it wasn't the sexual connection, it was the . . . the affection. That was the valuable part of the bond."

"So because this Hot Rain decided the fine you paid him for Long Shadow's death just didn't give him closure, he sent Charles to do something equally painful to you."

"Yes."

"And Charles got to Shreveport, kept his ears open, found out about me, decided my death would fill the bill."

"Apparently."

"So he heard about the shootings, knew Sam is a shifter, and shot Sam so there'd be a good reason for him to come to Bon Temps."

"Yes."

"That's real, real complicated. Why didn't Charles just jump me some night?"

"Because he wanted it to look like an accident. He didn't want blame attached to a vampire at all, because not only did he not want to get caught, he didn't want Hot Rain to incur any penalty."

I closed my eyes. "He set fire to my house," I said. "Not that poor Marriot guy. I bet Charles killed him before the bar even closed that night and brought him back to my house so he'd take the blame. After all, the guy was a stranger to Bon Temps. No one would miss him. Oh my God! Charles borrowed my keys! I bet the man was in my trunk! Not dead, but hypnotized. Charles planted that card in the guy's pocket. The poor fella wasn't a member of the Fellowship of the Sun anymore than I am."

"It must have been frustrating for Charles, when he found you were surrounded by friends," Eric said a little coldly, since a couple of those "friends" had just clomped by noisily, using a trip to the john as a pretext to keep an eye on him.

"Yes, must have been." I smiled.

"You seem better than I expected," Eric said a little hesitantly. "Less traumatized, as they say now."

"Eric, I'm a lucky woman," I said. "Today I've seen more bad stuff than you can imagine. All I can think is, I escaped. By the way, Shreveport now has a new packmaster, and he's a lying, cheating bastard."

"Then I take it Jackson Herveaux lost his bid for the job."

"Lost more than that."

Eric's eyes widened. "So the contest was today. I'd heard Quinn was in town. Usually, he keeps transgressions to a minimum."

"It wasn't his choice," I said. "A vote went against Jackson; it should have helped him, but it . . . didn't."

"Why were you there? Was that blasted Alcide trying to use you for some purpose in the contest?"

"You should talk about using."

"Yes, but I'm straightforward about it," Eric said, his blue eyes wide and guileless.

I had to laugh. I hadn't expected to laugh for days, or weeks, and yet here I was, laughing. "True," I admitted.

"So, I'm to understand that Charles Twining is no more?" Eric asked quite soberly.

"That's correct."

"Well, well. The people here are unexpectedly enterprising. What damage have you suffered?"

"Broken rib."

"A broken rib is not much when a vampire is fighting for his life."

"Correct, again."

"When Bubba got back and I found he hadn't exactly delivered his message, I rushed here gallantly to rescue you. I had tried calling the bar tonight to tell you to beware, but Charles answered the phone every time."

"It was gallant of you, in the extreme," I admitted. "But, as it turns out, unnecessary."

"Well, then . . . I'll go back to my own bar and look at my own bar patrons from my own office. We're expanding our Fangtasia product line."

"Oh?"

"Yes. What would you think of a nude calendar? 'Fangtasia's Vampire Hunks' is what Pam thinks it should be called."

"Are you gonna be in it?"

"Oh, of course. Mr. January."

"Well, put me down for three. I'll give one to Arlene and one to Tara. And I'll put one up on my own wall."

"If you promise to keep it open to my picture, I'll give you one for free," Eric promised.

"You got a deal."

He stood up. "One more thing, before I go."

I stood, too, but much more slowly.

"I may need to hire you in early March."

"I'll check my calendar. What's up?"

"There's going to be a little summit. A meeting of the kings and queens of some of the southern states. The location hasn't been settled, but when it is, I wonder if you can get time off from your job here to accompany me and my people."

"I can't think that far ahead just at the moment, Eric," I said. I winced as I began to walk out of the office.

"Wait one moment," he said suddenly, and justlikethat he was in front of me.

I looked up, feeling massively tired.

He bent and kissed me on my mouth, as softly as a butterfly's fluttering.

"You said I told you you were the best I'd ever had," he said. "But did you respond in kind?"

"Don't you wish you knew?" I said, and went back to work.